MALICE IN

MINIATURE

Also by Jeanne M. Dams
in Large Print:

The Body in the Transept
Holy Terror in the Hebrides

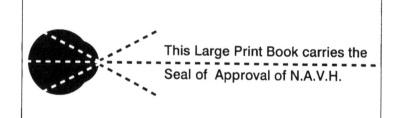

MALICE IN
MINIATURE

A Dorothy Martin Mystery

Jeanne M. Dams

Thorndike Press • Thorndike, Maine

Published in 2000 by arrangement with
Walker Publishing Company, Inc.

Thorndike Press Large Print Senior Lifestyles Series.

The tree indicium is a trademark of Thorndike Press.

The text of this Large Print edition is unabridged.
Other aspects of the book may vary from the original edition.

Set in 16 pt. Plantin by Minnie B. Raven.

Printed in the United States on permanent paper.

Library of Congress Cataloging-in-Publication Data

Dams, Jeanne M.
    Malice in miniature : a Dorothy Martin mystery /
Jeanne M. Dams.
        p.   cm.
    ISBN 0-7862-2408-8 (lg. print : hc : alk. paper)
    1. Martin, Dorothy (Fictional character) — Fiction.
    2. Women detectives — England — Fiction.   3. Police
spouses — England — Fiction.   4. Large type books.
    I. Title.
PS3554.A498 M35   2001
    813'.52—dc21
                                          99-058956

This book is dedicated
to the people of
St. Paul's, whose
friendship and
encouragement over the
years have been very
precious to me.

ACKNOWLEDGMENTS

If you want to see Brocklesby Hall in all its fantastic glory, visit Harlaxton Manor near the village of Grantham in Lincolnshire. This amazing Victorian edifice is now used as a foreign extension campus by the University of Evansville, my mother's alma mater, and when we visited there many years ago I swore somebody had to write a book about it. So now I have. At least I've used its architectural details freely, though I've made no attempt to reproduce the elaborate floor plan, and I've run up rooms of my own as it suited my purposes. I hope it's not necessary to add that there is no museum of miniatures at Harlaxton, nor anyone who resembles any of my characters in any particular. Most of the miniature houses and rooms Dorothy has explored are also fictional, alas! As a dollhouse enthusiast myself, I would love to see a Louis XIV house like the one housing Marie Antoinette's tea set, but no French miniature houses of that period are now known to exist.

I have, throughout the book, let my English characters refer to dolls' houses and the Americans to dollhouses, not to confuse you, the reader, but to preserve the customary usage of each country.

I owe a debt to so many people who provided information for *Malice in Miniature* that it would be impossible to name them all, but I would particularly like to thank the owners of dollhouse shops all over both America and England, who allowed me to browse their stock, ask innumerable questions, and now and then buy some tiny thing I couldn't resist.

1

It was a wet, blustery Monday afternoon in early November, the gray sky full of scudding clouds, leaves rushing through the air and sticking to the windows as the chill wind flung them there. I sat snugly in front of my fire, drinking tea in the cozy comfort of central heating and close-fitting windows and doors.

"They've made a good job of the house, Dorothy," said Alan, echoing my thoughts, as he so often does. It isn't unusual, after years of marriage, for a couple to communicate without words — but Alan and I, for all our gray hair and creaky joints, had been married for only a little over a month.

To each other, that is. I thought about my dear Frank, who had always known exactly what I was about to say, and smiled. I could remember him without pain, now. Our many wonderful years together would always be a part of me, a part, even, of my relationship with Alan. Like Tolstoy, I hold to the theory that all happy marriages are alike. Because Alan and I had each been happily married, we had been able to settle into the new bond with scarcely a ripple. Even the renovations to my seventeenth-century house, now (mercifully) nearly finished, had scarcely disturbed our bliss.

Secretly, foolishly, I tapped the wooden leg of my chair, just in case it was tempting fate to be so happy, and grinned at my new husband. "They've done a good job *so far*. At least the weather stays outside now. No floods in the upstairs hall, no gales through the parlor. Now if we can come up with a true miracle, an English plumber who understands something about showers . . ."

"Ah, yes, the standard American complaint about our plumbing. What's wrong with a proper English bath, I'd like to — What was that?"

Both cats woke from their sound sleep on the hearth, four ears swiveling in unison, four eyes wide with alarm as the pounding continued.

"Sit still; I'll go. Probably Jane, as it's the backdoor, though what she'd be doing out in this weather I can't imagine." I struggled out of the embrace of my favorite chair and hurried through the kitchen. The loud knocking sounded frantic. "All right, all right, I'm coming!"

I opened the door on the wettest, most bedraggled-looking human being I've ever seen. "For heaven's sake, Ada Finch! Come in, come in, and we'll get you dry. What brought you out —"

"Oh, madam!" she said, interrupting me. She leaned against the door frame, panting to catch her breath, one hand pressed to her ample bosom. "Oh, madam, 'ee never done it! You've got to find out 'oo did, so as they'll let 'im go, which they'd never a took 'im in if they'd 'ad so much sense as they were born with, but them p'lice — savin' yer presence, sir —"

The last remark was addressed to Alan — Alan Nesbitt, chief constable for the county of Belleshire and hence the city of Sherebury, who had joined me in the kitchen, looking mildly astonished. He now came to the door and ushered in the dripping Mrs. Finch, who allowed us to take her coat and then dropped into a chair at the kitchen table, still talking.

"— and if 'ee did 'ave it in 'is pocket, 'ee never put it there, did 'ee, which 'ee told 'im, over and over again, but 'ee wouldn't listen, not a nob like 'im, all 'igh and mighty, I'll 'igh and mighty *'im*, I will —"

I opened my mouth, but Alan shook his head slightly. "Better let her get it out of her system, whatever it is," he murmured under

11

Ada's unceasing flow of words. "She'll run down eventually, and then perhaps we can get some sense out of her. Meanwhile . . ."

His head tilted toward the Aga, the vast kitchen range I was learning to use, and I obediently moved the kettle to the hottest burner. Alan was quite right. Whatever ailed my voluble friend, a cup of tea would help.

"— and wot I want to know is, wot are you goin' to do about it?" Ada stopped talking at last, skewered me with a fierce glare, and then dissolved into sobs, her head on her arms. I patted her shoulder, uttered meaningless, soothing noises, and, when she began to quiet, put a cup of strong, sweet tea in front of her as Alan pushed one of his man-sized handkerchiefs into her hand.

She raised her head and sniffled. "Ta," she said to both of us impartially, blew her nose, and took a large gulp of tea.

"All right, now, Ada, I'm afraid we didn't get quite all of that; you're a little upset. Could you start over again from the beginning and tell us everything? It's Bob in trouble, isn't it?"

It was a reasonable guess. Not only is her grown-up son, Bob, the only important " 'ee" in Ada's life, but he and trouble are not always strangers. Bob's an honest man, but his drinking, which cost him his marriage and brought him home to Mum, still leads him into difficulties from time to time. This one must be a doozy; I'd known Ada to break down in tears only once before, when she discovered a dead body in the Town Hall — which circumstance, it must be admitted, might shake even the most stoic of us.

She put down her teacup and glared at me again. "It's not 'is fault this time!"

"Of course not. Now tell us, slowly, with all the details."

She hesitated, looking from me to Alan. Well, he can be tactful when required.

"So glad you're feeling better, Mrs. Finch. Will you excuse me? I have — er — some letters to write." He winked at me and disappeared.

"Which it's not," said Ada with a hint of her usual manner, "that I don't trust 'im, but once a p'liceman always a p'liceman is wot I say, and wot 'ee don't know won't 'urt 'im. Nor yet it won't 'urt me nor Bob."

I shook my head at that. "I tell my husband most things, Ada. If there's something you don't want him to know . . ."

She shook her head. "No matter. Wot *you* tells 'im, as from 'is wife, is different to wot *I* tells 'im. I'm the public, and 'ee'd 'ave to take notice, official-like. Wiv you it's" — she eyed me coyly — "only pillow talk."

I couldn't help laughing at that piece of Jesuitical reasoning, and we both relaxed a little. "Okay. Just as long as you don't expect me to keep things from him. Now, to be perfectly honest, I didn't follow a single word of what you said before, so you'll have to start all over."

She was collected now, and paused for thought before she began. "The short of it is, Bob's been 'ad up for stealin'."

I stared at her, genuinely shocked. "But he'd never do such a thing! Even if he was — umm —"

" 'Ee could be drunk as a lord, and 'ee'd never take nuffink as didn't belong to 'im," said Ada flatly. "You know it; the 'ole town knows it. But they found it on 'im, y'see, and then that old —" She stopped abruptly, seeking a euphemism for whatever scathing epithet she considered unfit for my ears. " 'Im wot runs the place," she finally amended, " 'ee said as 'ow 'ee'd 'ad 'is eye on Bob, an' 'ee thought 'ee'd been pinchin' this and that for weeks."

I waved a hand in the air, confused. "Wait a minute, Ada. I'm still not sure I know what you're talking about. Was it someone Bob works for who made the complaint?"

Bob is a jobbing gardener who works for a

number of households in town, mine included. He's a hard worker with true genius for his job; it took him only a few months to transform the weed patch in back of my house into the beginnings of a dream garden. But when he goes off on a toot he often comes back, sober and repentant, to find that some of his employers have lost patience and hired someone else.

I hired him when I lived alone, and I still need him badly. No matter how hard I try, I can't make anything grow except couch grass and dandelions, and Alan is too busy for dedicated gardening.

"The 'All," said Ada obscurely, in answer to my question.

"Excuse me?"

"Brocklesby 'All. 'Is new job. Didn't 'ee tell you?"

"He doesn't talk much when he's here — except to tell me I'm watering too much, or not enough, and ask what to plant." The latter was purely a formality, though I didn't tell Ada so. Bob intends to plant my garden with whatever he wants, and quite right, too, but he is always punctilious about consulting me. I gravely agree to his suggestions; he then puts the already purchased seeds or plants in the ground. We both enjoy the ritual.

Ada nodded, poured herself another cup of tea, and settled back to explain in full. It took a while, what with my interruptions for clarification and her elaborate digressions, but what it amounted to in the end was simple, mystifying, and somewhat disquieting.

Brocklesby Hall, it turned out, was a big country house a mile or two outside Sherebury; I vaguely remembered hearing the name. As these things go in England, it wasn't an old house. There had been a very old manor house on the site, some parts of it pre-Conquest — "built before the Frenchies come and took us all over" was Ada's way of putting it — but when that family died out in the early nineteenth century, the land was bought by a nouveau riche merchant named Brocklesby. "Beer" was Ada's brief explanation of his wealth. He had proceeded to tear down the old house, leaving only a few picturesque bits of wall for instant ruins, as was the fashion in those days. In its place he had erected a fantastic testimony to what bad taste, allied to a huge bankroll and a monstrous ego, could perpetrate.

Not that Ada put it that way, of course. She had long admired the place as the grandest house in the neighborhood, bigger and more elaborate even than the manor house where the ancestral squires of Sherebury had lived, and when Bob went to work at the Hall she had basked in reflected glory and acquired guidebooks and a set of postcards, which she now proceeded to take out of her carryall and show me. I got the idea very quickly.

The house was built with fifty bedrooms (pure ostentation, that sounded like; Ada said Brocklesby had been a bachelor who almost never entertained), countless drawing rooms and ballrooms and galleries and halls, and one bathroom. Nobody, except possibly the servants who had to look after them, had counted the fireplaces, or the windows.

Every surface, every angle that could possibly bear carvings or embellishments had been so adorned; those that couldn't had been painted or gilded. Ceilings were fitted out with carved plaster and peopled with hovering nymphs and cupids cavorting among painted clouds. Staircases, inside and out, were guarded by lions — stone ones, and wood, and plaster. Nowhere was the eye allowed to rest and draw breath, so to speak; everywhere it was urged on: Yes, but just look at *this!*

"It's — amazing," I said weakly, when she had finished showing me the pictures, head cocked to one side to invite comment. "I can't imagine how I've missed seeing it."

"You want to go out in the summer when the gardens is at their best. At least . . ."

She trailed off, her face threatening to crumple again, and I hurried into the breach. "Yes, well, so Bob got a job there. Who does he work for? Who owns the house now?"

"It's a Brocklesby, still, though I don't know as 'ee didn't change 'is name to that when 'ee come into the inheritance. 'Ee's a cousin of a cousin or somefink. The old geezer wot built it never 'ad no children — wot 'ee would own to — so it went to 'is brother's son, and it's been like that, down the years. 'Ardly never passin' straight down, but sideways, like. They don't run to marriage in that family. They all 'as their peculiarities, like, and this one — Sir Mordred, 'ee is — 'ee's the most peculiar of the lot."

Mordred? What a very odd name. Perhaps I'd misunderstood; Ada's accent broadens under the influence of stress. I'd ask Alan later; just now I was more interested in Sir Whatever's eccentricities. "Peculiar how?"

" 'Ee plays with toys. A grown man, and 'ee's sixty if 'ee's a day, spending all 'is time with fiddly little bits o' dolls' furniture and that. That's wot 'ee does to keep the 'ouse runnin'. They all 'as to 'ave somethin', don't they, to draw the tourists. They turns it over to the National Trust, or builds a zoo on the grounds, or claims it's 'aunted so the coach tours'll come. And Sir Mordred, 'ee 'as this collection of dolls' 'ouses, so when 'ee comes into this 'uge old 'ouse, 'ee brings 'em all in and sets up a Miniature Museum, and charges five quid a 'ead to see 'em."

"Five pounds! That's a lot, just to see a few dollhouses."

"Well, and there's the 'All itself, isn't there? And it ain't only a few bits. 'Ee 'as 'undreds of 'em, I reckon, all with furniture, and rugs and curtains and crockery and that, and some with dolls, too, queer stiff little 'uns. I seen some of 'em. Bob showed me. They was out in one o' the barns, where the old — where Sir Mordred was workin' on 'em, repairin' 'em and that. But we never touched nuffink, and Bob, 'ee don't know 'ow that tea set come to be in 'is pocket!"

We had come to the crux of it, finally. "Ah, a tea set. That's what Bob is accused of stealing, then? It seems like they're making a lot of fuss over a toy."

"It's old," said Ada. "Couple of 'undred years. Severs."

I blinked. "What severs what?"

"Severs china. You know. French."

19

It took me a moment, but I got it. "Oh, Sèvres! My word, you mean a miniature Sèvres tea set? I didn't know they ever made miniatures. How small?"

"I only seen it out in the barn, that once. It were in a 'ouse wot was being worked on. I'd reckon the tray is so big." Ada held her fingers about three inches apart. "And there's a china pot and sugar bowl and milk jug and all, and cups and saucers and even little silver spoons."

"Hmmm. Well, it sounds interesting, anyway. And it was found in Bob's pocket? What made anyone look?"

"I dunno. 'Ee didn't tell me when 'ee rung me up. 'Ee just said they found it, and said as 'ee were pinchin' it, and called the p'lice. But 'ee never!"

"Well, that's all right then," I said briskly. "You don't need to worry. We know Bob didn't really take it, so he'll be fine."

"But 'ow did it get in 'is pocket?" Ada wailed. " 'Ee says 'ee never put it there, and 'ee's never lied in 'is life. 'Ee 'as 'is faults, as I won't deny, but a liar 'ee ain't."

"That's the question, isn't it? And, Ada, I hate to say it, but the only answer I can think of is, somebody wanted to get Bob into trouble. So the question really is, who? And why?"

2

"That doesn't necessarily have to be the case, you know," said Alan. We were sitting at the kitchen table that evening, finishing pie and coffee and rehashing Bob's dilemma.

I had finally managed to reassure Ada, promised I would look into Bob's difficulties as soon as I could, and sent her home somewhat comforted. I had offered to drive her, but she had refused.

"You 'ates to drive; I'll be all right on me own."

"Maybe Alan —" I began, but she shook her head.

"Ta, but I don't want me neighbors to see me comin' 'ome with a p'liceman. It's one thing for Bob to be in jail. 'Ee's been there before now, sleepin' it off. But I never 'ad no truck with no p'lice, and when all's said and done Mr. Alan's a p'liceman, even if 'ee is ever so 'igh up."

Alan, although as high in rank as one could get in police administration, and very near retirement, is indeed a policeman. I smiled now, thinking of Ada's equating him with a constable on the beat, likely to disgrace her by association — Alan, who was on a first-name basis with the Dean and the Lord Mayor, among other Sherebury luminaries.

"What's funny?" he asked.

I told him, and he smiled, too. "She's right, though. A policeman I am and a policeman I remain, no matter how many years I've spent away from a beat. And I say again, you may have got hold of the wrong end of the stick. It's far more likely that someone else was stealing the tea set, had it in his hand, lost his nerve for some reason, and shoved it into Bob's pocket."

I frowned. "Alan, I really don't think so. Did I forget to tell you the thing was out in one of the barns? Apparently Brocklesby has set up a sort of workshop out there for repairing the houses and furnishings. They'd need work constantly, I should think, as tiny and fragile as they must be. But the thing is, what would anyone who didn't belong there be doing in the barn? The security must be pretty good, if the collection has any genuine value. The insurance people would require it, or they would in America, anyway."

"Oh, British underwriters are quite as security-minded as American ones, I assure you. Especially in recent years, since so many of Lloyd's underwriters lost their well-stuffed shirts in various disasters. So you're right; it makes a big difference that the theft was from a nonpublic area. But what could anyone have against a harmless soul like Bob Finch? He's surely never hurt anyone in his life."

"No, even in his cups he never picks fights, according to Ada. Just gets a bit lively and sings, she says. Maybe he kept someone staying in a pub awake too many nights." I smiled a little, trying to rid myself of a nagging sense of unease.

"Or piled up too big a tab for the publican's liking," Alan suggested gravely. "Or offended a brewery owner by drinking too much of the competitor's product. Although it is a trifle difficult to imagine what benefit any of those affronted parties would derive from Bob's arrest and incarceration. Dorothy, nothing makes sense, to be brutally honest, except to suppose that Bob lost his head and actually took the wretched thing!"

"And that makes no sense either," I argued, "even if one were prepared to suppose Bob would have done such a thing, which I am not. What would Bob do with a miniature tea set? He has no children. His mother is far too practical to want any such thing. And as for profiting from it — assuming it has some substantial value, which seems unlikely — how could Bob sell it? Let's suppose, for the sake of the argument, that it's rare enough to be worth a lot. In that case it'd be known to any dealer. Nobody reputable would touch it, and if you're going to suggest that Bob is involved with a network of professional fences, I simply refuse to listen!"

I finished a little more heatedly than I had intended. Alan grinned and put his hand over mine. "Always the defender of the underdog, aren't you, my dear? Very well, Bob is as pure as the driven snow, and as his mother says, 'ee never done it. That gets us back to where we began. Who did, and why?"

"At the moment, I don't have the foggiest idea. I only know I don't like the smell of it. I really think I'll have to go out there and get the lay of the land, and then maybe I can come up with some ideas. It sounds like an incredible place."

"It must be seen to be believed." Alan pushed his chair back from the table and stretched. "And even then, the mind boggles. I've not been since I was a boy, when the old sinner asked my family to tea for

24

some reason, but I distinctly recall having nightmares for weeks afterward. I do hope, my love, that you don't expect me to accompany you."

I squeezed his hand and stood up to clear the dishes. "Not on your life; you'd cramp my style. Once a p'liceman, always a p'liceman, remember? People see you coming and instantly try to remember how many parking tickets they've ignored, or wonder if someone saw them driving that night when they were a little sloshed. Nobody would say a word to me if you were around. No, but I would appreciate your driving me out, if there are more than two roundabouts between here and there." Driving in England is *my* nightmare; I've lived here well over a year now, but it doesn't seem to get easier.

"Driving lessons, first thing in the new year," said Alan firmly. "Until then, of course I'll drive you, and come to fetch you as well. I doubt anyone at the Hall would recognize me, but I'm delighted to have an excuse not to go." There was a pause. "I suppose you'd like me to see what's being done about Bob, meanwhile?"

I ignored the hesitation. "Ada and I would be very grateful," I said demurely, trying for an impish smile. It was evidently close enough; Alan grinned, stood, and gathered me up in a bear hug, and what we did for the rest of the evening has no bearing on this story. The dishes did not get washed.

In the morning Alan went off to his office as usual, but phoned a little later to say that Bob had not been charged, after all, partly because the police were inclined to believe his story, and partly because Brocklesby, with a change of heart, had decided he preferred not to pursue the matter. "He was upset at the time, he said, but the little trinket came to no harm, and perhaps some mistake was made, after all. And Bob had always been a good worker, and he was prepared to overlook the incident."

"Alan, that's very odd!" I said. "Why did he make such a fuss about it to begin with, then? And Ada mentioned something about his suspecting Bob of other thefts as well. You'd think he'd follow up. It's good news, I suppose, at least for Bob and Ada. But I'm still going to go out there. Something's going on, and I want to find out what."

"I must say," Alan remarked, "it's something of a relief to find you looking into something as frivolous as the theft of a toy instead of your usual murder and mayhem. I just hope — well, never mind. I asked my secretary to check the hours of the museum;

it's open every day but Monday from ten to six, and they serve tea. Shall I run you out after lunch, and meet you for whatever miserable fare they offer, at about — say, four or so?"

"Museum food — ugh! We can take a look, anyway, but if it's too awful we'll go to Alderney's." The tea shop in the Cathedral Close is one of our favorite places, a constant threat to my efforts to keep my plumpness from turning to plain old fat. On the days that I volunteer at the Cathedral Bookshop I'm all too apt to stop in at Alderney's for a bite before and/or after work. One of these days all those cream cakes are going to do me in. It might be wiser to have thin sandwiches and stale scones at Brocklesby Hall, after all.

The rain had stopped, but threatened to begin again at any moment. I was beginning to understand that the only predictable factor in English weather is its unpredictability, but these past few days we did seem to have settled into a stormy pattern. I poked my head out the door and squinted at the sky. Maybe there was time before the next downpour to carry out the next step in my plan. I shrugged into a sweater and trotted across my back garden to Jane's kitchen door.

Jane Langland is my best friend and chief source of information in Sherebury. It would be unkind to call her a gossip. The word implies a certain mean-spiritedness, a delight in the retailing of others' failings and misfortunes, and Jane doesn't have a mean bone in her body. She has, however, a keen interest in her fellow humans, and an encyclopedic knowledge about Sherebury and its inhabitants. She's a warm, sensible sort of person, so people confide in her. And although she respects those confidences, when I, as a newcomer, need to know about someone, she passes along tidbits, benignly filtered through her compassion and deep understanding of human foibles.

She opened the door before I got there. "Dorothy. Been expecting you. Cup of coffee? Just made some."

I never ask Jane how she knows things almost before they happen, but this time, grinning at the look on my face, she volunteered the information.

"Saw Margaret this morning at Matins."

Which explained everything. Margaret Allenby is the wife of the Dean of Sherebury Cathedral. Ada Finch cleans her house for her twice a week, and since Ada talks every minute, she would have told Margaret all about Bob's problems, including my

28

promise to look into them. Margaret often attends the weekday services in the cathedral, and so does Jane — so do I, for that matter. The place is next door, after all, and the choir is well worth hearing even if there were no other reason to go.

"So you want to know about Brocklesby," said Jane, setting coffee down in front of me.

"Among other things," I admitted. "How's Bob?"

"Hungover," said Jane succinctly.

"Oh, dear. I suppose he went on a real bender when the police sent him home. Only to be expected, really." I picked up my cup and took a sip. "My word, you make good coffee, Jane. My American friends think the English only know about tea."

"Used to be so. Coffee like dishwater. One thing we learned from the French. Credit where credit is due," she added with determined fairness. "All right, Mordred Brocklesby." She shook her head. "Odd sort of duck. Whole family is odd."

"Are there a lot of them, then? I had the impression they were a bit — scattered."

"Are — or were. Old Mordred is the last of the lot. No children, no brothers, no cousins — or no male ones, anyway. He was an only son of an only son, and his great-grandfather had just the one other boy."

"Who would have been," I said, frantically doing genealogical tables in my head, "Mordred's great-uncle — right?"

"Right. He was the one who owned the Hall before Mordred. Died at age ninety-seven. Talk was, he didn't want to leave the Hall to anyone. Had plans to turn it into a home for cats, but died before he could get through the bureaucratic maze."

"A cats' home? He liked cats?"

"Hated 'em. Hated his neighbor worse. Woman had asthma, terrified of cats."

"But that's awful! He could have killed the poor woman if he brought a bunch of cats into the neighborhood!"

"Mmm. Wanted to buy her property, enlarge his own. She wouldn't sell. Her estate might have."

"And he had the energy to engage in all this plotting and scheming and — and sheer malice — in his nineties? Amazing!"

"Family's always been long-lived. Flourish like the green bay tree."

"I can't imagine why he thought a feud was worth it, though, at his age. Oh, well. So Mordred inherited. Ada thought he changed his name when he came into the estate, but she also thought he was a more distant relation than he was, so I suppose she's wrong."

"Not exactly. He'd given up the name, but he had to take it back when he inherited. Been calling himself Pendragon."

"Surely not!"

Jane nodded, jowls quivering. Jane bears a distinct resemblance, in both appearance and manner, to the late Sir Winston Churchill, or else to the bulldogs she loves — if there's a difference. "Mordred part is real." She made a face. "The mother had a fixation on the Arthur legend, passed it on to her son."

"What an inheritance! But why such a nasty sort of name? I'm not thoroughly checked out in Arthuriana, but surely Mordred was the one who betrayed Arthur and spoiled everything in Camelot, wasn't he?"

Jane nodded. "Apparently Mum liked the villains best. Or else didn't like her children. There was a sister, too, named Morgana, but she died or something."

I shuddered at the idea of naming a daughter after a witch. "What did he get knighted for? Mordred, I mean. Ada said he was a 'Sir.' "

"Distinguished Service to the Arts," said Jane without so much as the ghost of a smile. Deadpan is the essence of British humor; it took me several months of living in Sherebury to be sure when someone was being funny.

"Yes, of course, but really . . ."

"His father made a packet in buttons or crisps or something — can't recall — and Mordred's devoted his life to spending it on dolls' houses. Donated so many of them to the V and A they had to do something for him."

"The Victoria and Albert? I didn't know they went in for that sort of thing." When Frank was still alive we used to enjoy going to the big London museum on our visits to England, but I didn't remember seeing any toys there.

"Not the V and A proper. Museum of Childhood, run by the V and A. Toys, dolls, largest collection of dolls' houses in the world — now."

"Oh. Okay, so Mordred became Sir Mordred because he gave them a lot of stuff. He must be a collector on a really huge scale — Ada says there are hundreds of houses at the Hall."

"Exaggeration. Few dozen houses, barns, whatever, I'm told. Lot of what they call room settings — boxes with a glass front, tiny furniture inside."

"And Brocklesby really spends all his time collecting this stuff?"

"And looking after it, and repairing it, and making it. Good craftsman, they tell me."

"Well, I can believe what everyone says about his being odd. I can't wait to see him in person. What's he like?"

Jane shrugged. "Don't really know him. A Londoner, only lived in the Hall three or four years. Don't care for the Hall myself. Never go out there."

"Why not? It looked interesting in Ada's pictures, if somewhat grotesque, architecturally speaking."

"Grotesque is the word. Just don't like the place, is all."

She shut her mouth firmly, and I looked at her in astonishment. Jane, as solid and sensible a person as I know, is not given to unexplained antipathies. "Oh, come on. You can't stop there. Is it haunted, or what?"

She shrugged and looked embarrassed. "There's an — atmosphere. If you believe in that sort of thing. Probably because everyone who's owned it has been unpleasant. Still contention and — mischief."

There was something in the way she said the word that resounded of the Litany. *From all evil and mischief; from the crafts and assaults of the devil . . .*

"What *do* you mean?"

She shrugged again. "Probably nothing.

33

Seeing bogeymen in my old age."

"Jane, if you see bogeymen, the rest of us need to be put in an asylum for not seeing them." I looked at her hard, but she would say no more. Eventually I gave up. "Well, I'm going out there this afternoon, unseen terrors or not. I'll report back."

"Yes. Be careful."

It had not been a reassuring conversation.

3

It was pouring pitchforks and hammer handles, as my Hoosier father used to say, when Alan came home for lunch.

"Shall we defer the Brocklesby Hall expedition?" he asked over his bowl of chili. Alan has developed a taste for American food, thank goodness, since it's what I know how to cook.

"Certainly not!" I replied indignantly. "You know perfectly well I want to go, never mind the weather."

"I had a suspicion, though it's not the best sort of day for a place like — however. You'd best put on wellies. If I remember correctly, the car park isn't paved."

To be on the safe side I donned not only Wellington boots but the full set of rain gear: yellow slicker, or oilskins as the English say, and the accompanying floppy yellow plastic hat. I looked like a large, elderly version of Paddington Bear. The hat certainly wasn't my usual style, but I wasn't about to risk one of my more frivolous creations in this weather.

It was a wise decision. Alan dropped me off as close to the door as he could, but I still had to slog through a good deal of mud, and the rain was pelting down. I rang the bell and waited.

The wait was long enough for me to conjure up a fine case of the horrors. From what little I could see of the house through the driving rain, it would have made a wonderful setting for a Gothic novel. The door itself, heavily carved, should, just about now, swing open on creaky hinges, and a Mrs. Danvers type should say, "Yes?," with a rising inflection, a lifted eyebrow, and a tone of infinite menace. I actually tried the handle, and was foolishly relieved when the door was properly locked. Telling myself not to be silly, I rang again.

The person who eventually answered did not in the least resemble the baleful housekeeper of *Rebecca*. She was young, pretty, and out of breath. "I'm so sorry! I was in another part of the house. We didn't really expect any visitors on such a frightful day."

"This is the Miniature Museum, isn't it?"

A fussy little man had bustled into the anteroom where I stood dripping, and now he winced visibly.

"Please!" he said in a high, pained voice. "Museum of Miniatures! We do have a min-

36

iature museum, indeed, rather a splendid one, with as fine a collection of original artwork as you will ever — but do come in! Your coat and hat will do nicely on the rack, thank you, and the boots — er — I'm afraid I have no slippers to offer you —"

"It's all right, I brought shoes. If there's a chair —"

"My dear lady! Of course, of course! Do forgive me!" He nodded imperiously to the young woman, who scurried away and came back with a folding chair.

I studied my host covertly while I accomplished the awkward business of changing out of very muddy boots. That he was my host I had no doubt. There is an indefinable look of calcified enthusiasm, a slightly demented glitter in the eye, that characterizes the truly fanatic collector, and this tubby little man, with his rather long, flyaway white hair and his pudgy but delicate hands, had all the stigmata. I wasn't sure whether he looked more like the first assistant elf in Santa's workshop, minus the beard, or one of those little cartoon demons with horns, tail, and red tights. The elf, I decided, but something of a thorn in Santa's side, perhaps. He would be good at working on tiny objects, but not fond of taking orders.

I stood, properly shod, and extended my

hand. "You must be Mr. — er — Sir Mordred Brocklesby, and my name is Dorothy Martin." Alan and I had agreed that it was more practical for me to keep my old name when we married; when an American marries an Englishman there are enough legal complications without a name change thrown in. And I'd been Dorothy Martin for over forty years; I wasn't sure I could adjust to Nesbitt. "I live in Sherebury," I went on, "but I've never managed to get out here to the Hall before. I certainly could have chosen a better day, couldn't I?"

"Not at all, not at all," said the elf. "I shall be pleased to devote myself entirely to you. I am indeed Mordred Brocklesby, and I am delighted to meet you." There was something so condescendingly regal about his manner I was half-surprised he didn't refer to himself as "One." I would have liked to meet the young woman, too, but Sir Mordred plainly considered her a part of the furniture. So I smiled at her and paid my admission fee while Sir Mordred studied the ceiling, apparently finding the exchange of money in his house to be indelicate.

He wasn't shy, however, about turning the house into a museum. Chattering away in a fluting alto, he led me through a doorway into the great hall of the house. "As you will see, I have devoted my house, and indeed my life, to the preservation of the art of the miniature. I refer, of course, not to small paintings, as the term is often used, but to dolls' houses and their appurtenances. You are interested in miniatures?"

"I confess, I know very little about them. I am interested in architecture, though, and I've heard a great deal about this house."

I raised my head as I spoke, to examine the carved and painted ceiling with its huge crystal chandelier, and ran smack into Sir Mordred, who had stopped dead in his tracks. I started to apologize, but he waved his hands in agitated fashion.

"No, no, it was my fault, but, my dear lady! I do *beg* of you not to mention this house in the same breath as the word 'architecture.' This is not architecture! This is a nightmare, an unharmonious horror, a travesty! Just *look* at it!" he wailed, pointing dramatically.

I obediently looked. He was pointing to the staircase, and it was worth looking at. I had never seen anything like the plaster work that adorned that staircase and its ceiling. Draperies, tasseled ropes, garlands, cherubs, satyrs, nymphs, the odd lion here and there, all in white and gold, and all jostling for space amidst the carved wood and marble beams, balusters, railings, and stair treads, not to mention an occasional mirror or trompe l'oeil window.

There was something oddly unpleasant about the effect. Were the proportions wrong? I didn't know enough about such things to be sure. Perhaps it was the leering expressions on the statuary, or the unexpected angles, or the streaky, rather warped mirrors. Or, more likely, I was still in my Gothic fantasy and was imagining the whole thing.

I blinked and looked back at Sir Mordred. "Yes. Well."

He nodded, satisfied. "If it were not for the space demands of the museum, I should never live here — never. Now you must allow me to show you some genuine architecture. Just through here, and I should advise you to avert your eyes from the visual discord on all sides."

We passed into a dark corridor which, ignoring Sir Mordred's advice, I studied with a sort of horrified fascination. The prevailing color scheme was dirty cream and faded blue, with murky touches of burgundy and bilious green. The ceiling was coffered, the walls were paneled below and bordered above, the arches —

Sir Mordred opened a door whose handle

was so ornate it must have been excruciating to grasp, and said, "Voilà."

The contrast could not have been greater. The room had been stripped down to plain white walls, dark plain wainscoting, dark floor. The modern track lighting looked extremely out of place until I shifted my gaze to what it was illuminating, and forgot everything else.

The entire center of the room was filled with one object behind a glass barrier. It was a model of a house, an enormous country mansion built to impress, to overwhelm, like Brocklesby Hall itself. But there the resemblance ended. This one was elaborate, yes, but gloriously, magnificently symmetrical. Towers, turrets, colonnades, windows all had a sense of rhythm, a feeling almost of poetry. The whole was executed with incredible attention to detail.

I peered through windowpanes no larger than my thumbnail, and saw draperies, tables, lighted lamps. As my amazement grew, so did a vague sense of familiarity. I looked up at Brocklesby, slightly dazed. "But this is incredible! I don't think I've ever seen such delicate workmanship. And surely it's —"

"Blenheim Palace." Brocklesby's face radiated pride and satisfaction. I've seen exactly the same look on a cat's face when it has killed something truly spectacular. "Half-inch scale. My crowning achievement."

"You don't mean to say you made this beautiful thing yourself!"

"The entire structure. I had a great deal of help with the furnishings, of course."

He moved to a wall, turned a key in an inconspicuous keyhole, and the exterior shell of the house — roof, walls, even the front steps — rose, attached to the ceiling by thin cables. The ground floor of the house lay revealed, decorated and completely furnished, down to a table set with an elaborate dinner for twelve — plates, cutlery, napkins, flowers, fruit in a silver epergne, soup in a china tureen . . .

I've never been to Blenheim, and have seen pictures only of the exterior, but I hadn't the slightest doubt that Sir Mordred's version was accurate to the smallest detail. My eyes moved from one room to another, marveling. The fireplaces were surmounted by overmantels holding lovely, tiny ornaments, and hung above with portraits, obviously in oil. Tiny tapestries adorned the walls, tiny statuary filled the corners. A gorgeous marble staircase led up to the next, hidden story.

"I have not yet furnished the upper stories

completely, alas," said Brocklesby. "I possess neither the skill nor the equipment to make such things as the silver tableware, or the crystal, nor am I an artist in oils or silk, and as you can imagine, these exquisite little things are very expensive to purchase. Unfortunately, I am not made of money, so I must go slowly. Nor have I been able, owing to considerations of space, to duplicate the kitchen and stable wings, nor the Marlborough Maze. One day, one day!" His eyes glittered as he turned the key again and the shell of the house gently subsided into place.

"As the gem of the collection, my Blenheim is normally the last display to be shown to the public, but I really could not let you suffer for one more moment the aesthetic indigestion induced by the architectural obscenity in which I am forced to live. Now, if you will follow me, we shall move to the proper beginning of the tour."

"But I shouldn't take your time," I protested. "I'm sure you don't usually show people around yourself." Actually, having to some extent taken the measure of Sir Mordred, I wanted to meet the rest of the establishment.

"You are quite correct. My time is fully occupied with the continuing efforts of acquisition, maintenance, and restoration. I hire several young people — university students, for the most part — to serve as guides. But I told them, or rather my curator, Mrs. Cunningham, told them not to come in today. They are paid by the hour, and there was simply no reason to waste the money on a day when we would have few guests. Miss — er — the young person who opened the door to you had already left her home for work, so I've set her to doing other chores."

There was real annoyance in his tone, and I marveled not only at the fact that he didn't know the poor girl's name, but at the ruthless thrift sometimes employed by the wealthy. That may, of course, be one reason why they're wealthy and I'm not.

Oh, well, might as well make the best of it. If I was to be honored, or burdened, with Sir Mordred's undivided attention for the rest of the afternoon, I'd find out what I could — guilefully. Until I had a better idea whether this was a case for Miss Marple, Sherlock Holmes, or Mata Hari, a devious approach seemed wise.

Flattery was almost always a good way to begin. "Well, I got the best of the bargain, then. I'm sure you know far more about the collection than any of the hired help."

He giggled, and expanded visibly. "I should do, shouldn't I, since I built or acquired every stick of it myself, over the course of the last thirty years. Now in this first room are the oldest houses of the collection, some of them quite crude, but of very great historic interest.

"This first house is German, probably made in the mid-sixteenth century, shortly after the very first dolls' house on record, the Duke Albrecht house. That one is no longer in existence, so that mine is quite possibly the oldest dolls' house in the world — certainly older than the 1617 Hainhofer farmyard or the 1600 Nuremberg house; in any case, the contents of that one are not all original. This is not the earliest known collection of miniatures, of course. For that we would have to go to the Egyptians and their models of boats, houses, furniture, and so on, made for the royal tombs. You can see some of those in the British Museum; none, unfortunately, are in the hands of private collectors."

Unfortunate, presumably, because that way Sir Mordred would never be able to buy them.

We went on from room to room of the mansion, seeing everything from complete dollhouses to cabinets with small furniture arranged on the shelves. German houses, Dutch houses, English houses. There were the room settings Jane had described, everything so perfectly to scale that I forgot I was looking at miniatures. There were wooden houses with rather primitive furniture, tin houses with the furniture painted on the walls. There were farms and stables and garages and shops, zoos and circuses, and one exquisite little church.

Sir Mordred prattled on enthusiastically about dates, owners, and historic significance. I stopped listening and simply gazed in astonishment. It had never before occurred to me that dollhouses could be so detailed, so crammed with minute objects. The kitchens, especially, fascinated me, with their dozens of plates, pots, ladles, molds, utensils, all in copper or pewter or brass, all shining.

"How in the world do you keep them polished?" I asked, interrupting a scholarly lecture on the Nuremberg guilds of the eighteenth century.

"Keep them — oh. The metal objects. They are lacquered, I am sorry to say. It is not proper practice, from the standpoint of verisimilitude. Mrs. Cunningham scolds me, but there is no other way to preserve them from oxidation. They can be polished only with very harsh chemicals, which is unthinkable, of course, or a polishing cloth, which would be impracticable, given their size and the quantity of objects we have. Now, as I was saying . . ."

He droned his way on, but eventually we arrived at the crossing of two hallways, with a few chairs against the walls. Sir Mordred had progressed to the subject of English miniatures. I ignored his hand, pointing the way down yet another interminable corridor, and sank into a rather hard chair, barely managing to suppress a sigh. He stood, still talking, bouncing on the balls of his feet. "Of course, the finest English house is unavailable to the private collector: Queen Mary's Dolls' House, on display at Windsor Castle. You really must see it. It is overelaborate, true, and quite new, twentieth century, you know, but there are some very fine pieces — furniture, books, and so on — especially commissioned for Her Majesty.

"And speaking of very fine houses, you are American, are you not, my dear lady?"

An unnecessary question; my accent is unmistakable. I nodded, with a questioning frown.

"Do you live anywhere near Chicago?" He pronounced the *Ch* as in cheese.

"I live in Shferebury now." I'd already told him that, but people don't always pay attention. "I used to live in Indiana, not too far from Chicago." About 200 miles, but I never say that; to an Englishman accustomed to an island something over 700 miles long, 200 miles doesn't sound like "not too far."

"Ah, well, then you must know the Thorne Miniature Rooms and Colleen Moore's Fairy Castle." He looked so expectant that I hated to disappoint him. His face crumpled when I shook my head.

"I'm afraid we — my late husband and I — didn't get in to Chicago very often." A lie, but well-meant.

"But surely you know the Chicago Art Institute!"

"Yes, of course."

"And you truly didn't know that it houses a very fine collection of miniature room settings? Nor that the Museum of Science and Industry has perhaps the most elaborate dolls' house in the world?" Overcome with shock, he sank into a chair, shaking his head.

"Have pity on my ignorance, Sir Mordred! I thought dollhouses were something for children to play with; I didn't know they could be works of art."

He beamed and forgave me. "We must see to your education, then. When we finish with the museum, perhaps you would care to see my work in progress. I don't usually show my workrooms to the public, but —"

I jumped at it. "Your workrooms! How exciting! Do you have some marvelous new project going?"

"Not at the moment, alas. Routine maintenance, for the most part. The antique houses, you see, need constant care. They tend to come to bits as glues dry over the years, so I must rehang wallpaper, relay floor coverings, replace table legs, and so forth. In addition, many articles of furniture have gone missing, some by the natural attrition of the ages and some, I regret to say, to pilfering."

"Really?" I packed as much incredulity into the word as I could muster. "I wouldn't have thought that was possible, what with the barriers and so on. And surely not worth the trouble and risk. I mean, as fascinating as these little things are, they can't be worth all that —"

I stopped at the look of horror on Sir Mordred's face. His eyes bulged; his cheeks turned purple. I thought he was ill.

"Are you all right? Shall I —"

"My dear madam!" he gasped. "I cannot

believe . . . you *do* want educating! I am forbidden by my insurers to divulge the value of my collection, but if I tell you that I have seen items of miniature furniture offered for sale in London — new work, mind you — at close to one thousand pounds —"

It was my turn to gasp.

"— you may have some idea of the value of exquisite antique miniatures. I think I may be allowed to give you one small example. I have in my collection" — he hesitated a moment and then went on — "a French tea set, Sèvres porcelain with silver spoons, complete and in perfect condition. It was made in 1770 as a wedding present for Marie Antoinette. I — um — feared that it had gone missing, and had that been the case, I should have had to make a — well, let us simply say, a very substantial claim on my insurance. Not, of course, that the tea set would have been replaceable at any price — it is documented to be the only one of its kind in existence, not to mention its history — but you do see, don't you?"

He had gone on talking long enough for me to get my breath back. "Sir Mordred, I'm — I'm flabbergasted. I simply had no idea! But what a good thing it wasn't missing after all! Had it been misplaced, or — ?"

"No, no," he said quickly. "A misunderstanding, quickly cleared up. But as I was saying, most of the missing furnishings have simply disappeared over the many, many years that the houses have been in existence. It does leave the rooms rather bare in some instances, and so, for the sake of the children who come to see my treasures, I attempt to fill in the gaps with pieces of my own manufacture, in the proper period, of course. I am very careful always to mark them conspicuously with my own hallmark, so that there will be no question in future about their provenance." He sat up, reached into his breast pocket, and drew out a small object. "This is one I've only just completed for one of the eighteenth-century French houses. I was about to put it in its place when you arrived."

He dropped an object in my hand and I marveled. It was a clock, a grandfather clock in an elaborately carved case, about seven inches long by an inch or so in cross section. At the top a fretwork of wooden lace surrounded the carefully painted and gilded clock face with its minute Roman numerals and tiny, fragile hands. Below, weights hung from slender golden chains and an elaborate pendulum swung free.

I handed it back to him, afraid to hold it,

awe stamped on my face.

He smiled. "It doesn't keep time, of course. I'm not a watchmaker. I might have put in a quartz movement, but I rebelled at the anachronism. The hands are properly mounted, however, so I can set them to any time I choose. Shall we say teatime?" He adjusted the hands with one delicate finger to four o'clock.

"Now, my dear lady, perhaps we should continue. There is a great deal still to see, the miniature museum, and —"

A door banged somewhere nearby. Sir Mordred stopped talking as if a switch had been flipped, peered down the hall, and then stood, quickly replacing the little clock in his pocket. Heavy footsteps sounded and a woman appeared at the corner.

A hundred years ago she would have been described as "a fine figure of a woman." Today the kind term would be "queenly"; of unkind terms there are many. Tall, with iron-gray hair pulled into an uncompromising bun, she was dressed in unrelieved black, which may have been intended to minimize her rigidly controlled bulk. It certainly did nothing for her sallow complexion.

"Ah, Mrs. Lathrop." Sir Mordred's voice came out in a squeak. "May I present Mrs.

52

— er? This is Mrs. Lathrop, my house-keeper."

"Dorothy Martin," I said, smiling.

She inclined her head perhaps half an inch, then turned to Sir Mordred and favored him with a smile that displayed a superbly crafted set of white, even teeth. "You have not, I trust," she said in a voice whose steely quality was not quite hidden, "forgotten we were to meet this afternoon about the dinner."

"No. No, indeed! I was just taking my leave — you must forgive me, Mrs. — er — Martin, a matter of a fund-raising function, I must —"

"Of course." My smile was just as wide as the gorgon's, and my teeth, if not quite as perfect, had the advantage of being original equipment. Acting on mischievous impulse, I loaded my voice with honey and put my hand on his arm. "I don't mean to detain you, but let me just ask you where I could learn more about miniatures. I'd like to be less ignorant by my next visit. Are there shops, or maybe the library . . ."

"But, my dear Mrs. Martin, you must use my own library." He gave my hand a little squeeze. "It is open to anyone who wishes to do research, and you will find it most complete. You're welcome to browse now, if you like, and Mrs. Cunningham will be happy to help you. It's just off the great hall, to your left as you enter from the corridor."

"That's in — let me see, which direction —"

" 'Ullo, 'ullo, 'ullo!" The nasal voice reverberated from marble surfaces, creating unpleasant echoes. "Naow, this *is* cozy, innit? All one 'appy family, are we?"

I removed my hand from Sir Mordred's arm and looked at the interruption.

He was youngish, in his late twenties I guessed. His hair, what there was of it, was dead white, sticking straight up in spikes. The left half of his head was bald. He wore a large safety pin in one ear, a black ring in his nose, and a silver stud in his lower lip. His leather vest flapped unbuttoned over a naked, hairless chest; torn and filthy jeans hung low enough to reveal a large portion of grayish shorts. An odor of unwashed flesh and marijuana surrounded him; the cigarette he was smoking at present, however, smelled more conventional.

"What are you doing here, Claude?" Sir Mordred's voice rose to an agitated squeak. "I thought you were in London. And smoking is not allowed in the museum; you know that. There are signs —"

"Aaoow, ever so sorry, I must've forgot,"

said Claude in a high, affected voice, blowing smoke in Sir Mordred's face. "Come to visit me lovin' mum, 'aven't I?" He smirked at Mrs. Lathrop. "Me and mum need to 'ave a little chat, don't we? Alone," he added pointedly, dropping the fake Cockney for a moment.

I know when I'm upstaged. "Yes, well, I'm sure I can find the library, thank you so much, you've been most . . ." I gabbled, and beat a rapid retreat.

4

I waited until I was out of sight, around a corner or two, before I paused to regroup.

I didn't really want to see the library. I had, truthfully, developed an interest in dollhouses, but not so great a one that I wanted to spend the rest of the afternoon reading about them. I'd intended, mostly, to irritate Mrs. Lathrop, and I hadn't achieved even that unworthy ambition; the egregious Claude had provided far more irritation than I was capable of in my very worst efforts.

However . . .

It wasn't even three o'clock, and I didn't intend to look at yet more dollhouses for an hour. For one thing, I was developing a fine case of museum feet, and for another, I didn't want to run into Claude when I was alone. Call me a coward, but young thugs have always terrified me, and though Claude wasn't all that young, his thuggery looked as though it had survived the aging process remarkably well. The library sounded like a safe haven; I couldn't imagine that scholarly pursuits came high on Claude's list. And Mrs. Cunningham might be glad of a little company on a dreary day.

In other words, she might be persuaded to talk. So far I had learned very little of interest. True, Claude looked capable of any amount of skullduggery, but there wasn't much point in identifying a villain until I knew for certain that villainy was afoot. For that certainty, I needed more information.

I set out to find the library.

It took some searching. Brocklesby Hall was not laid out in any logical fashion, or if it was, the logic escaped me. Corridors seemed to appear in the oddest places and lead nowhere in particular. I hadn't paid much attention when Sir Mordred was shepherding me around, and now I couldn't get my bearings.

It finally occurred to me, as I turned down a corridor I had certainly traversed at least once before, that the original eccentric Brocklesby had built himself an instantly old house, as he had caused instant ruins to be erected in the gardens. A genuine manor house would have additions here and there, new wings tacked on over the centuries; therefore, his house would have wings everywhere, and in various styles, at that. This particular one was done in high Gothic, with pointed arches everywhere and sinister little gargoyles leering nastily from dark corners.

The effect was not comforting. I shuddered. Jane had a point about this house.

Just when I had decided I was doomed to roam the house forever, like poor Charlie on the MTA, I rounded a corner and found myself in the great hall, next to a set of heavy oak doors sporting carved books as decorations. Library, I deduced brilliantly, and pushed down on one of the brass griffin handles.

It was a big, gloomy room, octagonal in shape and Gothic, again, in design. Perhaps on a brighter day the narrow lancet windows would have admitted some light, but not much, since they were almost entirely obscured by heavy velvet draperies of a color I couldn't determine. Books in dark bindings lined the walls from floor to high ceiling; bookshelves filled most of the floor space as well, with a few tables and chairs crammed in. The green-shaded lamps on the tables and the heavy brass chandelier hanging from the ceiling provided just enough light for me to see the desk in the center of the room and the person seated behind it, her eyes fixed on a computer screen.

If I had entertained a mental image of Mrs. Cunningham, curator for a bunch of dollhouses, this person didn't match it. No untidy gray hair or granny glasses, no sensible suit with a frilly white blouse, not even a three-year-old Laura Ashley print. This woman couldn't be anywhere near thirty yet, and her no-nonsense white shirt, a couple of sizes too big for her, was hanging over a pair of blue jeans. Her hair was untidy enough, certainly, but it was a bright shade of copper. And she wore no ring. Divorced, I gathered.

I cleared my throat. Not even looking up from her work, she spoke indistinctly around the pencil clenched between her teeth. "Sorry, this part of the house is not open to the public. The lavatories are through the corridor to your right, then down the stairs. Follow the signs." She consulted the card in her hand and clicked the mouse.

"Thank you," I said apologetically, "but I think I'm in the right place. This is the library? And you are Mrs. Cunningham?"

She looked up, curiosity alive in her blue eyes. "I am. And you are . . . ?"

"My name is Dorothy Martin, and Sir Mordred said I could do a little browsing in here. I won't interrupt your work, if you don't mind my poking around."

"Oof!" She pushed the mouse aside with an explosive little sigh. "A pleasure to meet you, and I'm delighted to be interrupted. It's boring work I'm doing at the moment, trying to get this new program up and running, and I feared no one would pop in today and I'd be chained to this computer. I'm Meg." She held out her hand and grinned. The freckles on her nose crinkled appealingly.

"Dorothy then, please," I said, returning the hand and the smile, "and you were very nearly right. I took a wrong turn somewhere and thought I'd be lost till my bones bleached. This is quite a house."

She raised her eyes to the ceiling and ran both hands through her hair (which didn't improve its appearance). "A madhouse — in every sense of the word. You're American, aren't you?"

I admitted it. "And you're surely Irish."

The grin grew broader. "Exactly one quarter. Except when I'm mad and it all comes to the top. I'm an O'Brien by rights; my father's father was from Wicklow."

"But I know Wicklow! My late husband and I visited there once on a brief tour of Ireland. Beautiful, beautiful country."

"It is that. Terribly poor, though. Are you

over here on another visit? Not the time of year I'd have chosen; the weather . . ." She gestured to the windows; the rain streamed down.

"No, actually I've moved to England and remarried. I've lived here in Sherebury for well over a year, in fact, but I somehow never made it out here to the Hall. I agree I chose an awful day."

"Well, now you're here, what can I do for you? Is there anything special you were looking for, or do you just want to see what's here?"

I hesitated. I could bluff Sir Mordred, but this woman looked intelligent — and perceptive. I opted for honesty, at least modified honesty. "I'll come clean. I'm here under false pretenses."

She laughed delightedly. "All right, then, let's see. Are you a CIA spy, looking for secrets hidden in dolls' houses? Or are you trying to sell me something? I warn you, I've no money at all, personally, and Sir Mordred won't spend his on anything but miniatures."

"Neither of the above. It's just that I'm not really here to use the library. I don't know a thing about miniatures, and I probably wouldn't understand your books. I ducked in partly to find somebody to talk to in this mausoleum, and partly to escape a couple of unpleasant characters."

She quirked her eyebrows. "Not dear old Mordie? He's more than a trifle odd, certainly, but . . ."

"He certainly is. Are all miniature collectors like that?"

"No, he's an aberration. Most of them are perfectly delightful people, adults who haven't forgotten what it was like to be a child."

"I'm glad to hear it. Sir Mordred was my introduction to the breed, and . . . anyway, he didn't bother me. It was the housekeeper and — I don't know if you've met her son —"

Meg's grin vanished. She sat bolt upright and slapped both hands on her desk, hard. *"Damn!"*

"Oh," I observed mildly. "You *have* met him, then."

She didn't even smile. "I have. And to know him is to loathe him." A thought seemed to strike her; she bounded out of her chair. "Where did you see him? In the car park?"

"No, in the house, but don't expect me to know where. This place is worse than any maze I've ever — no, wait, I *can* tell you. We were — let's see — we'd just left the room with the miniature circus, I think. There's a sort of lounge there, where two hallways cross?"

Long before I'd finished talking she had loped across to the door and turned a large key. "Right. What's he doing here?" she demanded.

This was an extraordinary conversation to be having with a total stranger. "He said he'd come to talk to his mother, but he sounded — oh, it was probably my imagination, but he sounded almost threatening, somehow." I shuddered. "I was scared stiff of him, actually. I ran like a rabbit."

"And quite right, too." She sighed and sat back down at her desk with a plop. I glanced at the locked doors and then back at her.

"Oh, *Lord!*" she said, running her hands through her hair again. "I don't need this, I thought he was safe away in London, I —" She broke off and looked at me doubtfully. "Look, I'm sorry. I go off the deep end sometimes. This is my problem, not yours, and I'm probably making too much of it."

"Well, I'm not sure of that. Claude looked to me like a first-class heel."

"If he is, it's the only thing about him that's first class," she said emphatically. "He's not even a particularly successful crook, but he's good at making trouble. Every time he's in the house there are ructions of one sort or another. Oh, I can deal with him; I just don't like the idea of him sneaking up on me. That's why —" She jerked her head toward the door. "Anyway, I didn't mean to lock you in. If you want to go —"

"Thank you, but if I'm not bothering you, I'd just as soon stay. To tell the truth, the more locked doors there are between me and that not-so-juvenile delinquent, the better I like it." Well, that *was* the truth, if only part of it. I reminded myself that I was there for a purpose, from which I had so far been distracted. Was there a way to keep her talking without being too obvious about it? "Besides, my husband is meeting me here later, so I might as well stick around. But I really mustn't keep you from your work." I glanced at the screen. Ah, that was it! "A new program, you say?" I asked innocently.

I know almost nothing about computers, but I do know that people who are good at them can't resist telling you all about whatever they're doing. Meg, who could change moods faster than anyone I'd ever met, positively leapt at the distraction.

"Yes, it's a new cataloguing system for the collection, and it's going to make things much easier, once I get all the revolting data entered." She swung around to her desk.

"Look, I'll pull up a template for you. See, the fields are already set up and labeled; all I have to do is fill them in. Here's one that's completed, with the cross-references to the individual items . . ."

She clicked away with her mouse, layering one incomprehensible display atop another.

"Yes, I see what you mean," I lied earnestly. "Very impressive, indeed. I can see how entering the data must be tiresome, though, with so many thousands of separate items."

"That's the snag, of course, especially when Sir Mordred keeps on changing —"

She stopped abruptly, and I chuckled.

"It's all right, you don't have to say it. Even I had the impression Sir Mordred was — shall we say — tampering with history a little now and then. I always thought museums did as little restoration as possible."

Meg sighed gustily. "*Proper* museums. But here, I'm afraid — not that the work isn't well done; he's extremely skilled. And of course it's *his* collection, so in a way I have no right to complain. But as curator I can't help being annoyed when an eighteenth-century baby house is fitted out with as many twentieth-century reproductions, or antiques from another source, as miniatures that came with the house originally — and nothing to show which are which. The guides do tell people, of course; it's part of their speech. At least, they do if I'm told. Sometimes he puts things in the houses, things he's made or bought, and forgets to tell me."

She reminded me of a kitten, young and fluffy and extremely serious about her own importance. I hid my smile. "He did strike me as being somewhat absentminded. Did he tell you about the clock?"

"Clock?"

"He's just finished a grandfather clock for — let's see, I think he said one of the French rooms. I forget which century."

"A long-case clock," Meg corrected automatically, shaking her head with exasperation. "Probably for the Marie Antoinette house — he's nearly finished restoring it. He would have told me eventually, I suppose. He's always frightfully apologetic and promises never to do it again."

"It's a beautiful piece of work."

"Yes, it would be." She sounded depressed.

"He also mentioned some thefts," I said tentatively.

"Nonsense! He's simply lost things and doesn't want to admit it. I've never believed in the thefts; the security is too good." She frowned at the screen, entered a word or two, and looked back up at me.

I was forced to take the hint. "Heavens, my dear, I said I wouldn't take up your time and I've done nothing else. You won't mind if I look around?"

"I do have to get this done, I'm afraid, though I'd rather talk. Feel free." She waved an airy hand and bent back to her work.

I wandered to a bookshelf and pulled down a volume at random. Taking it to a half-hidden table, I sat down and tried to think.

I'd gotten all I could out of Meg for now, it seemed, but friendly relations had been established, and I could find an excuse to try again. And if I were to accomplish anything, I'd certainly have to try again. So far I had very little material to ponder. In fact, the afternoon had produced no information except that Mrs. Cunningham didn't believe in any thefts, and that she disapproved of her employer and feared his housekeeper's son. The latter was probably irrelevant, since Claude had presumably been in London when the incident with the tea set occurred. Oh, yes, the tea set, that was another piece of information: It was worth a lot of money. But, I reminded myself, mostly because of its historical background, which also made it virtually unsaleable.

I gave it up. Inspiration might strike later. Meanwhile, Alan would be another half hour at least, and my book was copiously illustrated and unexpectedly interesting. I read on . . .

The knock on the door, when it came, startled me considerably; I dropped my book. The knock came again, louder.

With a glance my way, Meg went to the door. "Yes?" she said. "Who is it?"

I was also apprehensive about the answer. From my secluded corner I could hear no more than a murmur through the heavy oak panels, but Meg's shoulders relaxed and she opened the door. A man slipped inside.

Surely I only imagined that the room became a little brighter when he entered. Maybe it had something to do with the look on Meg's face. Certainly the man's face was as dark as any thundercloud.

"He's gone," he said briefly. "Back to London. I thought you'd want to know. Now listen, Meg —"

She gestured toward me in my corner, just a nod, but the man lowered his voice. I retrieved my book and studied the two of them over the top of it.

He looked like a gardener. I would have bet he was Bob's boss, probably doing odd jobs inside on a day like this. His checked shirt and worn corduroy pants and tanned face spoke of the earth and the sun; his huge hands were made for handling a spade. And not only his hands were huge. He was constructed on a large scale altogether, including his deep voice, which was rising again.

". . . won't have it, I say! How can you —"

Meg said something, briefly and very quietly, that shut him up completely. He shot a furious glance in my direction; I ducked down behind my book and heard the door slam.

I stood, a little creakily — the chair was very hard — and walked across the room.

"That, I gather, was a friend of yours," I said.

Meg glared at the door through which he had passed. "Friend, ha! He can be so —" She shook her head in angry frustration and took a deep breath. "Anyway, Claude's left, thank God, so you can stop pretending to read that book, and leave." She clapped her hand to her mouth. "Oh, I didn't mean that the way it sounded! Please don't —"

I laughed; I couldn't help it. "My dear girl, I, too, suffer from the habit of speaking first and thinking second. It isn't exclusively the province of the Irish, nor, I'm sorry to tell you, of the young. I know what you meant, and I was about to leave anyway. It's almost four o'clock, and my husband is joining me here for tea. So I'll scoot for the tearoom, if you can show me —"

"But you can't!" she said, dismay in her voice. "It isn't open today! With the terrible weather, we — Mordie said I should put off the tearoom volunteers . . ."

"Oh. Oh, dear. Well, then, I'd better go out and wait for Alan, so he won't bother to come in."

I peered out the window. I could see, through the trees, a pond that was rapidly becoming a lake.

"Yes, but it's pouring, and — look, I've an idea." She hesitated for a moment, then made up her mind. "Mrs. Hawes, the cook, does tea for the staff. Why don't you and your husband join us? There'll be plenty of food, if you don't mind eating in the kitchen."

"Well —"

"Please. I'd enjoy your company, and anyway, I do *not* want to have to deal with Mrs. Lathrop alone. I need to try to keep the right side of her, and with guests, she won't be quite so . . ."

That settled it. I hated to disappoint Meg, whom I was beginning to like a good deal, but tea and polite conversation in Mrs. Lathrop's company — no thank you. I started to refuse the invitation, when somewhere in the distance I heard the shrill summons of an electric bell, and Meg brightened.

"That'll be your husband, I'm sure, and you wouldn't want to push him out into the wet again, would you now?"

She smiled, and those Irish eyes did it. She managed with a melting glance to convey that she would be devastated if I turned her down, and overjoyed if I accepted. I gave in. Alan would provide moral support, after all, and I might get in some useful conversation, even with the gorgon around. I went out to tell my long-suffering husband what was going on.

"I don't know what Sir Mordred is going to think of this arrangement," I said in an undertone. Alan also looked dubious as Meg led us to the kitchen.

It was a cavernous room in the semi-basement, the high windows admitting little light even on the best of days, one suspected. On a rainy November afternoon, the atmosphere was so shadowy I was sucked back into my horror movie fantasy. I half-expected to see great torches stuck up in iron brackets on the walls, or sconces with

71

dripping, sputtering candles. They might, at that, have been an improvement on the electric lights, single bulbs dangling from the ceiling on long wires, their dim rays obscured by little paper shades in an unfortunate blue-green that turned the air the color of dirty water.

We need not have worried about Sir Mordred's opinion; he was not, it seemed, to be present. "Oh, no," said Meg, her eyes raised expressively heavenward. "He takes his tea in his office. A bit lonely if you ask me, but he's far too grand to mix in with the rest of us. No, with so few here today it'll just be Mrs. Lathrop and us. And Richard, of course." Her eyes dropped. "Do be careful; the floor is a trifle uneven I'm afraid."

We were shown to a large round oak table, covered in the kind of plush cloth I thought had gone out of fashion at the end of the last century. Its color, somewhere between moss and mud, fit nicely into the prevailing decorating scheme. I stole a glance at Alan, who shrugged eloquent shoulders behind Meg's back and held out a straight, hard chair for me.

"They're more comfortable than they look," Meg said in an undertone. "Wicker seats, and unless you're unlucky enough to land one of the frayed ones, not too bad. And," she went on in a suddenly louder voice, "I'm sure Mrs. Hawes is giving us something marvelous to eat."

The lady in question clumped to the table as Meg finished speaking, a huge tray in her muscular arms. The sound she made as she put it down just escaped being a grunt.

"Not what I'd have done if anybody had bothered to tell me we were having guests," she said, frowning portentously.

The tray was laden with sandwiches, scones, and a large fruit cake from which a few slices had been invitingly cut. We hastened to voice appreciation, and Meg attempted to placate. "But you've given us a feast, as usual, Mrs. Hawes."

She sniffed. "And far more than is needed, as nobody bothered to tell me most of the staff wasn't here today, neither." In heavy silence she brought another tray, with a teapot and its satellites, as well as large bowls of strawberry jam and clotted cream.

"I did mention something to Mrs. Lathrop," Meg whispered, "but —"

Mrs. Lathrop chose that moment to make her entrance. The murky atmosphere did nothing to flatter her; nor did what was obviously a full-blown snit. Pushing the kitchen door open so hard it slammed against the wall, she approached the table, lips pressed together, breath coming in heavy gusts.

"I seem," she said glacially, "to be intruding. I was under the impression that this was staff tea, but I gather it is a party."

Alan stood courteously; I tried to smile. Meg, however, straightened up and met the steely glare with lifted chin and a glare of her own. The Irish was coming to the top.

"These are my guests, Mrs. Lathrop," she said, the edge in her voice daring the housekeeper to speak. "Sit down and let me pour you some tea and introduce Mr. and Mrs. — Martin, I believe it is? This is Mrs. Lathrop, Sir Mordred's housekeeper."

"We've met," I said sweetly. I would have gone on to correct Alan's name, but he stepped on my foot and said, "I'm delighted to meet you, Mrs. Lathrop. Thank you for letting us share this excellent tea." He extended his hand, smiling blandly. Mrs. Lathrop hesitated, then half-surrendered to his charm.

"Hmmph," she replied graciously, plopping down in her chair with an audible creak of corsets. "A better tea than you'd have got at that tearoom, I will say that for Mrs. Hawes. And free as well." She clamped her excellent teeth down on a ham sandwich.

I met Alan's eye and then looked quickly away before we both disgraced ourselves.

The food was delicious, but the atmosphere was not conducive to enjoying it. I'd downed one sandwich and was reaching for a scone when several more people came into the kitchen. Most of them headed for the other table, where Mrs. Hawes presided. One of the young women was the one who had opened the door to me; the other two, who looked like teenagers, I assumed were maids. But the last one in the door was the giant in checked shirt and old cords who strode to our table and sat down without a word to anyone.

Meg looked at him the way she might have greeted a cockroach in her scone, but her manners were excellent, even when her heritage was showing. "Richard," she said, widening her mouth in a splendid imitation of a smile, "I'd like you to meet Mr. and Mrs. Martin. This is Richard Adam, our gardener."

He glowered at both of us, nodded curtly, and helped himself to several sandwiches, which he proceeded to devour in silence.

I cleared my throat. The sound echoed in the vast room. "Who is the young woman over there in the red sweater?" I asked brightly. "She opened the door for me, but I never caught her name."

"That's Susan — Susan Eggers," answered Meg. "She's a university student, one of our best guides. She lives in Little Denholm, so she'd left for work this morning before I could ring her and tell her not to come in. Mordie was annoyed, but agreed she could help me with the computer project. I've had her running about all day checking accession cards against the collection." She laughed, without much amusement. "It helps — somewhat — with the problem we were discussing earlier."

She had spoken in a low tone, but Mrs. Lathrop caught the last remark. She chewed industriously and swallowed before taking a deep breath that visibly lifted her imposing bosom. "If," she said ponderously, "you are once again referring to Sir Mordred's lovely work, I wonder if it's quite appropriate for an employee to pass judgment on her employer's habits." She took a healthy swig of tea. "Of course, as a mere employee myself, perhaps it is not my place to judge."

Really, conversation was hard going in this crowd! I cast about for something to keep the ball rolling, and hit on the two maids, eating their food in subdued fashion under the eagle eye of Mrs. Hawes at the other table.

"Are the two girls your only help in the

house, Mrs. Lathrop? Aside from Mrs. Hawes, I mean? This seems a very large house to run with so few . . ." I ran down. Mrs. Lathrop's gray gimlet eyes were regarding me bleakly.

"The young persons to whom you refer are indeed the sole indoor *staff* whom I *supervise,* madam," she replied. "I do not, of course, know what sort of household you are accustomed to in America," — she made it sound like a third-world country — "but in the household of a gentleman like Sir Mordred a housekeeper does not do the dusting herself. I'm sure you will excuse me." She picked up several scones, dropped them into her pocket, and stalked off, once more banging the kitchen door against the wall. It swung creakily for several seconds after she left, back and forth, back and forth.

"Goodness," I finally said when I was sure she wasn't coming back. "It's a wonder the door has survived. What set her off, Meg? Was it calling the maids 'girls'? I didn't mean anything demeaning, it's just that they're so young. Or is a small staff somehow a reflection on her status —"

"No, no," Meg said, her shoulders beginning to shake. "No, it was your calling them 'help.' It implied that she, Mrs. Lathrop, actually did some of the work herself, whereas —"

She succumbed to a fit of silent laughter, finally blowing her nose and wiping her eyes. She looked furtively at the other table and almost collapsed again.

"Look how scandalized Mrs. Hawes is! She'll tell Mrs. Lathrop I laughed at her, and then the Lathrop may really get me sacked. At the very least, she'll make sure life won't be worth living around here for quite a while."

"And when was it ever?" growled the gardener. He pushed back his chair with a loud scrape and followed Mrs. Lathrop out the door.

5

"Well, what did you think of all that?" I demanded as Alan and I made our way back up the long Brocklesby Hall drive.

He was silent for a moment, frowning as he eased the car up the muddy, rutted lane. "I've not changed my opinion of the house," he said at last. "Quite definitely nightmare material. And — there are undercurrents, wouldn't you say?"

"Tidal waves, I'd call them. Not being given to English understatement." I told him about Claude, and Meg's fear of him. "It would be a help to know why," I said, glancing meaningfully at his profile. "She implied he'd been in trouble — I assume with the police. I wouldn't mind knowing where he was yesterday, either."

Alan nodded. "I could find out, probably, at least about his record. What else struck you?"

"Well, the household is an odd sort of setup, don't you think? Sir Mordred must be a real tightwad to run the place on such a mingy little staff."

"I suspect he spends every penny on that collection of his."

"Oh, yes, Meg said as much, come to think of it. You know, Alan, I'd forgotten how passionate collectors can be, and how single-minded. It's almost frightening. I'm sure he loves his miniatures more than anything else — or anyone."

"Mrs. Lathrop thinks so, too," said Alan, nosing the car out past the huge clumps of dripping rhododendrons and craning his head both ways before turning onto the main road.

"Mrs. Lathrop! What d'you mean?"

"Didn't you notice? If there does not beat beneath that ample bosom the throbbing pulse of unrequited love, my years of training in observation have been in vain."

"Goodness! What *have* you been reading, Barbara Cartland? You could just be right, though, even if your prose has turned somewhat purple. I thought that little outburst of hers was just a demonstration of authority, but it makes more sense your way. And it could be one reason why she's so hateful to Meg — who represents, to Mrs. Lathrop, the collection, the rival for Sir Mordred's affections."

Alan smiled indulgently at my piece of two-bit psychology and slowed down for an especially large and threatening puddle that stretched across the narrow road.

"But really, Alan, what an unlikely romance! I'm not at all sure he's interested in women, for one thing, and when I saw the two of them together, he acted scared half to death of her." I started to giggle. "Oh, Alan, if you'd *seen* him! He's about half her size. The picture of them in a tender embrace — his arms wouldn't go around her, and his nose would end up somewhere near her —" I collapsed in helpless giggles.

"At any rate," I said when I could speak again, "if *la belle* Lathrop cherishes a secret infatuation for the lord of the manor, she's wasting her time being jealous of Meg, who's in love with the gardener."

"That's one *I* didn't notice."

"Aha! You didn't have the advantage I did, though — you didn't see them quarreling together. But that involvement aside, Meg made it discreetly obvious that she has very little use for Sir Mordred. She's conscientious about her job, and he's absent-minded, always forgetting to tell her about new acquisitions. He also offends her ideas about proper curatorial practice by actually fixing houses that need fixing, and replacing furniture that's disappeared.

"By the way, apropos of nothing, why

didn't you want them to know who you are?"

"Obeying your implicit commands, my dear. As you said, people dry up in front of a policeman."

"Oh, yes, I'd forgotten. Well, but they didn't exactly stream with information for me, either. I got a sort of basic picture of the peculiar inhabitants of Brocklesby Hall, but I didn't learn a thing about 'The Case of the Missing Miniatures.' "

I settled comfortably into telling Alan all about it. One of the very nicest things about a good marriage is having someone to tell all about it, whatever "it" is.

"Sir M. took me around the museum himself, and I admit I did find it intriguing. The only dollhouses I've ever seen have been rather crude, just toys for children. I'd never realized they could be so detailed, with such fine workmanship. Some of the room settings are so perfect you forget you're seeing something small. They need a thimble or something in a corner to remind you of the scale.

"Anyway, I've got half a notion to buy a dollhouse and start furnishing it. It might be fun. Do you suppose one of your granddaughters would like such a thing as a Christmas present?"

I thought I was being subtle, but Alan grinned at me. "Michelle is the youngest, as you know perfectly well. She's thirteen, and interested only in horses and dogs, according to Beth's latest bulletin. Boys will be entering the field any day now, but dolls' houses — no. You're looking for an excuse to go back to the Hall."

"Well — they must have a shop, all museums do, and poking around *would* give me a chance to ask a few more questions. I honestly think I'd enjoy the project, though. I can probably buy a house there, but I'll have to try to make most of the furniture and stuff myself, because he — Sir M. — said it's terribly expensive. Almost a thousand pounds for the best pieces. A *thousand pounds*, Alan — and for modern work!"

Alan whistled.

"And listen to this. The tea set Bob was accused of stealing is historical — owned by Marie Antoinette, no less — and it's apparently worth a *lot*, although Sir M. wouldn't tell me how much."

"Did he mention the tea set, or did you?"

"He did, more or less in passing. We were talking about the value of the collection, and he brought it up just as I was trying to think of a way to work it into the conversation. Difficult, since I wasn't supposed to know about it. Anyway, I tried to get him to talk about the supposed theft, but all he would say was that it was a misunderstanding. No details."

"What about the other pieces he claims have been stolen?"

"He did just allude to them, but in general, nothing specific." I frowned, trying to remember. "I was about to pursue it, as I recall, when the gorgon appeared on the scene, and then nasty Claude, and I forgot about it. But I honestly don't see how it could be done, stealing, I mean, and incidentally, neither does Meg. All the houses and room settings and so on are — sort of fenced in, with glass or plastic, and there are alarms. I expect the alarms could be defeated somehow — they always can, if a thief knows enough about technology — but surely nobody would bother to do all that and then take one tea set, or whatever, no matter how valuable the piece might be. They'd clean out the whole shebang, or just steal house and all."

"Hmmm. Then it either had to be done from the workrooms, or — you didn't see them, did you?"

"No, Sir Mordred offered, but that was something else that got sidetracked. Come to think of it, that offer was an odd thing, from a security standpoint. I'm a total stranger."

"But an American, don't forget. A certain kind of Englishman often dismisses Americans as negligible." He smiled blandly, his eyes fixed firmly on the road, and ignored my punch at his arm. "Actually, it doesn't altogether surprise me that he made the offer. It fits in very nicely with my second thought."

I waited until he had negotiated a particularly hairy double roundabout. "Okay, I'll bite. What second thought?"

"That puts me one ahead again, Sherlock! I think — in fact, I'm reasonably sure, now I've seen the setup — Sir Mordred is stealing the miniatures himself."

"But — oh. For the insurance, you mean?"

"Probably. I don't think the economy he practices in the running of his house is entirely a matter of eccentricity. The place looks to me as though it needs a large infusion of cash; Sir Mordred may have decided he had a clever way to find some. He planted the tea set in poor Bob Finch's pocket to plant *him* in the minds of us overworked and none-too-bright policemen, so that when a major theft was discovered, we'd have a ready-made culprit. He was even ready to show his workrooms to you, an innocent American, so that you could testify, later, to how easily something could be taken away from them. Quick conviction, no complications, large cash deposit to the credit of his precious museum."

"Ye-es," I said slowly, thinking hard. "His mind might work that way. Stupid people often assume others are no brighter than they are. And of course he, of all people, would know exactly where to sell the stuff. He couldn't sell it openly, but I'll bet there are unscrupulous collectors in the miniature world just as there are in the world of full-scale art, people who'll buy what they want and no questions asked. And Sir Mordred would know who they are."

"Exactly."

I lapsed into a brooding silence. We had reached home before either of us spoke again.

"I suppose you're going to have to look into it."

"I'll notify the Fraud Squad, certainly. They can investigate quietly into Sir Mordred's recent insurance claims and report back."

"It seems almost a pity," I said, pausing before getting out of the car. "He's rather an interesting little man, in his peculiar way, and he hasn't hurt anybody. Except Bob, and that only briefly."

"And his insurers, don't forget them. So many people think of insurance fraud as a victimless crime, but it actually damages everyone whose rates go up. Or who can no longer find insurance, because no one will take the risk."

"You're right," I said with a sigh. "And it's a sleazy sort of crime, anyway. Nasty, underhanded, slinking — especially when an innocent like Bob Finch is set up to take the fall. I guess I don't like Sir M. so well after all. But — you will check out Claude Lathrop, too, won't you?"

"I'll try, though I doubt he's involved in this particular caper. He sounds a nasty bit of work, though, and I'd just as soon have his measure if he's to be lurking on my patch."

I got out of the car and dashed through the rain into the house while Alan maneuvered the car into the tiny garage. When he had come in and dried off, he poured us both a chill-chaser dose of Jack Daniel's and we settled in front of the fire in our favorite squashy armchairs.

"There's a flaw in your reasoning," I said suddenly.

"Yes?"

"We've talked about what a wild-eyed fanatic Sir Mordred is about miniatures. Could he bear to part with anything in the collection, even for lots of money?"

"Good point. Perhaps his cash-flow problem is temporary and he planned to buy them back later when things were better. Or perhaps he didn't plan to spend the money on Brocklesby Hall, but on another whatnot of some sort, still more marvelous than the ones he had to dispose of."

"Maybe. But here's another thing. If he needs money and is willing to get it by getting rid of stuff, why doesn't he just sell it openly? It belongs to him, after all. Why the sneaking around?"

"Ah, that's an easy one; you're not thinking, my dear. The insurance company would pay him full insured value — *and* he'd have whatever he managed to get for the things from his — er — customer. He'd probably realize only a fraction of that if he sold the items at auction."

"Umm." I took a sip of my drink. "Alan, this isn't as much fun as I thought it would be."

"Crime isn't often fun, love."

"No, but this one ought to be. I feel cheated. I mean, a weird old house filled with dollhouses, Santa's helper, the theft of

88

a tiny tea set — it sounds like a cross between Nancy Drew and the Brothers Grimm."

"Ah, yes, but you're forgetting that the Brothers Grimm —"

"— were pretty grim," I finished with a groan. "That one wasn't funny the first time somebody said it, which was a *long* time ago."

Alan heaved himself out of his chair, topped up our drinks, and kissed me, which is a very effective way to deal with a pout.

It took nearly a week for all the information Alan had requested to be assembled. English police are very thorough and methodical. I also gathered from Alan's cryptic remarks that the Fraud detail were more interested in investigating actual cases than possible ones, and that if it hadn't been the chief constable asking they might have taken a good deal longer.

Meanwhile, there were plenty of things to keep me busy. Friday was November fifth: Guy Fawkes Day, that odd English celebration of the occasion, in 1605, when Fawkes and a group of rebellious Roman Catholics almost succeeded in blowing up Parliament. I'd never taken part in the festivities before; Frank and I had never happened to be in England on the day, and last year, my first as an English resident but also as a widow, I hadn't felt much like crowds and fireworks. This year, however, Alan and I entered amiably into the spirit of things.

The atmosphere felt a good deal like Halloween back home, with children coming to the door and demanding, "A penny for the Guy." In the evening the Guy — an effigy of Guy Fawkes — was to be burned in the park down by the river, and a modest display of fireworks would be set off.

It was a mild night, for November, and dry for a change. Since we'd both be doing some drinking, Alan had his driver take us to our favorite riverside pub, the King's Head.

"Sorry you drew the duty on a festive night, Carter," said Alan to his driver as we got out.

"It's all right, sir," he said, smiling. "I'd as soon be driving you as patrolling the park and the streets. There'll be a good deal of rowdying tonight; I'm teetotal, and happier away from it. I'm sorry I can't get you closer, but the traffic —"

"This is splendid. You needn't hang about; we'll not be going home till the fireworks are over."

"Right." He touched his cap. "Enjoy your evening, sir — madam."

We strolled arm in arm through the crowds already thronging the riverbank. Cries still resounded of "A penny for the Guy!" Now and then an illicit firecracker went off with a pop, though seldom near us. Most Sherebury residents know their chief constable by sight.

One group of children was chanting, "Remember, remember, the fifth of November, gunpowder treason and plot. I see no reason why gunpowder treason should ever be forgot!"

"Such a strange little rhyme," I murmured. "One would think they — you — would want to forget the incident. The Gunpowder Plot wasn't exactly England's finest hour — on either side. We Americans don't celebrate our traitors."

"We celebrate the fact that the plot was foiled," Alan retorted. "Anyway, you Americans have no sense of history, probably because you have no history to speak of. What's two hundred-odd years — look, there's a friend of yours."

It was Meg Cunningham, standing on the strip of grassy riverbank. She was next to a car, her arm around the shoulders of a little girl, and hovering over them was the unspeakable Claude.

I stopped dead and clutched his arm.

"But, Alan, that's Claude! And I don't think — can't you —"

"I can't interfere with a man who's doing nothing but talking," he said reasonably. "I can, however, watch."

He leaned against a convenient tree. We weren't far away, but the tree shadowed us from street lamps and bonfires and the light streaming from the pub. I kept my hold on his arm and strained to hear.

There was a good deal of background noise, and the occasional firecracker. But Claude's voice was elevated by alcohol. ". . . wouldn't like to give me a lift home later on, would you, sweetheart? Shouldn't be on me bike, should I, with a skinful?"

"I'm leaving now." Meg spoke quietly, but with a steely clarity. "I must get Jemima to bed."

Jemima, who looked to be about seven, paid no attention to this outrageous remark. Her eyes were on the sparklers being waved by nearby children.

"Not staying for the fireworks? Pity, that'd be, wouldn't it, Jemima?"

He reached out a hand to Jemima's head; the little girl jumped and shrank from his touch. Even from where we stood, I could see Meg's expression. "Don't you touch her!" she breathed furiously. Pulling

Jemima close, she reached for the car door, and Claude put a hand on her arm.

Alan moved smoothly and very fast. He disengaged himself from my grasp and joined the little group; I trailed belatedly in his wake.

"Good evening, Mrs. Cunningham. How nice to see you again. Chief Constable Alan Nesbitt, and of course you remember my wife, Mrs. Martin. And this must be your little girl?"

Claude simply evaporated. I didn't see him go, but when I glanced around, he wasn't there. Meg, shaking with fear or fury, or both, said something unintelligible and bundled Jemima into the car, the child protesting in a high, keening wail that made me give her a sharp glance. Alan, with a gesture, summoned one of the strolling constables to deal with the traffic; the car pulled away and disappeared, and Alan offered his arm again.

"Shall we have a drink?"

"I could use one, after that."

The King's Head was crowded, but Alan is an Important Person. A tiny table was made available for us, and Alan eventually returned from the bar with abstemious half-pints of our favorite ale.

"You are remarkable, you know?" I

touched my glass to his. "You didn't even have to *do* anything. Just being there — and of course, throwing your title around."

"I've blown your cover, as they would say on your side of the Atlantic."

"They haven't said that for years, and this is my side of the Atlantic now," I said softly. Our eyes met, and for a moment the rest of the room didn't exist.

"Ooh, sorry, luv!" A drop or two of beer landed on my sleeve, and a quickly produced handkerchief dabbed at it. " 'Ere, let me scrub that orf you — ever so sorry, dear, it were that clumsy lout of a son of mine —"

"Never mind, Ada, it'll wash out, and we'll all smell like beer before the night's over, I expect. How are you, Bob?"

I eyed him judiciously, but he seemed cheerful and reasonably sober. His cheeks were red, but not his nose — yet.

He tipped an imaginary hat at me and winked. "Me mum's keepin' me on the straight and narrow. A fine thing, w'en a man carn't 'ave 'isself a drop or two wivout 'is womenfolk carryin' on —"

"Excuse me, *may* I be allowed to pass?"

The icy tones were all too familiar. Mrs. Lathrop stood, haughty amidst offending elbows, with little Sir Mordred beside her, looking miserable and holding two glasses. I was reminded of a battleship and its attendant tugboat.

Bob obligingly moved aside an inch or two — all that the space allowed — but Ada stood her ground, her face upturned pugnaciously to Mrs. Lathrop's.

" 'Ullo, Emma. 'Ave a drink wiv us? You an' yer boss, that is to say, if 'ee likes?"

Mrs. Lathrop pursed her mouth and looked at a point on the far wall. "How do you do, Ada. We have other plans."

She sailed majestically past, pulling Sir Mordred after her, and Ada chuckled roguishly. "She don't like to be reminded we was girls together," she confided. "Fancies 'erself too good for the likes of us now. But she don't want to make a scene in front of 'im, neither."

"An' bad luck to 'er. *And* 'im." Bob raised his glass in a sour toast.

I didn't want to see the burning of the Guy. The religious prejudice inherent in the history of the practice grated on me; much as I love English tradition, parts of it can be distasteful. So we found a couple of chairs for the Finches and Alan bought another round while the crowd thinned out. I saw Richard Adam enter the pub, look around, and leave.

"Lookin' for Meg Cunningham," was

Bob's comment. " 'Ee's sweet on 'er."

"I'd noticed that," I replied. "I would have thought they'd have been together tonight, but we saw her earlier, and she was alone with her daughter." I didn't need Alan's kick under the table to limit the story; I gave him an indignant look, and he grinned and buried his face in his beer. "Anyway, he won't find her here tonight; she took Jemima home."

"Ar," said Bob in a profound male comment on the inexplicability of female conduct, and we finished our beer amiably and went out to watch the fireworks.

6

The next Monday evening Alan came home with news. We were drinking our after-dinner coffee when he dropped his little bombshell on the kitchen table.

"The reports came in today."

I didn't have to ask which reports he meant. "And?"

"I don't know whether you'll be disappointed, or the reverse. I'm not sure how I feel about it, either, except that I seem to have made rather a fool of myself." He ran a hand down the back of his neck in a familiar gesture. "The insurance report was negative."

"What does that mean?" I asked, confused.

"It means that they came up with nothing at all. Sir Mordred has made no claim against any insurance policy he holds on the museum. None."

"But . . ."

We looked at each other.

"Maybe," I said, feeling for an idea, "maybe he just hasn't gotten around to it yet. Maybe he's been hiding away a few little things just to pave the way for something big that he plans to blame on Bob."

"Possibly. If so, we've put a spoke in his wheel. Our people are very discreet, but the fact we've been asking means the insurers will be very careful indeed about any claim Sir Mordred should happen to make in future. And no doubt word of our inquiries will filter back to him. If he *was* planning to pull off a major theft, he's not likely to now."

"That makes me feel better. I think. Or maybe we were entirely wrong, and the Bob incident was just some sort of mistake. A tempest in a tea set, as it were."

Alan groaned dutifully. "Maybe." He shook his head. "And as for Claude . . ."

"Oh, yes, dear little Claude."

"Not so dear. He's even nastier than I'd supposed. He's never actually been convicted of anything — too clever by half — but he has an impressive pedigree of charges. Vicious little crimes, all of them. His favorite weapons are intimidation and a flick-knife; his victims women and the elderly. And of course that's an actionable statement, since he's officially innocent." He paused.

"And — is there anything in this roster of noncrimes that involves Meg Cunningham?"

I prompted, a little afraid of what I might hear.

"Attempted rape."

I stared at him, appalled. "Oh, Alan, how terrifying — and the little girl —"

He covered my hand comfortingly with his huge, warm one.

"Nothing like as bad as it might have been. It happened about a year ago, at the Hall. Apparently Claude was living with Mum — she lives in, you know — and caught Mrs. Cunningham alone somewhere in the maze of corridors. The notes on the case are somewhat formally written, but I got the impression Richard Adam charged onto the scene like a roaring bull and scared the liver and lights out of young Claude. My sources say he hasn't been seen about the Hall since, until last week. He's been living in various squats in London, and he was apparently there on the Monday. I couldn't, of course, ask for a full investigation; the Metropolitan Police are as shorthanded as we are, and no crime has actually been committed."

"Well, no wonder Meg is scared of Claude. He shouldn't be allowed to hang around terrifying that poor woman. Can't anything be done to make him go back to London?"

"My dear, you know the answer to that. I've done what I could — ordered a sporadic patrol of the Hall, one constable making himself very conspicuous at irregular intervals, in the hopes of discouraging friend Claude. There's nothing more we can do, legally, even if we had the resources — which we do not."

Alan shook his head in a dismissal of the subject, stood, and said, "Can I help wash up?"

It was over the dishpan that he sprang his other little surprise. "Dorothy, I hadn't wanted to tell you until I was sure, but I'm going to have to be away for a few days, starting on Wednesday."

I looked up in dismay from the pot I was scrubbing.

"They want me to go to Bramshill for a briefing. You remember, I was to take over there in September, before those hitches developed. Now they're talking about it again, and I need to take a detailed look at the situation before I make up my mind. My own position has changed, of course."

The Police Staff College at Bramshill is a beautiful estate in Hampshire where senior officers are sent for special courses. Alan had, the previous summer, been offered the job of commandant, a very great honor even on the temporary basis they proposed. Then various matters arose that meant the old commandant had to stay on for a while, and then, of course, Alan and I married and settled down in my house. I had managed until now to avoid thinking about moving to a house which, while about the same age as my Jacobean cottage, was a world apart. I wasn't at all sure I was prepared to live in a country manor with peacocks on the terrace, a famous herd of white deer in the park, and at least one notable ghost.

Alan looked at me a little anxiously, his hands frozen on the dish towel and wet plate. (I don't know why men can never talk and work at the same time.) "I shan't be gone long, my dear, probably a week, two at most. You'd be welcome to come with me, of course, but I'm having to make do with a student room. I gather the commandant's quarters are being cleaned and renovated, and aren't yet ready for new occupants. The last chap was a bachelor, so . . ."

"Yes, I understand. That isn't what's bothering me." I rinsed the pot and started on another. "I'll miss you, of course, but there's always the telephone. No, it's just that I'd almost forgotten about Bramshill. I suppose we have to go, but I'm not terribly happy about it, to tell the truth. Moving, just as we've gotten settled here, and — oh, having to play the official hostess and all that . . ."

"Getting cold feet, are you?" His tone was light on the surface, but I could hear the worry underneath.

We had never talked about the problems inherent in a marriage like ours, an unknown American marrying a well-respected Englishman with an extremely responsible and sensitive job. We had both known trouble might crop up. English society still regards many professional jobs as requiring the wife to be the second, unpaid member of the team, and she is expected to be diplomatic, selfless, ready to drop her own agenda at a moment's notice, and highly skilled in protocol. I possess none of those qualities. I am stubborn, blundering, and very involved in my own affairs, and though I could easily handle large dinner parties at home in Indiana, I know nothing whatever about the finer points of social behavior in a foreign country.

I had hoped, with Alan close to retirement, that the problem might not arise. Now it loomed, large and terrifying.

"In a word, yes." I dumped out the dishwater and gently took the towel and still unwiped plate from Alan's hands.

"Oh, sorry. Look, I haven't definitely accepted the appointment, you know." He ran a hand down the back of his neck. "If you truly would rather not —"

"Alan, I've never even seen the place. I'm certainly not going to say I won't go just because I'm scared stiff of the whole idea. And anyway, I don't want you to base your decision on my — my cowardice. You go ahead and go, and decide whether it's something you want to get into. Maybe next weekend I can visit. There must be an inn or something within spitting distance."

He grinned. "Yes, I'm sure we can find suitable accommodation somewhere, and a visit would be an excellent idea. I think you'll like the house when you see it. But you do understand that I don't require self-immolation from my bride. If you don't want to live there, I shan't take the post, and that's flat."

"Yes, well, we'll see then." But I went to bed determined not to let my feelings show again. I was not about to make his career decisions for him, and this was an important step. Anyway, it was a temporary position, and surely I could stand anything for a few months.

There was little fuss about Alan's departure. His years as a widower had taught him to fend for himself, so he packed neatly and methodically, arranged matters at the office to run without him for a little while, and had Police Constable Carter call for him very early Wednesday morning.

I had, of course, ignored his injunction not to see him off, but by the time I struggled out of bed and stumbled downstairs he had brewed his own coffee, boiled an egg, and made toast. I sat at the kitchen table feeling useless. Once we had commented that it looked like turning into a fine day for the run to Hampshire, there seemed little to say. Alan's mind was plainly on the days ahead, and it was something of a relief when he gathered up his luggage, gave me an absentminded kiss, and was gone.

"He didn't have to leave so early," I said resentfully to Samantha, who sat in the kitchen, her blue Siamese eyes following my every move. "It's only sixty miles or so. Well, maybe eighty, the way your stupid English roads run. And there's no point in thinking, miss, that just because I'm up you're going to get an early breakfast. I'm headed back to bed."

I closed the bedroom door to keep out the cats, who persist in thinking that the first sign of human activity, at no matter what hour of the morning, means food. It was only six, and pitch dark, and I had no intention of doing anything useful for hours.

But I couldn't sleep. It wasn't just the steady stream of high-pitched complaint from Sam, joined now and then by deeper wails from Emmy, my big British Blue, who also beat a tattoo on the door with well-practiced front paws. I'm used to ignoring feline impatience, and earplugs are a great boon. No, it was my own restlessness that kept me awake and tossing until the stars began to lose their brilliance and the eastern sky to take on a pearly luminescence. The cats had long since given up and gone back to sleep themselves, but I lay amidst rumpled bedclothes and worried.

Part of me hoped that Alan would find Bramshill unattractive, and would come home determined not to accept the job. He didn't, after all, enjoy administration all that much. He looked back nostalgically to the days when he was, as he put it, a real policeman, actively involved in solving crimes. This job would be pure administration, with not a crime in sight.

It would also, the other part of me argued, be a real plum, the capstone to a distinguished career, Alan's crowning achievement. He might even be knighted; it was not an unknown honor for absolutely brilliant policemen, and it would be well-deserved.

Good grief! Was I ready to be Lady Something-or-other? I didn't even know if an American could be! It certainly didn't sound very democratic, and could I ever learn to respond when someone addressed me that way, or would I look around to see who they were talking to?

That thought finally got me out of bed. If I had nothing better to do than worry about my hypothetical reaction to a hypothetical title, it was time I found something.

Dawn was well past when I sat down at the breakfast table with my third cup of coffee. I had fed the cats and myself (in that order), tidied up the kitchen, and was now wondering what to do for the rest of the day. It was not one of my days at the Cathedral Bookshop. The house was clean. The plumbers weren't due to show up to make estimates on the remaining work until next week — if they came then. Two previous appointments had been canceled, English plumbers being, unfortunately, not much different from the American variety.

I was free, in fact. I could do anything I wanted. I could take the train up to London and do some shopping, or call my friends the Andersons, Americans who have lived for years in a lovely Georgian house in

Belgravia. They would probably be available for lunch or tea or the theater or something. Or there were always the museums. I love museums, and London has dozens and dozens of them, including many small ones I've longed to see but somehow never had time to visit.

Or, the thought insinuated itself between sips of coffee, there was always the museum on my very doorstep, or not far from it. I'd said I wanted to buy a dollhouse; why not seize the day? I was still far from satisfied about the Bob Finch incident; if the opportunity arose for a few leading questions . . .

And I certainly needed something to take my mind off Alan and Bramshill.

After a look at the bus schedules, and some stern conversation with myself, I decided to drive to Brocklesby Hall. My lack of mobility, with a perfectly good car at my disposal, was nothing short of ridiculous. I knew the way, it wasn't far, the weather was gorgeous, and no woman of sound mind and body who'd been driving for nearly fifty years had any business being intimidated by little things like roundabouts and the wrong side of the road.

Besides, whispered a little voice at the back of my mind, which I tried to ignore, *if you have the car you can get away quickly.*

Nonsense, of course. But there *was* something about that house . . .

I put on an entirely proper hat, a sedate blue felt with just one restrained feather, and arrived on the dot of ten o'clock. I had to wait to be admitted. Two school groups, just arrived, were being unloaded from buses, along with harried teachers and helpers. Crowds of children milled around the front door, wriggling and chattering like a cageful of monkeys. I hoped there were enough guides to deal with them today; I cringed at the thought of what unsupervised children could do to the delicate displays.

But the museum had evidently been forewarned. When I finally got inside, the children had been organized into several small groups, each in the charge of one adult from the school and one neatly blue-blazered guide. They were listening quietly while a fiftyish woman in tweeds explained procedures and rules. I stood listening and admiring. She was a real pro. Without once raising her pleasant voice or uttering threats, she made it clear that this was going to be an interesting experience, but also that any child who made a nuisance of itself in any way would deeply regret it. The groups then dispersed in different directions, still quiet and orderly.

"Remarkable," I said to the young woman selling tickets, someone I hadn't seen before. "They were acting like fugitives from a zoo, outside."

"Yes, Mrs. Butler is brilliant with the children."

I frowned. "I was here a week or so ago and didn't meet her. Does she just work part-time?"

"Oh, no, she's the new director of education. She's only been here two days, actually, but she's made a great difference already. The school groups are *much* easier to cope with! Now, did you want to tour the museum? There will be children everywhere, I'm afraid, but —"

I made an instant decision. "No, actually I came to use the library. Last time I came Sir Mordred gave me permission; I've become interested in miniatures and want to learn more about them. Mrs. Cunningham knows me."

"Oh, well, that's all right then. Can you find the library?"

"Yes, I can get lost in this place in five minutes, but I think I can manage to make it across the great hall."

"Do you know, I've been working here for six months and I still can't find my way about? I don't like the house anyway; it's creepy. But the dolls' houses are marvelous."

She opened the door into the great hall, smiled at me, and went back to her post. Well, at least I wasn't the only one to find endless corridors and leering cupids a little frightening.

Voices, presumably of children or guides, could be heard faintly, coming from various directions as I stood in the great hall. They echoed oddly off the hard surfaces and became a sort of clanging buzz, from everywhere and nowhere, resounding in my head. I wondered if the house had the usual quota of ghosts. True, it was on the young side for that sort of thing, but if there were ever a house designed to inspire macabre legends, it was this one.

I shook my head to dislodge the nonsense, and opened the library door.

I had expected the room on this sparkling day to be a little less dark and gloomy than the first time I had seen it, with a monsoon in progress. Perhaps it was, but only a little. The velvet draperies — I could see today that they were a dispirited brown — shut off most of the sunshine that wanted to penetrate, and something was blocking the bottom of one window. As before, dim electric lights were lit. I searched for Meg, hoping she was in one of her "up" moods, and finally saw her in a far corner, poring over some sort of large book with someone who looked, in the twilit atmosphere, to be male.

"Yes?" she said, looking in my direction and voicing the inquiry I'd long expected in this house. It didn't have the properly sinister inflection, though.

"It's Dorothy Martin," I said, advancing. "Wouldn't you think Sir Mordred could afford some higher wattage lightbulbs?"

"Wouldn't you now?" she agreed, her eyes dancing as she came toward me. The male person followed her, clutching his book. "Mrs. Martin, this is John Thoreston, our accountant. He might be able to answer your question." She was trying hard not to laugh.

"Oh, dear. How do you do?" I said, extending my hand and smiling ruefully. "Open mouth, insert foot. Didn't I say, Meg, that one never outgrows it? I hope I haven't offended you, Mr. Thoreston."

"Er — not at all," he muttered, looking very ill at ease, while Meg nearly choked on a giggle.

"Anyway, I'm sorry I interrupted, Meg. I just wanted to drop in and say hello. Please do go back to — whatever you were doing."

I loaded my voice with inquiry. Meg didn't let me down.

"No, we had finished, actually. We were just cross-checking my accession records against the account books. Sir Mordred had asked some questions," she went on. Her sniff spoke volumes about her opinion of Sir Mordred's meddling.

"I wouldn't have thought he'd have a clue. He doesn't strike me as the practical type."

"I doubt he can read his bank statements, let alone a proper set of books," said Meg with fine scorn. "And as far as I can tell, everything is in perfect order, which is one in the eye for him!"

"Er — quite," said Mr. Thoreston, gulping. His prominent Adam's apple rose and fell. "Er — if you'll excuse me —" He clutched his ledger and fled.

"Not a very self-possessed young man," I commented.

"A right twit," said the curator crisply, shaking her head with impatience. "Not bad at his job, actually, but scared of his shadow. If he had good sense he'd find another post; he's paid half nothing. I hope he doesn't, though, for we'd be hard put to find anyone to take his place. Nobody likes being hovered over by a banty cock who doesn't know how many beans make five. Now then." She took a deep breath. "Is there anything I can do for you, or are you just browsing?"

I grinned. "Not today. I really did just come in to see you. How's Jemima? Did she get over missing the fireworks?"

She grinned back. "We did a few sparklers and Roman candles at home, but they were a poor substitute for the real thing, I'm afraid. Of course, firecrackers —"

She stopped abruptly.

"Of course, they wouldn't have much appeal, would they? All they do is make a bang." I watched her face. "Jemima is deaf, isn't she?"

The smile vanished with that disconcerting, lightning mood change of hers. She looked at me warily. "How did you know?"

"I was a teacher. There was a deaf child at my school for a little while, oh, a long time ago now, back when they were trying to 'mainstream' children with some kinds of disabilities. His parents got him into a school for the deaf after a couple of months, and I believe he went on eventually to a Ph.D. in something or other, but I never forgot the sound of his cry, that atonal wail of someone who can't hear his own voice. He cried a lot, poor dear; he was only seven, and terribly frustrated."

"Yes, so was Jemima till I found the school

she's in now." She hesitated. "Look, I don't mind you knowing, but I hope you won't talk about it. I don't want — there are some people I'd rather didn't know about her."

"Claude, for example."

"Definitely Claude," she said. "It'd be one more thing he could hold over me. A threat to her —" Her expressive eyes darkened; she set her chin firmly and changed the subject. "And speaking of threats, do tell your lovely husband I'm grateful to him. I've been kicking myself for going off the other night without a word, but I was —"

"Don't worry about it. I would have been in hysterics, myself. Has that miserable excuse for a human being gone back to London yet?"

She shuddered. "I don't think so, but he's been coming and going a good deal lately. I haven't seen him since Friday, but his mum is nervous, so I gather he's about. If he turns up here, I'll —"

I clucked sympathetically. "There's nothing the police can do, you know. I asked. Except that Alan did set up patrols of the area around the Hall. Only occasional ones, but I thought it might make you feel better to know someone's keeping an eye on the place. And on Claude."

She didn't exactly smile, but those remarkable eyes softened and warmed. "It does. Thanks."

"All right, then. Now. There is something you can do for me, come to think of it. Do you have any books about making miniatures? They'd have to be written for the all-thumbs set, though."

"Getting hooked, are you? I think we have just what you want."

She pulled several books off the shelf, and sat me down with them. It didn't take me long to succumb to their fascination. Once one got used to looking at things in one-twelfth scale (the most common standard for miniatures — an inch to a foot), everyday objects took on new meanings. A large thimble was an admirable wastebasket. Beads and bits of metal from discarded jewelry were re-worked into perfume bottles or lamps. Toothpicks could serve as parts of chairs or stairways, and tiny scraps of cloth were useful in all sorts of ways. I let my imagination roam. A small house to start with . . .

"Excuse me, Dorothy."

I looked up from the small world in which I had become immersed.

"Were you planning to eat lunch, or are those books sufficient nourishment? Because I'm about to go have mine, and I have to lock up."

"Gosh, I'm starved, now that you mention it. What time is it?"

"Nearly one."

"Heavens! I thought I'd been reading for about half an hour. Time to call it a morning, then. There's one book I'd like to take home with me, though. Do they circulate?"

"I'm afraid not, and Mordie is a real fusspot about it. But they stock some good books in the gift shop. It's just next to the tearoom. I'll show you the way."

We went through the maze of corridors to a part of the house I'd never seen, past yet more rooms full of tiny things. The halls were quiet; apparently the school groups had departed. Near the end of one hall was a conservatory, burgeoning with tropical-looking plants, palms and monstrous succulents looking, to my eye, more like predatory animals than plants. Not a room I would care to enter alone.

Across the hall was a large room filled with small, brightly new houses and furnishings, obviously the shop.

"The tearoom is just beyond, if you're brave. Are you all right, then?"

"Fine, thanks. I don't suppose you'd care to join me?"

She grinned, looking much more like herself. "Not in there, and not today. I've an errand to run. But yes, one day I'd like that. Enjoy your lunch — if you can."

I watched her cross the hall purposefully and enter the conservatory. I would have made book on whom she hoped to find there.

7

The tea room was every bit as appealing as museum eateries usually are. I ate two thin sandwiches that tasted mostly of cardboard and mustard, drank some tea quickly before it ate its way through the paper cup, and repaired to the shop. The choices there were considerably more enticing; they were also expensive. It was the kid-in-a-candy-store syndrome. I agonized over the difference between what I wanted (nearly everything) and what I could afford, and finally bought not one book but three, a kitchen stove and sink, a set of bathroom fixtures, and, blowing the budget completely, a lovely six-room thatched cottage.

I stuffed my credit card back in my purse before meltdown set in and looked with dismay at the house I had just acquired. "I don't have the slightest idea how I'm going to get that to my car. Not to mention where I'll put it when I get it there."

"That one will fit in most boots," said the clerk, a round, pleasant woman in her thirties. "And we can find someone to carry it out for you."

"It won't fit in *my* boot unless I leave the lid up," I retorted. "And as I drive a Volkswagen, with the boot in front, that would make driving a little awkward."

"Oh, dear, it would, wouldn't it? We could deliver it, perhaps . . ."

"No! I want it right away; this is a good time for me to get started working on it."

The clerk smiled gently. She evidently had some experience with children, of whatever age; she knew perfectly well I wanted to get my purchase home immediately so I could gloat over it. "It is a lovely little house, isn't it? A few scraps of chintz would make the most delightful curtains."

I nodded eagerly. "And rag rugs, don't you think? Or maybe braided — there are patterns in one of the books, and I have lots of leftover yarn."

"Such fun to plan it all!" said the clerk sympathetically. "As good as a real house, I always think, and less trouble. And though I oughtn't to say so, working here, I'd always rather make my own furnishings. Far more satisfying, to my mind."

We smiled in complete accord. "I intend to try, anyway. I don't have many talents except patience — and stubbornness — but I'll take a stab at it. Most of the materials are free, that's one mercy. But I do want to get started, so if we can get the house to my car, I'll cram it in somehow."

To my delight, the man she found to carry my purchase was Bob Finch. "Oh, you're back to work, then!"

"For the past week," he replied laconically.

"Good. I was afraid . . . listen, can we talk?" I whispered conspiratorially as he trudged down the path to the parking lot, my huge purchase cradled easily in his short, sturdy, brown arms.

Bob grunted. He always reminds me of one of those gnomes people buy as garden ornaments — weathered, compact, and silent. " 'Ee's gone to Lunnon," he said briefly. "There's only 'Er Worshipfulness, and she's 'avin' 'er nap after 'er dinner." He was too polite to spit in my presence.

"Well, then. There hasn't been any more trouble, has there? Sir Mordred has behaved well about your coming back to work?"

Bob shrugged. " 'Ee apologized. I keeps meself to meself; 'ee don't bother me. An' 'ee's been gone since Monday. An' 'er — I don't pay no mind to 'er."

"So you're all right?"

He shrugged again. His mother is the one who does the talking in the family, perhaps because it's hard to get a word in edgewise when she's in full spate.

"Well, I'm sorry to say I haven't been able to find out anything very significant about your — er — unpleasant experience, but I don't *think* you'll have any more problems. If Alan and I are right, whatever dirty work may have been afoot, there isn't likely to be any more. Here's my car. Do you think we can squeeze the house in?"

We were struggling with it when Richard Adam appeared from around the corner of the house. He frowned at Bob.

"So that's where you've gone. I need your help with the pruning."

"We'll be finished here in a minute," I said with a would-be conciliatory smile. He growled something, turned on his heel, and strode off.

"Goodness! Is he always so surly?"

Bob wedged the last awkward corner of the house into the backseat and closed the car door. "Nah. 'Ad a row last week wiv 'is ladylove."

"Oh, dear, another one?" I opened the driver's door and got in. "Over what, this time?"

" 'Im."

I wish Bob weren't so fond of pronouns. It makes his conversation distinctly cryptic.

"Sir Mordred?" I ventured doubtfully.

121

"Nah. Told yer 'ee were in Lunnon. 'Im." He jerked his head to one side and I saw, through a patch of bushes, the gleam of a big silver motorcycle zooming up the drive. The snarl of its engine reached my older ears a moment after Bob had heard it, as Claude took a corner in a spectacular skid that flung clods of mud over the shrubbery. The bike roared off toward the back of the house and disappeared.

"He didn't see us," I said with relief. I was not at all eager for another encounter with dear little Claude. "But what do you mean, they quarreled over him? Surely Mr. Adam doesn't think —"

"An' will that be all, madam?" said Bob in a loud, artificial voice as Mrs. Lathrop opened the front door and strode forward with a grim face that boded no good for either of us.

I started the engine.

"Just a moment, Mrs. Nesbitt," said the housekeeper, holding up an imperious hand. I sat helpless, pinned in my car by the conventions, as she approached ponderously and put her hand on the frame of the open window.

"I wish," she said stiffly, "to apologize for not welcoming you properly when you first visited. Of course, I could hardly know who you were, since you chose not to use your real name."

"Dorothy Martin is my real name," I said, every bit as stiffly. "I kept it when I married Mr. Nesbitt. If I'd known that my husband's position mattered to you, we would have mentioned it. I didn't realize that you mete out your hospitality on the basis of a guest's social prominence. Excuse me."

I rolled up the window, nearly catching her hand, and peeled out of the driveway almost as gracelessly as Claude, consigning Mrs. Lathrop and all her works to perdition. Pestilential woman! I was childishly disappointed; she'd ruined my pleasure in my new dollhouse. I drove so furiously on the way home that I forgot to worry about the roundabouts.

It wasn't Mrs. Lathrop's snobbery that bothered me most, nor even her rudeness. I'd actually been far more impolite than she, and (I admitted without a shred of guilt) I'd enjoyed it. No, what really irritated me was the loss of my precious anonymity, and with it my freedom of movement. If I'd had any hopes that Alan's encounter with Claude had gone unreported, I was now disabused of them. From now on all Brocklesby Hall knew who I was, and my most innocent inquiry about miniatures would be viewed with deep suspicion. Soon it would enter Sir Mordred's tiny mind that I had been less than candid with him on my first visit to the museum, and he would start wondering what I was up to.

No, correction: He would wonder what the wife of the chief constable was up to. Dearly as I loved Alan, it was galling to be viewed as nothing more than an extension of his job and personality. Not only did it make me less than a person, it also put a considerable limitation on my sleuthing activities.

Was it time for me to hang up my deer-stalker and calabash and take up water-colors? Or miniature-making?

What a sweet, appropriate hobby for an old lady, I thought, making a face as I pulled the car into my sorry excuse for a driveway and considered how to deal with the house Bob and I had wedged into the backseat.

"Need a hand with that, do you?"

It was Jane, come to my aid. A never failing help in time of trouble, that's Jane. My hat askew, we wrestled the bulky, awkward thing out of the car and into the house, and Jane said, "Where?"

"On the kitchen table for the moment, I guess. Actually, I never thought about it. Oh, dear! It really is a problem, isn't it?"

It was. The little house was nearly three feet wide, maybe half as deep, and over two feet high. If I was to work on it, painting and wallpapering and hanging curtains and so on, I needed space around it. And in my ancient cottage there was very little extra space, and certainly no workshop.

I must have looked crestfallen, for Jane grinned at me. "Buy in haste and repent at leisure, eh?" She tipped her head to one side, considering the matter. "A good, sturdy table, now. I've a folding one I never use. What's in your spare bedroom?"

"A lot of junk, mostly."

"Let's have a look."

Left to my own devices I would have dithered over the junk. Jane made short work of it, appropriating some for resale in aid of one or another of her good causes, ruthlessly stuffing the rest into plastic bags for the rubbish bin. I insisted on keeping the box of gaudy old costume jewelry to turn into dollhouse oddments, but nearly everything else went. By the end of the afternoon we had the twin bed pushed into the corner and the dollhouse ensconced in the middle of the room on Jane's table.

I made Jane stay to supper, and over cottage pie and salad I told her about my morning at the Hall. She sighed (rather theatrically, I thought) at my account of the tangled relationships between Meg Cunningham, Richard Adam, and Claude.

"Getting yourself involved in other people's lives again," she said. "Sure to lead to trouble."

"I've noticed," I said wickedly, "that you pursue a deliberate policy of noninvolvement, yourself. Stand by and watch your friends hang themselves; never lift a finger. Right?"

She suddenly became very busy fending off the cats, who, as usual, were weaving themselves around her ankles, ready for any stray tidbits of attention or food that might come their way. She petted them absently and put her plate on the floor while I waited.

"Oh, well," she said finally, resignation in her tone. "Daresay you can fend for yourself."

"With a little help from my friends," I agreed. "For instance, tell me about that witch of a housekeeper. I had thought Sir M. probably brought her from London with him, but Ada says they knew each other when they were both girls."

"Sherebury born and bred," Jane agreed. "Mother was gentry, but married an innkeeper's son, good-looking, plausible fellow — went through money like water. By the time Emma came along they were headed for trouble, and then young Lionel . . . Linford . . . Lawrence — getting old, can't recall his name — anyway, he went off to war and never came back. Emma more or less had to bring herself up; mother went to pieces when she got the news about her husband and was never good for much after that. Not good for a lot before that, if you ask me.

"Soon as she was old enough, Emma went into service as a superior sort of house-keeper-cum-factotum, and managed to do fairly well for herself even in those days of postwar austerity. Better as the country began to recover. Buried a couple of hus-bands — butlers — worked at some respect-able houses. Bullies her employers into thinking she's indispensable."

"She certainly has Sir M. bullied. Alan thinks she's nourishing a secret passion for him."

Jane sighed. "What fools these mortals be! Myself, I'd as soon cuddle up to a Pe-kingese. Sooner. Even the silliest dogs have some sense; silly men, never."

She refused dessert and went home, and I spent the evening with my dollhouse, plan-ning decorating schemes, hunting up soft old scraps of cloth to make into curtains. The cats were just as interested as I, jumping in and out of the house and playing with my scraps. They also complained about Alan's absence, running down the stairs to find him and then up again to inform me that he wasn't there. He called just as I was climbing into an early bed.

"So tell me all about Bramshill," I said when I had nestled myself comfortably into the pillows.

"It's a pretty complex operation," he said. "I've taken courses here over the years, naturally, but I never fully realized the scope." He detailed the breadth of College activities. "I certainly wouldn't care to be responsible for the day-to-day running of the College as a permanent job. But what they want me for, principally, is to overhaul the overseas aspect of operations, the advanced training of foreign police officers, before they hand it on to the next chap."

"Well, you've got the experience for that, certainly. All that time you've spent in Washington, and Brussels —"

"And Nairobi and Hong Kong and New Delhi, et cetera, et cetera. Yes, I think I could make a contribution. But I need to learn a good deal more about the details before I take on the job. And of course I want you to look the place over thoroughly. You'll like the manor house, I think. The tapestries in the drawing room must be seen to be believed."

"Have you come across the ghost yet?"

He chuckled. "I'm told the poor lady seldom leaves the main house, and has so far totally avoided the students' blocks. Perhaps if you come for the weekend she might condescend to materialize for you; they've found a guest room in the house for us. I'm free almost all of Saturday and Sunday; can you get away, do you think?"

"I don't see why not. Give me directions and I might even try driving."

"I shouldn't, if I were you. You'd have to go through London or around it, in that ghastly traffic, and there are fairly decent trains from Waterloo. You want to go to either Winchfield or Hook; I've looked up the times for you . . ."

I wrote down his detailed instructions. "Okay, so I'll call you from Waterloo Station Saturday morning, when I figure out which train I can catch, and you'll meet me. Got it. Meanwhile, I miss you, and the cats do, too. You should have seen them, looking for you all over the house."

"Tell them I'll bring them a peacock feather to play with. The beasts are molting; their feathers are everywhere. And as for you . . ."

I ended the day feeling much happier than I had at its beginning, but my sense of well-being was shattered shortly after breakfast the next morning.

"Mrs. Martin, it's Derek Morrison here. I don't know if you remember me —"

"Of Town Hall fame! I met you over a corpse, with poor Ada Finch just recovering from hysterics. How are you, Chief Inspector?"

"I'm getting along splendidly, thank you, but I'm afraid Mrs. Finch is not doing quite so well. She's here at the police station and asking for you. Her son, Bob, has been brought in for questioning."

"Not more thefts at the museum!" I wailed.

Inspector Morrison cleared his throat. "Unfortunately not. There's been a murder."

I ran out the door without even putting on a hat. Panting, I arrived at the police station in the High Street to find Inspector Morrison waiting for me in the front hall.

"Tell me," I demanded.

"Mrs. Lathrop, out at Brocklesby Hall, died early this morning. It seems clear that she was poisoned, and Bob may have been involved. That's virtually all I know at the moment.

"I think you should see to Mrs. Finch straight off; she's on the verge of collapse. There's a matron with her, of course, but I don't think she'll calm down until she talks to you. I won't come with you; I'd be worse than no help. And I need to get back into the fray, but I wanted to brief you myself. The constable will direct you; I'll find you in a bit."

"Does Alan know?"

"Not yet." Morrison looked grim. I gathered he wasn't looking forward to passing the news along to his boss.

He left me in the care of an attractive young policewoman who took me to a small office on the next floor. Ada Finch was seated on a bench, her head in her hands, sobbing her heart out while the matron tried to comfort her.

I sat down on the bench next to Ada, gathered my wits about me, and spoke sharply.

"Ada, stop crying this minute and tell me what's happening!"

It was a risky move that might have sent her over the edge into full hysterics, but I was gambling on Ada's lifetime of deferring to "the gentry," hoping that my sternest schoolteacher voice would act on her reflexes.

To my great relief, it worked. Ada sat up

obediently, hiccuped, and accepted the wad of tissues I thrust into her hand.

She looked awful. Her bright blue eyes were swollen, her nose red from crying, her hair hanging in strings. I wanted to hug her, but sympathy at this stage would probably send her right off again. I hardened my heart, and when she finished blowing her nose and looked up at me dismally, I used my flintiest voice.

"That's better. I must say you've disappointed me, Ada. I'd expect you to fight back, instead of melting like this. Now, what kind of a mess has Bob gotten himself into this time?"

What with her misery and her anger — mostly directed at me — Ada wasn't terribly coherent, but I could get the details later from Morrison. My only goal just now was to get the poor woman calmed down.

". . . and never mind what the bloody p'lice say, 'ee never done nuffink!" she concluded, glaring at me fiercely.

"I expect you're right," I said mildly. "Unless there was some sort of silly accident. Was he — umm —"

" 'Ee never drinks on the job, as 'oo should know better than you! An' 'ee knows 'is plants. 'Ee never put nuffink in there wot didn't belong!"

Her lower lip jutted out; her eyes snapped. Much better. Maybe now I could actually get some information.

"I think you'd better tell me all about it, Ada. All I know is that she was poisoned."

"An' no loss to the world, neither! Just like 'er to cause trouble even by dyin'."

That was just Ada venting her spleen, but it was dangerous talk, with the matron listening to every word. I put my hand over hers, squeezed, and said, "Tell me what happened."

She pulled herself together, and when she spoke again, it was to the point. "I don't know, only wot they told me, as wasn't much. She takes — took — this tea, see, when she 'ad a bellyache from eatin' too much. Not proper tea, but 'erbs and that. Peppermint, an' 'oo knows wot." She sniffed meaningfully. "It'd poison anybody, I'd think!

"So she 'as a bad turn last week, an' uses up all 'er mixture. An' she tells Mr. Adam as 'ow she needs more, an' 'ee tells Bob wot to get from the garden, an' 'ee gets it. An' last night she drinks it, and this mornin' she's dead. An' 'ee never 'ad nuffink to do wiv it!"

She embroidered on that familiar theme for some time before I was able to extricate myself. Before I left, she made me promise to do what I could for Bob. I tried not to sound overly hopeful, but she had talked herself into believing that it was all a mistake, like the other time, and that I would soon clear it up. Her faith in me was touching, but terrifying, especially after I'd talked to Inspector Morrison.

"We're a long way from making a charge, but it's serious enough, I'm afraid," he said somberly. We were standing in the hallway, swirls of activity going on around us. "It isn't just the gathering of the herbs, or even the fact that Bob disliked Mrs. Lathrop. That motive would apply to everyone in the house, apparently. But it looks as though there might be a much stronger one, as well." He looked miserable as well as tired. "Mrs. Martin, I'm truly sorry. Bob's always been a respectable sort of man, apart from his drinking, and I take no pleasure in saying this, but it seems at least possible that he is, after all, a thief. There is no reason not to tell you that there was a plastic bag hidden behind some palms in the conservatory. It had Bob's fingerprints all over it, and it was full of miniatures."

8

I went home feeling very depressed, and very much alone. There was no point in trying to call Alan. He would call me when he heard the news from Morrison; till then I could only confuse the issue. In any case, I wasn't certain I was looking forward to talking to him, because I was sure I knew what he was going to say.

I don't know what Alan's first wife was like, but I had gotten the impression that she had been a lovely woman, intelligent and cultured, and quite happy to serve as Alan's helpmeet in the conventional way. I wasn't like that. I was American and prickly about independence. I'm not a feminist, exactly. I like men, on the whole, but I also like to follow my own pursuits, and Frank never tried to stop me. But Alan — Alan was protective. Oh, it wasn't his fault. He was brought up in the English gentlemanly tradition, and it was charming when it was a question of helping me into a car, or carrying something heavy. Interfering with my activities was another matter.

This wasn't the first time I'd gotten mixed up with the investigation of a crime, and on the previous occasions Alan hadn't been very happy about my involvement. True, once he'd gotten over his professional indignation at the idea of amateur meddling, and discovered I could actually be useful, he'd mellowed a little, but I knew he was deeply concerned that I might, someday, get into trouble I couldn't get out of. And now that we were married, it would be much worse.

He was going to try to keep me out of this investigation, I was sure of it. We would quarrel, and there is nothing so miserable as a long-distance quarrel. I moped.

The day was very long, and the weather was changing again. Clouds began to gather. The barometer began to fall. I should have been trying to help Bob somehow, but I couldn't make my brain work. And what was the point, when Alan was going to stop me in my tracks?

I tried for a little while to work on my dollhouse, but the weather had made my arthritic hands stiff and clumsy, and the project had somehow lost its appeal. There was nothing tempting on my bookshelves; my library consists largely of mysteries, which pall when one is involved in the real thing, and we hadn't yet unpacked most of Alan's books. I jumped every time the phone rang (two wrong numbers and the plumber, putting off his appointment yet again).

Alan called, finally, as I was pushing my supper around my plate.

"Well," was his greeting.

"Yes," I said. There was a pause. "Are you going to come home?"

"I don't think so. Morrison is perfectly competent, and in a way, I'm personally involved, since Bob works for us, so it's best I keep my distance."

Another pause.

"Are you still coming on Saturday?" he asked, finally.

"I don't know. It depends on what happens tomorrow, I suppose."

"Yes, of course."

It was horrible that we could speak only in formalities. I gulped down the lump in my throat. "Alan, I — you do understand that I have to support Ada?"

A sigh came over the line. "I understand what you think you have to do. I'm not entirely sure I agree."

"She's a friend, Alan," I said a little desperately. "She thinks I'm Miss Marple and Sherlock Holmes put together. She trusts me, and she — I'm sorry, but she doesn't trust the police at all. It's a class thing, I suppose, but there it is. I can't just abandon her." I stopped, perilously close to tears.

"Dorothy, I do see your point of view, but — look, we can't discuss this properly on the telephone. You will try to come on Saturday, won't you?"

"I'll try," I said. "Call me late tomorrow and I'll let you know."

"Very well. Good night."

I put my plate on the floor and let Sam and Emmy fight over it. I couldn't have choked down another mouthful.

The next day, Friday, I woke with a headache and no inclination at all to get out of bed. The sky was as gray as my mood, and the bedroom was cold. Yesterday had been so warm I hadn't turned on the central heating, but the weather, as it had threatened yesterday, had changed during the night. Now it was very Novemberish.

" 'A damp, drizzly November in my soul,' " I said aloud to Emmy, who jumped on my stomach and showed no interest in literary allusions. She was hungry, and so was Sam, and they told me so in ringing tones.

"All right, all right. I don't suppose you've ever heard of Moby Dick anyway. You'd think he was cat food."

At last I'd said something that made

sense. "Cat" and "food" are two of the words they know. Emmy nudged my cheek with a cold nose by way of encouragement, and Sam wailed in my ear. I got up.

It was too early to call and see how Ada was doing, too early to go to the police station and check on progress, even if they would tell me anything, which was doubtful. I dressed fast, turned on the heat, made some coffee (after feeding the cats, of course), and sat letting hot, fragrant caffeine warm and cheer me.

It took some time for the bells to penetrate my consciousness. The drizzle in the air muffled the tone, of course, but I had become so used to living with the sound of the cathedral's bells that I often didn't hear them, even on bright, crisp days when they chimed out clearly.

I looked at the clock. Five minutes till Matins.

I pulled on a hat at random, grabbed my umbrella, and streaked across the Cathedral Close, skidding through the arch in the choir screen just as the choirboys were filing into their stalls.

Margaret Allenby, the Dean's wife, moved over one place so I could sit at the end of the front row, and handed me the order of service for the day. I nodded my thanks and slipped to my knees for a moment before scrambling to my feet for the opening versicles and responses and the Venite.

I confess that I paid little attention to the service. I sat, stood, and knelt automatically, letting the beautiful old words and music wash over me. Here in the magnificent fan-vaulted choir, where little natural light penetrated on even the brightest of days, the November gloom seemed to matter less. The light of the choir's candles, of the beautiful brass chandeliers, of centuries of faith cast a warm glow of peace and good cheer.

But when old Canon Lovett had delivered the benediction in his kind, quavery voice, and choir and clergy had filed out, I turned to Margaret.

"Good morning, Dorothy. Lovely anthem this morning, didn't you think?"

"Beautiful," I said without a blush. I was sure it had been; it always was. "Margaret, do you have time for coffee?"

"Of course. My house is frightfully untidy, I'm afraid, but —"

"Heavens, I wasn't inviting myself over. I thought maybe Alderney's, if you don't mind walking in the rain."

"My dear Dorothy, perish the day an Englishwoman can't walk in the rain!" She gathered up her umbrella and followed me up the nave.

Alderney's is at the far west end of the Close, and we were both damp around the edges by the time we got there. The wetness was as much fog as rain, and had a penetrating quality unique, in my experience, to England.

It was late for breakfast and early for the morning coffee crowd; we had the place almost to ourselves, which was fine with me. We sat at a table in front of the fire and ordered coffee and Alderney's specialty, a kind of yeast bun with raisins that they serve doused with cinnamon butter. I waited until the waitress was back in the kitchen before planting my elbows on the table and my chin in my hands.

"Margaret, I need to talk to you."

"I rather suspected you might," she said mildly, and I smiled in spite of myself. "There, now, that's better! I thought you looked a bit seedy when you came panting in this morning."

"Very seedy. I badly need some advice."

"Then take some now, and get some food into you before you say another word."

I was sure I couldn't eat, but when our order arrived, the buns smelled so good that I took a tentative bite, and then proceeded to wolf down the whole rich, buttery pastry.

Margaret nodded with satisfaction. "You have some color back, now. You were gray as a ghost."

"I was hungry," I said with surprise. "Come to think of it, I didn't have any dinner last night."

"A great mistake, going without food," said Margaret crisply. "Saps the strength, lowers the resistance. Now." She leaned back and folded her hands across her stomach. "What's up?"

I waded in without preliminary. "You know about the murder at the Hall yesterday, of course, and that Ada Finch has asked me to — well, what she really wants is for me to prove that Bob didn't do it. She has an exaggerated idea of my abilities, and a very poor opinion of the police. And, of course, ordinarily I'd do anything I could, but — oh, everything's different now that Alan and I are married. People won't talk to me freely, and I don't think Alan likes the idea of my being involved. Well, I know he doesn't. He's away, of course, so we haven't talked about it at length, but he was very odd on the phone last night. Wary, sort of. And I can't bear the thought of anything coming between us, but I can't just let Ada down, either. And besides, I — I *want* to get into this."

I struggled to say what was in my mind. "Margaret, something's happened to me in the past few months. I've come alive again, somehow. After Frank died, I wasn't really a person for a long time. I was locked up in a cage, looking and talking like a human being, but actually being a robot. Everything was automatic.

"Do you understand at all what I'm trying to say? Somehow, now, the cage is open. I'm free, free to find out who I am, to redefine myself, and I'm finding out that I'm good at some very odd things. Like — well, like solving some kinds of crimes, silly as it sounds. This business, now. It's right up my alley, so to speak, and then with people I know and care about being involved . . ." I ran down, poured myself more coffee, and took a sip.

"Hmmm. Have you talked to Jane?"

"I can't, not about this. She has some peculiar notion about the Hall, and she doesn't like my going out there. She'll give me information when I ask, that's all."

"Jane has excellent judgment, you know."

I sighed irritably. "Does that mean you're going to tell me the same thing? Not to get involved?"

"I'm going to tell you no such thing. You must make up your own mind what to do.

It's your conscience that has to be satisfied, after all, no one else's. What I am saying is to listen to what Jane tells you, because it will be reliable information. And, Dorothy — don't sell Alan short. He's not an unreasonable man, not the sort to keep a woman caged up, or glorified on some sort of pedestal. He simply loves you."

"I know he does. And I love him. But I — oh, I don't know. I come, not just from a different country, but from a different world in many ways, and I'm used to being independent. And then there's his job. If I get into trouble, it's going to reflect on him, and . . ." I ran down again.

"Have you told him all this?"

"No. He knows."

"You'd be astonished at what people don't know until you tell them. My advice, for what it's worth, is that you defer any decision until you've talked it out thoroughly with your charming husband. Argue your point of view, and see what he says. And then think about it again for a good twenty-four hours, so you're not doing anything irrevocable when your mind is in a turmoil.

"Now I must run. I've a meeting of the Altar Guild in five minutes. I'll pray for you, my dear, and I'll ask Kenneth to, as well. Don't leave your umbrella behind."

She laid some money on the table and blew out the door.

Maybe it was the sensible, matter-of-fact advice, or the stabilizing influence of a centuries-old form of worship, or the prayers of a good woman. Coffee and food probably had something to do with it, too. At any rate, I left Alderney's with a plan.

First on the agenda was the phone call to Ada.

The voice that answered was male, and I instantly felt twenty years younger. "Bob! You're home!"

"Ar."

I waited for an explanation, but there was only silence, punctuated by heavy, adenoidal breathing. "That's good news!" I said brightly. "Have they arrested someone else, then?"

"Naow."

A further interval. "Bob, I actually called to talk to your mother. Is she around?"

"Ar." The phone was laid down with a bang, and eventually Ada's voice sounded.

" 'Ullo?"

"Ada, it's Dorothy. I was so relieved when Bob answered, but I couldn't get anything out of him. Has he been cleared?"

She gave a snort, unmistakable even over the phone. "Not so's you'd notice. 'Ere, 'old on a minute."

There was the sound of a door closing, and Ada came back on the line.

"I didn't want 'im to 'ear me. 'Ee's mopin' around like a sick turkey, feelin' sorry for 'isself."

"But why, for heaven's sake? If he's been allowed to come home —"

" 'Ee ain't out of the woods yet," Ada said somberly. "They didn't 'ave enough evidence against 'im to 'old 'im, but they told 'im not to leave town, and 'ee come 'ome yesterday, so today 'ee goes out to work, it not rainin' 'ard enough to matter, an' there bein' a pile 'o work to be done on two of 'is gardens before winter sets in 'ard."

She paused for breath. "An' they both told 'im they didn't need 'is services no more."

There was no adequate response. "I see," I said slowly, growing angrier the longer I thought about it. "Just because he's under suspicion. It isn't *fair*, Ada!"

"An' 'oo said life was fair?"

I couldn't think of anything helpful to say to that, either, and hung up feeling I had done no good. But instead of being depressed myself, I was gloriously angry, and in that mood I put on one of my most outrageous hats for moral support, flung myself in my car, and headed recklessly out to

Brocklesby Hall for the second item on my mental list.

Rain slowed the traffic, so I had time on the way to think out an approach. The museum would probably be closed. In fact, the whole place was probably designated a Crime Scene, but I might be able to wangle my way in. If being the wife of the chief constable was proving to be a handicap in some ways, surely I was entitled to use its advantages for all they were worth.

So I smiled pleasantly to the young constable on duty at the door. "Good morning. I don't believe we've met, but I am Mrs. Nesbitt." Never mind my preferred usage for now; this was a time for name-dropping. "I hope I won't be in the way, but Mrs. Cunningham needs some help in the library, what with all the confusion. May I use this door, or would it be better to go in the back?"

Poor man, he knew perfectly well that he should keep me out, but he couldn't quite face the possible consequences. Nor could he leave his post to make sure I went where I said I was going to. He smiled uncertainly, but my hat settled the matter. No one who would deliberately don an object featuring droopy chrysanthemums and velvet oak leaves could be taken seriously as a villain.

"I'll just ask someone to show you the way, madam —"

"Oh, never mind, I know the way. Thank you *so* much!" I sailed in, making a mental note to ask Alan to keep the poor constable out of trouble. I wasn't playing fair, and I knew it, but just at the moment I didn't care.

I hoped Meg was actually in the library. I had no idea whether she would be; she had been an excuse to get inside the house. I'd thought I'd offer to help, anything to lend some credence to my lie, and then slip out as soon as I decently could and poke around, trying to avoid the legitimate representatives of the law. My thoughts hadn't progressed any further than that.

Which was just as well, because the minute I laid eyes on the librarian I knew she was in genuine need of help. Her eyes were swollen; there was a sodden handkerchief on the desk in front of her.

"You poor dear, what is it? Has Claude —"

She jumped when I spoke, dabbed angrily at her eyes, and glared at me. "It isn't Claude. Claude's away; nobody's seen him since the murder. It's just — oh, everything is so miserable!" She picked up the handkerchief; I substituted a clean one from my purse and let her cry it out.

"Sorry, Dorothy," she finally muttered stiffly. "No excuse for that."

"My dear girl, don't apologize! One reason women have fewer ulcers and heart attacks is because society allows us to show our emotions. Well, at least American society does; you English . . ."

She blew her nose and sat up straighter. "Repressed and neurotic, that's us. Though my Irish means I *can't* always keep it in. Thanks for the handkerchief."

"Any time. Do you want to talk about it? You'd probably feel better. Or shall I go away and let you cry some more?"

Her eyes flashed at that. She was recovering. "Even I can't weep to order. But —"

"But you're worried about what I'll tell my husband. He's out of town at the moment, and I only tell him what I think is relevant. If you'll allow me that judgment, I'm a pretty good listener, Meg." I sat down and removed my hat.

Meg eyed it warily, blew her nose again, and began to speak in something like her usual incisive manner.

"You were right, at that. It does all go back to Claude. If only he were the one who . . ." She sighed and went on. "I suppose you know about — our past history."

"I know a little, yes." She winced and I

made haste to explain. "You mustn't think that these things are made public. It's rather a special case, since I had guessed that something was very wrong, and asked Alan to check on Claude. I haven't told anyone, and you don't have to talk about it if it tears you up."

"Not anymore. At least I thought it didn't. I thought I'd dealt with it. It happened over a year ago, when I first started working here. Claude was living here then, in his mother's part of the house. He was always hanging about, trying to chat me up, and I — well, I was pretty off-putting. He wasn't as disgusting then as he is now, but — oh, I hadn't been divorced very long, and I was supersensitive, I suppose. The fact is, I could never bear him. Perhaps if I'd been polite, anyway, he —"

"Stop blaming yourself. He's a blot on society and the sort who would victimize anyone. You're not the only one, you know."

"I did have some idea, actually. One hears things. Well, anyway, one day he —"

"We can skip that part. How is it he got away with it?"

"There was no proof of anything. I screamed and Richard came, and Claude pretended nothing had happened. I did make a complaint, but Claude had scarpered for London by the time the police got around to doing anything — sorry."

"It's all right. I don't identify myself with Alan's job. And even he knows he doesn't have enough men to do every job right. So then . . ."

"I decided not to pursue it. I need this post badly, for one thing, so I can't afford to antagonize Mrs. Lathrop. And then it's quite trying to relive that sort of thing, which I would have had to do if I'd decided to take him to court. And, of course, there was Jemima."

"She would have been about six then?"

"Nearly seven. She's eight now, but small for her age, and young, as well. I didn't tell her anything, of course, but she's always been perceptive about emotions. She knew I was upset. Neither of us was terribly good at sign language then, so I couldn't tell her much or console her very well, and I could see she was worried. That's one reason I dropped it. She'd only just begun in her new school, and it was so good for her I didn't want anything to upset her. Besides, I needed to put it behind me. I thought I had," she repeated. "I wasn't really afraid for myself, you know. It was just — if he'd ever come to my house — with Jemima there . . ." Her voice trailed off.

"And then Claude came back," I prompted.

She nodded; her face looked bitter. "Claude came back. I don't know why. I'd thought he was going to stay put in London. Certainly his mother didn't want him here."

"One can see why," I said emphatically. "Especially when she cultivated such an image of respectability. I was surprised to see him on Guy Fawkes Day. I thought he'd gone away again."

"He did, but he came back on Thursday. Last Thursday, a week ago. And that's what started all the trouble." She stopped and looked at her lap. The hard part was coming, then. I looked as attentive and sympathetic as I possibly could.

"He came to the library." Meg's hands were twisting in her lap. "I knew the minute he opened the door — he threw it back against the wall with such a crash that I screamed — and then he slammed it shut again and locked it."

"Meg!"

"Yes." The hands twisted; her breath came fast and shallow. "It was — bad. He's not a big man, but he can be very strong, and he was in a violent mood.

"He said — things —" Meg's unruly hands, of their own volition, moved to cover her ears. She became conscious of them, then, and clasped them fiercely in her lap. "I tried not to hear. Then he started walking toward me, slowly, and I backed up and backed up until I was against one of the bookcases, and he kept moving closer —"

Her voice broke.

"Meg, stop! I'm sorry, Meg. This is too awful for you. We'll take it as given that Claude is a violent louse, and —"

"No, you don't understand. That was only the beginning of it. Because, you see, Richard rescued me again."

"But how? You said the door was locked."

"He broke a window."

I looked up and saw that the obstruction I had seen, without noticing it, was a wooden panel fixed over the bottom half of one of the lancet windows.

"Good grief! He must have cut himself."

"Not badly. He was wearing heavy gardening clothes, and gloves. But he got a cut over one eye, and he looked like the wrath of doom when he came crashing in. He'd been in the conservatory and heard me scream, and just came running as fast as he could. And when he couldn't get in the door —"

"Yes, I see. A man of action, it would seem. What did he do to Claude?"

"He would have half-killed him, I think,

but I managed to unlock the door and Claude — left."

I laughed, a little shakily. "He's good at evaporating, isn't he? And you . . . ?"

"I got into a frightful row with Richard."

"But surely —"

"After he'd saved my life? Or my virtue, at least?" She opened her desk drawer and rummaged for a moment, then shook her head and shut the drawer with a frustrated bang. "I stopped smoking years ago, when I was pregnant with Jemima. At times like this I still forget.

"You're right, Dorothy. I owe Richard a lot. But that's part of the problem. I don't want to be obligated to him. He thinks what he's done for me, or our relationship — if you can call it that — gives him the right to order me about. I *won't* be told what to do, even by someone I love!"

I could certainly sympathize with her there. "So you were overwrought anyway, and when Richard tried to boss you around — yes, I see. Then you ran into Claude again on Friday. No wonder you were afraid."

"Not for myself, not even after what had happened. Claude's a coward; he'd never try anything on when he might get into real trouble. But with Jemima there — I confess,

I even kept wishing Richard would turn up, and then when your husband did — well, it was help with no strings attached, and I truly appreciated it. I'm afraid I was rude, I —"

"No, you weren't, and anyway, you thanked Alan, later, through me. You mustn't worry about it. But, Meg, it's probably none of my business, but what is Richard trying to order you to do?" I thought I could guess, but it was certainly time to stop talking about the egregious Claude.

My guess was wrong.

"He keeps insisting that I have to leave the Hall and find a job somewhere else. He wants to marry me, but we couldn't live on just his wages, and there's no other job in Sherebury that would work out for me at all. And now that Mrs. Lathrop is dead —"

She stopped abruptly. I looked at her and was silent.

"Oh, all right. Mrs. Lathrop was trying to get me sacked. She told Sir Mordred we didn't need a curator, that I was just a glorified librarian, and he could hire somebody part-time and save money. I heard her say it one day when she didn't know I was in the next room. Saving money wasn't the reason she wanted me out, though. She was jealous of me, I think. She was jealous of anybody who took up Sir Mordred's time and attention. But she's gone now, and I don't intend to give up a perfectly good job just because of awful Claude!"

"But, Meg, he's a real threat. Why do you have to stay in Shrebury?" I checked myself. "Oh — how stupid of me. It's Jemima, isn't it? She's doing well in school?"

She nodded, with a deep sigh. "We'd tried so many schools, ever since she was four. None of them seemed able to help her, and then we found this one, and they've done wonders. She's happy, she's made friends, she's learning. Dorothy, she's forgotten she has a disability, and I almost forget it, too. I can't spoil that; I can't —"

I'm pretty transparent sometimes. My face must have reflected my thoughts, because Meg stopped abruptly.

There was a little silence.

"Meg —" The words stuck in my throat, but I had to ask. I tried again. "This all happened a week ago, you say."

She nodded dumbly.

"I saw you two days ago, and you didn't say a word about it. You seemed to be in pretty good spirits, in fact, though Bob Finch told me you'd quarreled earlier with Richard. Why is it upsetting you so much now?"

"Because I — there's been a murder, for the love of — and what right have you —"

Her voice had risen. Neither of us had noticed the opening of the door.

"Excuse me, Mrs. Cunningham. Of course I would not for the world wish to interrupt your tête-à-tête, but if I could just recall your mind to your work for a moment?"

Sir Mordred stood in the doorway, his face fixed in a furious pout.

9

I was the first to recover, speaking, for once, with my mind fully engaged. "Sir Mordred, may I offer my condolences? I'm sure you must be devastated by the loss of such a capable housekeeper."

My careful tact availed me nothing. He muttered something to me and turned back to rant at Meg.

"I did ask you, if I recall correctly, to give me a complete and current list of the collection by lunchtime. It is now five minutes to twelve, and I am being badgered by the police for the list. May I ask if you have found time in your busy social schedule to make any progress at all?"

She had herself back under control. "I have been *trying,* Sir Mordred," she snapped, "but it isn't easy. The house is in an uproar, the computer catalogue is far from complete, and I am not a machine!" There was fire in her eye. "I'll do my best, but don't expect miracles. *And* I need some figures from John Thoreston, if he ever turns up. Have you heard from him?"

"I have not." Sir Mordred drew himself up to his full five feet five; his face grew an even richer shade of plum. "Nor do I expect to. I have been informed by the police that Mr. Thoreston is not in his rooms. Nor is his luggage. My accountant, it appears, has flown. Now may I ask when I may expect you to complete this work? Surely it is a simple enough task, if your records are in any sort of . . ."

Only a self-absorbed man like Sir Mordred could have delivered that staggering piece of news as an afterthought. Meg and I were struck dumb. Sir Mordred raved on until he eventually ran out of invective and stood there, drumming his fat little fingers on her desk, waiting for a response.

"Have you not realized," I said as gently as I could, "what Mr. Thoreston's disappearance may mean?"

He turned to me, directly acknowledging my presence for the first time. "I am not an imbecile, madam. I quite realize that my affairs will be in a shambles for some time, due to the thoughtlessness and incompetence —"

I interrupted him; I couldn't help it. "Sir Mordred, think! An accountant who vanishes often has a very good reason for doing so. I imagine that the police will confiscate the museum's books immediately, if they have not already done so. And have you further considered that an embezzler might have an extremely good motive for murder?"

And then Meg and I were very busy for a few minutes, opening windows and administering water and issuing soothing comments. I couldn't decide whether Sir Mordred was having a stroke, or a heart attack, or simply a fit of temper. He wouldn't let us call a doctor or put him to bed. Eventually I helped him to his office, where he slumped down onto a squashy old leather couch and waved me away.

"Quiet! I need quiet! Just go!"

I went.

I would have liked to question the police in the house about the missing accountant, but thought better of it. I was there under false pretences. The moment a policeman with some sense saw me I would be escorted off the property, with all due consideration, but very firmly. I preferred to leave in dignified fashion, on my own. I did stop back in the library for a moment.

"Well, he's settled, for the moment anyway. I think he'll be all right, but he's had a shock. I'd love to know what the police find in those books."

Meg shook her head. "I'm astonished about John. He was a wet fish, but I'd have sworn he was an honest man. He was certainly competent."

"Of course it takes a good accountant to cook the books convincingly," I pointed out. "I don't expect he's stolen much. He didn't look to me like a man of nerve and daring."

"No." She shook her head. "But he didn't look like someone who could kill, either." She sighed, but there was relief in her voice, all the same.

"You're right. Look here, the police don't appreciate my being here, but I'll stay if I can be of any help. I didn't mean to upset you before — I —"

"It's all right. I overreacted. Everything's in such a ghastly muddle, and I've been frantic, but I'll cope. It's better, now that we know who . . ."

"Well, then, I'll . . ." I trailed off awkwardly and slipped away.

I did say a few words to the constable at the door about Sir Mordred's collapse, and he promised to have someone look in on him from time to time. He would have promised to take over the nursing duties himself, I think, just to get me off the premises.

I saw Richard Adam on my way to the

parking lot. He was standing beyond the far corner of the house, intently studying a garden plot. The plants were gray, and sagging with rain; I couldn't see why he was so interested.

He saw me out of the corner of his eye, turned and looked at me for a quick moment, then deliberately walked away without so much as a nod.

Impatient of waiting until he called me, I put through a call to Alan as soon as I got home, but he didn't return it until I had sat down to a sketchy lunch.

"There have been developments," I said, hastily swallowing a mouthful of tuna sandwich. "I won't go into details on the phone, but things are looking up for Bob. I'm definitely coming tomorrow; you're still going to be able to meet me?"

"Absolutely. I'm so glad you can come." His phrasing was formal, and I could hear voices in the background, but the warmth in his voice was good to hear. "If the weather improves, I'll take you for a stroll through the deer park."

"How Jane Austen that sounds! I'm planning to catch the earliest possible train, but I'll call from Waterloo, because you never know what changes they'll suddenly decide to make. Weekend rail travel, you know."

"Just get here as soon as you can, my dear."

Only that, but I finished my sandwich with such appetite that I made another one.

By the time I got as far as London on Saturday morning, the weather had improved enough that I had great hopes of the deer park. The train, by some miracle, was actually running on time, and the sun was shining, if somewhat halfheartedly, when I arrived at Winchfield station.

It was some time before I could speak to Alan. Heedless of the stationmaster, who was looking on with great interest, he'd folded me into a bear hug so tight I could hardly breathe. When he released me he looked me over, top to toe, and gave a great roar of laughter.

"That hat, my dear, is the most ridiculous one I've ever seen you wear, and that is saying a great deal."

"Don't you like oak leaves? I thought it appropriate to a deer park," I said primly, "although it really could use a few ostrich plumes to suit the period."

"Jane Austen's characters wore simple poke bonnets. Unless, of course, you're intending to impersonate Mrs. Bennet."

I stuck my tongue out at him. "Oh, Alan,

it *is* good to see you. I didn't know I could miss anyone so much after only three days."

"Mmm." It was a typical male non-reply, but the look that accompanied it was entirely satisfactory.

"Have you had your breakfast, my dear?"

"Coffee, a hundred years ago. I thought I'd get a bite in Waterloo Station, but I barely had time to catch the train. I'm starving."

"Good. There's a charming little cafe on the way, where we can get a proper breakfast. I waited for you."

Anyone who worries about cholesterol would have a heart attack just thinking about a "proper" English breakfast. If there's something missing that is fattening and artery-clogging, I can't imagine what it is. Eggs, bacon, sausages, fried potatoes, fried bread, grilled mushrooms, grilled tomatoes. Badly prepared, it is a greasy nightmare, but when the cook knows his business it is food for the gods. I ate everything except the canned baked beans that, for some incomprehensible reason, often form part of the meal.

"All right, lead me to the deer park," I said with a groan. "I need to walk miles as a penance after that."

We drove for some time through the rolling Hampshire hills, still beautiful even with winter coming. The sheep were round with wool, the cattle sleek and healthy. Now and then a rabbit would disappear into a hedgerow, and for one lovely instant I saw a pheasant before he whirred up and was gone.

I didn't see the house until Alan had turned the car into the long, straight drive. Then it appeared before me in all its majesty.

The trees on either side of the drive had lost their foliage for the winter, and the bare branches did nothing to obscure the perfect lines of the manor. Made of soft pink brick and some kind of white stone, it rose serene and lovely.

And huge.

"Alan, this surely isn't — I can't — how could I ever —" I couldn't keep the panic out of my voice.

He patted my knee. "Don't worry. It looks enormous and confusing, but it sorts itself out quickly. You must admit it's beautiful."

It was. Compared to Brocklesby Hall . . . well, there was no comparison, really. This house was really old, built in a time when grace and proportion were paramount considerations. I would love being a guest here, strolling through the gardens, sitting by one of the fires that, judging from the forest of chimneys, warmed nearly every room. But *live* in a place like this? Me, a hick from Indiana?

Alan glanced at me and I forced a smile. "Perfectly beautiful."

I had the feeling I wasn't fooling him a bit.

He pulled the car into the prime spot reserved for the commandant and led me into the imposing front hall. It was as big as my whole house in Sherebury. On one wall a huge white marble fireplace crackled with a wood fire. Twin stone archways, flanked and surmounted by colorful coats of arms, led to another part of the house. The floor was of polished stone, the walls of polished wood. I clung to Alan's arm and tried not to gape.

A pleasant-faced young black woman in uniform was sitting at a desk to one side. She looked up and smiled broadly, at my hat, no doubt. Alan drew me nearer.

"Betty, allow me to introduce my wife, Dorothy Martin. This is Betty Atieno, who has volunteered to take you in charge for an hour or so. Unfortunately, I have a meeting in" — he looked at his watch — "in two minutes. Betty, if you'll deliver Mrs. Martin to the drawing room when you've finished, I'll join her there as soon as I can." He kissed me lightly on the cheek and strode off. I watched him go with the sensation of losing a lifeline in mid-ocean.

"Such a lovely man," said Betty, her ebony face lighting up with a smile. "We all hope he will come here. We would enjoy working with him. Now you must come with me and I will show you the house that may be your home for a time."

"Thank you. I'm afraid I feel a little lost. It's so big . . ."

"I, too, felt intimidated when I first came here. It is not like Kenya." She grinned, and I couldn't help joining her.

"Ah, that's where you're from. I wondered about that delightful lilt to your speech. I'm a foreigner myself, as you probably know. Do you like living in England?"

"I miss my home, yes, especially in the winter, but I enjoy my job and I like this estate. You will like it, too, Mrs. Martin, when you have found your feet. Do not worry."

Betty had missed her calling, I thought. She would have made a wonderful nanny. Meekly I allowed myself to be soothed and conducted on a tour.

The house had been turned into a working institution without a great deal of alteration. Certainly its beauty remained largely unsullied, but my appreciation was soon swamped by a return of panic, for in sheer size, Bramshill was as overwhelming as Brocklesby Hall.

Betty regaled me, as we turned one confusing corner after another, with the story of the ghost, supposedly a bride who, in a rather rowdy game of hide-and-seek on her long-ago wedding day, had hidden in the big chest that now resided in the front hall. She drew the lid down a bit too far and it locked. She was never found, and her restless spirit still, according to the story, walked the halls today.

I was skeptical. Ghosts that come complete with careful, logical explanations carry the scent of Hollywood, it has always seemed to me. Nevertheless, it was not a tale to inspire warm, happy feelings about the house. By the time I was deposited in the drawing room, I was feeling very New World, very small, and thoroughly daunted. Betty explained about the tapestries.

"They are old, and extremely valuable. We have a saying. 'In case of fire: women, children, and tapestries first.' And not necessarily in that order!" She showed me the cords that provided for a quick release of the hangings, so that they could be rolled up and carried off, and I realized she wasn't kidding. I shrank a little further into myself.

When Alan came to claim me I was hard put to maintain a smile, but he pretended not to notice. "Ready for that walk?" he boomed.

"More than ready," I muttered. "But I'll need to change my shoes."

My bag had been left in the front hall. I slipped into an old pair of tennis shoes and followed Alan out the door.

The sun had come out in full force, and the day was warm for November, but I was glad of my jacket. We walked briskly and silently, our thoughts interrupted only by an occasional scream from one of the peacocks. I jumped the first time; after that the screams were just irritating.

"Look," said Alan, touching my arm and pointing.

Three white deer moved like the ghosts of deer through the leafless skeletons of trees. They froze at some small sound and looked at us, motionless, then bounded out of sight.

"There's a bench over there, Dorothy. In the sun. Shall we sit for a bit?"

We sat and watched the woods for a little while, but no more deer appeared. Alan spoke at the same moment I did.

"Alan —"

"Dorothy —"

He gestured.

"No, you first."

"Very well. Dorothy, don't worry so. You've been edgy ever since we got here. Do I frighten you, now that you're burdened with me for life?"

"What an idea! No, you don't scare me, but this place does. It's all so beautiful and so English, and so unlike any place where I could feel at home. I hate to be such a — a coward and a killjoy, but I just can't get enthusiastic about living here. I'm sorry."

"My dear, there's no need to apologize! I hope you'll take a little longer to make up your mind, but if you decide in the end you don't want me to take up the appointment, I shan't. That isn't what I wanted to talk to you about, though."

"What, then — oh."

Here it came, I thought. He was going to call me off, tell me that a man in his position couldn't allow me to meddle any more in Bob Finch's problems.

Margaret Allenby had told me to let Alan see my point of view, but I was demoralized. "It's all right, Alan," I began dispiritedly. "I see your reasoning. Bob isn't the chief suspect anymore, anyway — I told you there were developments. I think —" To my horror, I couldn't keep my voice steady. I gulped, squared my shoulders, took a deep breath, and started over, on the proper tack this time.

"I've been thinking a lot about all this, Alan. You have a point, of course, but I think I do, too. Ada Finch is a friend, and she's begun to depend on me for moral support, and even for solutions to her problems. And maybe that isn't as silly as it sounds.

"The truth is, I'm an unashamed snoop, and people seem to like to talk to me. I can't help it if they tell me things, can I? Or if I start putting two and two together? I taught school for too many years not to know something about people and what makes them tick."

I had been studying my lap, but I looked up to see how Alan was taking this. He was looking at the trees in the distance, his face unreadable.

"Well, anyway, there it is. I think I can do some good, looking into Mrs. Lathrop's murder. Maybe I can even help the police a little. You're always saying you're under-staffed."

Still no response.

"Can't we work out some way that I can keep on poking around, without embarrassing you or breaking any rules? Alan, say something!"

He looked at me, finally, his face sober.

"Dorothy, I'm ashamed. I didn't realize you felt quite so strongly about it. I value your abilities, of course, and I don't want to stand in your way, but . . ." He ran his hand down the back of his neck. "The plain fact is, I worry about you. You constantly underestimate the potential for catastrophe. The police are trained to deal with dangerous situations; you're not.

"You think I'm concerned about regulations. I must consider them, of course, but my chief concern is your safety. My dear, I love you, and I couldn't bear . . ."

He looked away again.

"Well, at least we understand each other," I said after an uncomfortable silence. "Alan, a few weeks ago I promised to love, cherish, and obey you. I meant it. If you issue me a direct order —"

"Confound it, Dorothy, I'm not going to order you about! You're an intelligent human being with a will of your own; you've the right to make your own decisions. I suppose I'm being overprotective."

"Oh, Alan, you're not! Not really. You're just being — male. And English."

"I can scarcely help that," he said with a tiny smile.

"Any more than I can help being female

and American. And I don't want you to be any different. I just — I suppose I want to eat my cake and have it, too. Go my own way and lean on you when I need to."

He put his arm around me and drew me close. "Lean on me all you like, my dear. Let's leave it for now, shall we? I think we both need to do a bit more thinking. Meanwhile, I'll try to be a trifle less dictatorial and hidebound. And, love — it'll be all right. I promise."

We sat gazing at the trees, watching for the pale, lovely deer.

10

In spite of my reservations about Bramshill, and Alan's ambivalence about my activities, we enjoyed a pleasant weekend. We went to the village church on Sunday morning, and though the music was awful, compared to a cathedral choir and organ, the vicar was a charming man who conducted a dignified service and preached a good sermon based on St. Paul's letter to the Ephesians, the bit about husbands loving their wives. Perhaps because of that, or perhaps because a night together in a large, comfortable bed in the guest wing had strengthened our appreciation of each other, on Sunday afternoon we talked long and hard about Mrs. Lathrop's murder. By tacit consent we avoided controversy. I was careful to be non-provocative in my remarks, and Alan, in his turn, was scrupulously fair about dealing out information. He really was trying to unbend.

I brought him up to date on the disappearance of the accountant. "When I found out, it seemed obvious that he was the culprit, but I thought about it on the train coming down, Alan, and now I'm not convinced that Thoreston actually had anything to do with it. I'm sure they'll find irregularities in the books — that's why he's vamoosed — but he's not the type for anything more ambitious. He struck me, the one time I met him, as a sly, sneaky kind of person. He cringes, like Uriah Heep. Now a man like that might easily embezzle a few paltry sums, but would he have the steady nerves, not to mention the knowledge, to plan a particularly clever poisoning?"

"Means, motive, opportunity." My spouse intoned the classic trio like a mantra. "Look at it from a police point of view. The means and opportunity were at hand. From what I've been told, anyone in the house could have got at the herbal tea, though there's a limited time period involved.

"Morrison's kept me apprised of all the main points of the case, because of my personal interest. This, by the way, is privileged information; don't mention it to anyone.

"It seems Mrs. Lathrop asked for new herbs to be gathered on Wednesday, a week and a half ago, and Bob did as the head gardener, Adam, told him. She, Lathrop, allowed them to dry for a couple of days in a fruit desiccator, and then chopped them and put them away in her own particular tea caddy, which she kept in the kitchen. According to the cook, Lathrop was quite particular about mixing the herbs herself, though she trusted the gardeners to pick them."

"With her weight, I doubt if she would have enjoyed stooping over flower beds, especially in the sun."

"Perhaps not. At any rate, on the Sunday — a week ago — she indulged in a heavy meal and was struck with indigestion in the evening. She asked the cook to make her an infusion, drank it, and reported feeling better, although she drank a little more of the tea in the morning, a fresh infusion, just to be sure. She felt fine, then, until Wednesday night, when a meal of roast pork caused her fits again. She had a dose of the tea, but this time it didn't work quite so well. The cook implied that it was no wonder, the amount of pork she had eaten.

"So Lathrop got out of bed early in the morning, apparently still feeling uncomfortable. This time she went down to the kitchen and prepared the infusion herself, since the cook was in bed. That was when she became really ill, vomiting and thrashing about. She called for help, but the cook and Claude were the only ones in the house at the time, and they didn't know what to do. By the time the doctor came her heart was failing; she died a few minutes after his arrival."

"So. It sounds as if the tea was okay on Wednesday night, and not okay by — when?"

"The cook doesn't know for certain, since she didn't wake until Lathrop started screaming and throwing things, just before seven o'clock. It's fortunate, by the way, that the cook sleeps in a little room just next to the kitchen, or she'd never have heard anything in that great barracks of a house. She ought to have been up, of course, but it seems she was in the habit of sleeping late when Sir Mordred wasn't around, and letting Mrs. Lathrop get her own breakfast.

"Anyway, she assumes that Lathrop took about ten minutes to boil the kettle and steep the tea, and the doctor said the symptoms would make themselves known almost immediately after she drank the stuff. So that means she probably opened the caddy sometime between six-thirty and quarter to seven."

"So that looks like Claude, doesn't it?"

"Perhaps. Sir Mordred, as you remember, was in London. But of course the cook was there, though we have no reason to suppose she wanted Lathrop dead. And both Meg

Cunningham and Richard Adam have keys to the house."

"John Thoreston? Bob Finch?"

"No. Neither of them. But either could have hidden in the house until after it was shut up, done what needed to be done, and left. Several of the doors are self-locking." He waited politely for any further questions. I shook my head, and he went on.

"From the symptoms the poison is almost certainly an alkaloid, which means some sort of plant. Neither the autopsy nor the lab analysis of the herbal mixture left in the caddy has been completed yet, but the doctor's guess is monkshood, which seems a likely bet. Its active principle is aconite, which would cause the symptoms described. It's often grown as an ornamental in our part of the world; why not in Brocklesby's garden? So you see, Thoreston could have had both means and opportunity. And as for motive —"

"I know, I know. But the psychology is all wrong, it seems to me. Thoreston is the cornered-rat sort. He might bite in an extremity, but poisoning is not his cup of tea. So to speak."

Alan quite properly ignored that. "So you favor Claude?"

"Your guess is as good as mine — probably better. He's more vicious than Thoreston, certainly, but not anything like as intelligent, and certainly not a rural type. Would he even think of a plant as poisonous? Wouldn't an overdose of cocaine be more his style?"

"My dear, I don't know. He is vicious, as you say, and if he isn't precisely intelligent, he's quite clever enough to pick a few sprigs of a plant. But what motive would he have? I'm reasonably certain his mum was his chief means of support. Our information on him is a trifle sketchy, but nothing has turned up so far to indicate that he's gainfully employed. Why would he want to kill his meal ticket?"

"Well, I wish I could ask him, but he's vanished, too, probably run off to London in a panic. He's not the kind to stick around where there's trouble."

"Indeed. And as for Bob —"

"I flatly refuse to believe Bob guilty of anything worse than a weakness for his pint. Somebody planted that bag with the miniatures in it so Bob would be suspected. I wish it hadn't had his fingerprints on it, though."

Alan sighed heavily. "That's one of the reasons they turned him loose, actually. Morrison is no fool, Dorothy. That bag struck him wrong from the first. A trifle too convenient. And it was a bag that had held grass seed."

"Oh, of course. So Bob had handled it at one time."

"Exactly. No one likes the man as a suspect any more than you do, but when he's thrown at us, we must at least consider him."

"What a tangled mess." Privately I decided that I would spend Monday trying to do some untangling, but I thought better of telling Alan.

I left Bramshill on Sunday night, just in time to catch the last train back to Sherebury. After a couple of days in the manor house I had begun to feel somewhat more at home, but still not quite ready to commit myself to being chatelaine of such a dwelling. Alan and I left it at that. "We'll talk when I come home on Saturday," he said comfortably. "Don't fret about it, darling — or about anything else. We'll work it out."

Monday morning dawned brilliantly sunny, but very cold. A light rain the night before had left moisture in the air that condensed, toward morning, into hoarfrost. Every dry twig, every blade of grass glittered diamond bright. I put aside my worries; it was a morning to shout aloud for the pure joy of being alive. The cats caught my mood and raced around the house, rumpling the rugs and destroying various small objects in their wake. I couldn't scold them; I felt much the same way.

I rushed through my job at the Cathedral Bookshop. The gossip centered around Bob Finch, who was said not to be working at all, though so far staying sober. That strengthened my sense of purpose. I fixed a hasty lunch, ate it absentmindedly, and tried to think up an excuse for going back out to Brocklesby Hall.

Not that I needed to excuse my actions to myself. Alan had not forbidden me to continue, and I was stubbornly convinced I was in the right. However, I had to get past the Cerberus at the door, and that would require some fancy talking. I decided I might get by with offering again to help Meg in the library. Not only did I still have some questions for her, but she probably needed help. Thoreston's decampment had left her with some of his duties to perform, and she had more than enough to do already. Surely I could offer to take some of the more mundane library chores off her hands. Anyone with a working knowledge of libraries could read the shelves, for example, or file things. With that vague idea, and a bright red, morale-boosting hat, I set out.

The constable on guard duty this time was older than the poor boy I had conned on Friday, and made of sterner stuff. I explained my errand plausibly, I thought, and gave him my most winning smile. He steadfastly ignored the small red felt roosters bobbing on top of my head and repeated, "I'm sorry, madam. I have orders to admit no one except members of the staff."

"I see." Here was a brick wall; I would have to find a creative way around the problem. "Then perhaps I should call and ask Mrs. Cunningham to request my appointment as temporary staff. *Thank* you so much."

He looked at me suspiciously, but made no attempt to follow me to the parking lot which, fortunately, was around the corner, out of his sight.

It was also close to Sir Mordred's barn/ workshop, and there was more than one way to skin a cat. I paused by my car and surveyed the area. No one was in sight; the atmosphere positively reeked of peace and harmony. Somewhere in the distance I could hear the rattly hum of a lawn tractor. Richard was apparently taking advantage of the fine weather for one last mowing before winter set in. That really left only Sir M. likely to be outside, unless some police expert happened to be combing the herb garden. Well, Sir M. I could cope with. The police — I'd cross that bridge if I came to it.

There was a good, sturdy dead bolt on the barn door, so I was actually lucky that it was open and the lord of the manor was working inside. I've done a spot of breaking and entering now and again, in a good cause, but I'd never have been able to credit-card my way past that lock. Sir M. was fussing over some finicky job on the workbench when I came in, and jumped when I spoke his name.

"My dear Mrs. Nesbitt, I —"

"Martin. I kept my former name."

"Yes." There was no mistaking the disapproval in the monosyllable. "If you had only told me who you were when we first met, I should never have allowed you to take tea in the kitchen, as I understand you and your distinguished husband did."

"I guess I'm still not used to my married state. And it was a very good tea, so don't worry about it. You have a fine workshop here, Sir Mordred. I hope you don't mind my stopping in, but you did offer to show it to me once."

"Ah — yes. Yes, of course I did. And, in any case, I owe you a debt of gratitude for looking after me the other day. I must apologize for my behavior, but when you pointed out that Mr. Thoreston must be at the root of all my troubles, the shock, on top of all the other shocks . . ." He wiped his forehead delicately with a silk handkerchief. "You are most welcome to look at my humble work, dear lady. What would you particularly like to see?"

I didn't have a clue, of course. I was there to see what I could see, talk to him, and draw whatever conclusions presented themselves. "Whatever you'd like to show me. I love to see how fine craftsmen do their work."

A little of the best butter never hurts, but as my eyes wandered I could see that I spoke nothing but the truth. The room was untidy, but only in the way that an artist's milieu always is when work is being done. Tools that were not in use were clean and hanging neatly in their appointed places. The workbench, a fine smooth surface, had vises clamped to its edge, ranging in size from small to very small. There was a table saw, a drill press, a lathe, all somewhat smaller than the usual versions. Everything shone with care; some of the tools looked new. It was, in short, a fully equipped and very professional carpenter's shop on a reduced scale, and the bits and pieces that I could see lying around in various states of completion were extremely impressive.

Sir Mordred melted completely under my beams of appreciation. "Perhaps, then, you would like to see the steps in the manufacture of fine miniature furniture. As it happens, I have just begun a new Louis XIV desk . . ."

He showed me the processes and explained them in exhaustive detail. As usual with Sir Mordred, I soon felt I was learning a great deal more than I wanted to know about the subject, but there is no stopping a true enthusiast once he gets started. "And what is this in the corner?" I asked finally. "It looks like a small kiln. Do you make your own pottery?"

He smiled patronizingly. "I do, of course, but not in that kiln. That is for drying wood, when it is necessary to produce an aged effect in a short time. The pottery kiln is in the next room, where I store several kinds of clay, as well as the molds for various kinds of tableware, ceiling decorations, vases . . ."

I suppose it was interesting in its way, but it was also useless. I was trying to invent an excuse to make my escape when Richard Adam walked in the door, in the middle of a lecture on the various glaze effects produced by various techniques. "Salt-glazing, of course, is a very old — yes, Adam, what is it?"

"I've finished with the lawns, as you wished. Was there anything else? I should get to digging the bulbs while there's still some daylight."

His tone was almost rude, and little Sir M. looked distinctly annoyed. I seized the opportunity.

"I've kept you far too long, Sir Mordred. You obviously have responsibilities to tend to. Thank you so much for showing me what you do; I must be going."

I shot out into the daylight. The long shadows of evening were beginning to stretch out against the lawn, and birds were circling the small lake that dominated the back garden. One bird, coming in for a landing, took my breath away. From where I stood, about fifty yards away, it looked like an airplane, with a wingspan of at least six feet. I moved slowly across the grass, trying to be perfectly quiet, and I was nearly at the edge of the water when the great blue heron saw me, rose magnificently, and flew away. I followed it with my eyes, tilting my neck back and nearly losing my balance on the muddy shore of the lake.

As I looked down for surer footing, I saw it. I moved back then, slowly and carefully, like a cat backing up, until I stood safely on the grass where I could leave no more footprints, and studied what I had seen.

Something had been dragged across that little patch of mud at the edge of the lake, something heavy. The shoes that had slipped had been deep in the mud. And faintly, close to one of the footprints, was the slight but unmistakable print of a tire. Not a car tire, narrower.

A motorcycle tire?

11

If Inspector Morrison had been in sight I would have gone straight to him, but he wasn't. I didn't even know if he was here, or back at the police station, or out working on some other case, and I would be stopped if I tried to wander around the Hall looking for him. So I climbed in my car, drove home in reckless haste, and put in an urgent call to Alan.

He returned the call promptly.

"Alan, I've been out to the Hall, and there's something the police need to look into right away."

I detailed the marks I had seen at the edge of the lake. "If Claude is still missing . . ."

I didn't have to spell it out for him, of course. "I'll get on to Morrison myself, and then ring you back."

To my relief, he said nothing to curtail my activities. But why did he need to call me back? I'd told him everything I knew. Had he had second thoughts, or third or fourth? Would he call me off?

I sat by the phone with mounting apprehension and impatience, and snatched it up on the first ring.

"The tracks are new," Alan said without preamble. "Morrison said they checked the lake carefully on Saturday, on the principle of being thorough. It's a convenient place to get rid of anything one doesn't want found. There were no signs then of anyone having been near it. He's sending men out to the Hall immediately."

He cleared his throat. "You've been very helpful, love. It was clever of you to notice those tracks, and I'm glad you reported back immediately. There are — a few things Morrison told me that you might want to know."

I drew in a long breath. "Yes?"

"I'm meant to be in a meeting at the moment, so this will have to be quick. Three things: First, Thoreston was arrested yesterday in York, and has been brought back to Sherebury for questioning. Second, one of the gardens at the Hall does, in fact, have a fine stand of monkshood, and some of it appears to have been recently cut. Third, the head gardener is not being particularly cooperative. Morrison is sure he's lying about something, but can't tell what."

I didn't like Alan's last piece of news, and I was very, very glad he couldn't see my face.

"Well, that's all very interesting," I said cautiously. "By the way, what exactly did Thoreston do to cook the books? I'm not an expert on embezzlement."

He chuckled. "That's comforting to know. I shall rest easier, knowing my retirement account is safe. He did it the easiest way, ghost payroll. Brocklesby made it simple for him, not knowing the names of the casual employees."

"Just as I thought! Penny-ante, and not very imaginative. I can*not* see him as a murderer. No autopsy results yet, I suppose?"

"No, but Morrison has asked them to check specifically for aconite."

"And I take it Claude is still missing?"

"It looks," said Alan a trifle grimly, "as though you may have found him."

After I'd hung up, I sat and chewed the inside of my lip for some time, thinking furiously. Samantha didn't like it. She circled my feet with anxious little chirps and finally jumped into my lap and fixed her cross-eyed blue gaze on me.

"It's all right, Sam. I'm trying to decide what to do, that's all. No, don't lick my nose! Your tongue is rough and you have the most terrible tuna breath."

Satisfied that she had captured my attention, Sam settled herself into a purring

190

mound, and I stroked her thick, silken fur and thought some more.

If the tracks by the lake had been made sometime between Saturday and this afternoon, Monday, it was extremely unlikely that John Thoreston had anything to do with them. I got out a road atlas and made some mental calculations. York is a good long way from Shrewbury, 250 miles or so, I discovered, with London in between. True, it was motorway most of the way, and when the traffic is reasonable, motorways are fast — much faster, usually, than their official speed limit of seventy. The British, on the whole, pay even less respect to speed laws than Americans do. Offsetting that, however, were two facts. The first was that getting out of Shrewbury and onto the motorway involves a lot of narrow country roads, and the second was the fearsome traffic in and around London, which is guaranteed to produce delays. Not only that, but if I were John Thoreston, with cause to fear the police, I would take extreme care not to break any traffic laws.

Suppose that Thoreston had been in Shrewbury all the time, hiding out somewhere, and had, for some reason I didn't bother to question just then, killed Claude and dumped him in the lake. Now. If he were driving, I'd give him at least six hours to get to York. I didn't, of course, know that he had a car. If he'd had to rely on trains, with weekend schedules as unreliable as they are, it was anybody's guess. I was once delayed for two hours on a fifty-mile run, the excuses ranging from "the late arrival of the driver" to "debris on the line."

All right. Assume that he owned a car, or had stolen one. He might just have been able to kill Claude Saturday night, dispose of the body, and, late at night when traffic was lighter, get to York in time to be arrested on Sunday. That was if he had headed straight for York, with no deviations.

It was possible, but it seemed contrived, and wildly unlikely. Why on earth should he rush to York just in time to step into the arms of the police? It would have been more in character for him to wander, more or less aimlessly, after Mrs. Lathrop's death, knowing that his peculations would inevitably be discovered and trying to avoid the consequences. He might have ended up in York because he had some connections there, or maybe it just seemed a likely place to hide — a big city far removed from the scene of the crime. It was even possible that he didn't know about Mrs. Lathrop's death, that he had decided to run because Sir

Mordred seemed to be getting too interested in the books.

It was all guesswork, of course, until I knew exactly when Morrison's men had checked the lake on Saturday and found it innocent, and exactly when Thoreston had been arrested on Sunday, and whether he had a car. And those things, of course, were very well known to the police and therefore not matters about which I could profitably speculate.

The police would also be making exhaustive inquiries into Claude's movements. Where had he been since his mother's death? What had brought him back to Brocklesby Hall? When would someone, Thoreston or anyone else, have had a chance to kill him?

I tried to shift Sam; my right leg had gone to sleep. She growled in her sleep, gently dug her rear claws into my thigh, and stayed where she was.

The police would be coping with all these matters, and I was theorizing ahead of my data, as Sherlock Holmes pedantically warned never to do, but I thought my conclusions were warranted. I believed Thoreston was out of the picture, and Claude, by reason of being dead, was, too. It was just conceivable, I supposed, that Claude could have pushed his motorbike into the lake and walked off into the blue, but I could think of no possible reason for him to do so. And assuming he was dead, and Thoreston was not responsible for his death, I either had to posit two murderers at Brocklesby Hall or look for another suspect.

And who was there?

I reached for the telephone pad and pencil and made a desk of Sam's back. There weren't so many people left, unless one included the entire staff of Brocklesby Hall and the Museum. Any of them could have stuck around after the house was locked up and poisoned Mrs. Lathrop's tea, but why would they? I had no idea what might motivate the pleasant woman who ran the shop, or the women who volunteered in that lamentable tearoom, or the guides, or — no, it was hopeless.

I had to concentrate on the people I knew. Which meant:

Bob Finch
Meg Cunningham
Richard Adam

I chewed on the pencil for a moment and looked at the pad uneasily. Three names. One a good friend, one beginning to be a friend. The third I didn't care for much at all, but if he was the one, Meg would . . .

Meg is the best suspect, you know, whispered that nasty inner voice that torments me from time to time. *Meg is a mother tiger. She'd do anything to protect Jemima. The Lathrops were a threat to her. The Lathrops are both dead.*

I squirmed, mentally and physically, and Sam swore at me in feline Siamese and jumped down. She didn't, unfortunately, distract me from the painful idea I'd managed to keep at bay until now. Meg could have killed Mrs. Lathrop, easily. Claude would have presented more of a challenge, but Richard — oh, Richard would have loved dealing with Claude once and for all . . .

Horrified by the picture I had conjured up, I substituted one of Meg, weeping and miserable. Was that the face of a murderess? Or a conspirator?

Or, the nasty voice suggested, *a woman terrified for her lover?*

I wrenched my unruly thoughts back to the other name on my list. Bob Finch.

Supposing, just for the sake of the argument, that Bob had stolen some miniatures and Mrs. Lathrop had found out about it. Never mind how wildly unlikely the scenario was, but supposing. What would Bob have done then?

If he'd been drunk at the time — I modified that thought to *if he'd been exceedingly drunk* — he might, I supposed, have picked up a handy flowerpot and thrown it at her, or conked her on the head with a spade, or something of the kind.

Would he, by any stretch of the imagination, have bided his time, gone out to the garden, picked some monkshood, dried it and shredded it up and deposited it stealthily in Mrs. Lathrop's caddy full of herbal tea, for her to drink later and die in agony?

And would Mrs. Lathrop, meanwhile, have sat by, telling no one about Bob's sins, patiently waiting to be murdered?

I crossed Bob's name off the list while knowing it probably remained on the police list. I'd deal with that later.

That left Meg and Richard.

Alone or together. And Richard was lying to the police. And Meg was acting very oddly.

Where were Meg and Richard on the Wednesday night before Mrs. Lathrop died?

I knew as I wrote the question on the pad that it was pointless. The police had certainly already questioned both Meg and

Richard about their movements, just as a matter of routine.

No, there was no point in my going into that kind of thing. What I could do better than the police was find out about people, what worried them, what made them happy, what they were afraid of. I already knew quite a bit about Meg; it was time to find out about Richard.

I headed across the backyard to Jane's.

I tapped on the kitchen door and walked in, to be met by savory smells, assorted bulldogs, and the sight of Jane seated at the table, knife and fork in her hands and a book open by her plate.

"Oh, good grief, I'm sorry. I forgot it was supper time. I'll come back."

Jane looked at me sharply and pulled out the chair next to her. "Casseroled chicken. There's plenty; get yourself a plate."

I know Jane's kitchen almost as well as my own. I found a plate and cutlery, helped myself to chicken and vegetables, and let Jane pour me a glass of white burgundy. I hadn't realized how hungry I was until I put the first forkful into my mouth, then I applied myself single-mindedly to the business of eating.

"Apple tart?" she said after a while.

I looked down at my empty plate. "Oh,

Jane, I'm ashamed of myself! Eating you out of house and home, and without a word of thanks, even!"

"Nary a word of any kind," she said with raised eyebrows. "What's wrong?"

"What makes you think something's wrong?" I asked defensively.

"Forgot it was mealtime. So hungry you forgot to talk." She was ticking items off on her fingertips. "Forgot to be polite — you, of all people. Something's on your mind."

"You know me too well. I'd intended to be subtle about it. Yes, I'd love some apple tart, and some coffee if you're having some, and some information."

"The Lathrop murders?" She put the kettle on for coffee.

"Murders? Oh, then it was Claude in the lake!"

"You didn't know?"

"I guessed. I saw the print of a motorcycle tire near the lake, and called Alan. How did you find out, the cathedral-town grape-vine?"

"The news, about an hour ago," she said dryly. "Do you never watch the telly?"

"Hardly ever, and certainly not today. I was too busy worrying. Look, Jane, I think Meg Cunningham and/or Richard Adam may be mixed up in this mess, and it worries me. He's a surly chap, and I hardly know him, but I like her, and I feel sorry for her. What can you tell me about them?"

She took her time about measuring coffee into the French coffeepot, carefully pouring in boiling water, fastening the top on.

"Determined to keep on messing about in murder, then?" she said gruffly. It was not really a question.

"Yes, I am, Jane. You know all the reasons why."

"Know more than you think I do. Been talking to Margaret." She cut us wedges of pie, set them on the table, and sat down. "Suppose I may as well help, then. Might keep you out of trouble."

I didn't thank her, or give her a hug, or do any of the things I wanted to do. Jane is not a demonstrative person, and she hates to be praised. I sat eating the excellent pie, and waited.

"Meg Cunningham," she pronounced after she had pushed down the plunger in the pot and poured us cups of strong, fragrant coffee. "Don't know her except by hearsay. Lived in Sherebury just over a year now. Divorced, one daughter who's deaf, poor child. Suppose you know all that."

I nodded and sipped my steaming coffee.

"Hasn't much money," Jane went on.

"Lives in a council house. Ex-husband doesn't always pay his share of the expenses, and they're heavy. Special school, training for Meg in sign language — the lot. Makes ends meet, and keeps the house clean and tidy and the girl properly dressed and fed. Not much more than that."

"Does Richard help, at all?"

"Tries, they say."

"I suppose Meg won't accept his help. She's very independent."

"Except when it comes to the child, Jemima. She lets him help with her, not treats, but necessities she can't afford."

"Where does he live?"

"Cottage in the country, hard by Brocklesby Hall, nearly in Sir Mordred's back garden. It was his mother's; he's lived there always. Him I've known since he was a pup, taught him his sums when he was a boy. Not surly, exactly, but the stubbornest person, boy and man, I've yet met. Thinks because he wants a thing, it has to be that way. Has a good heart, mind, but knows what's best for everybody."

"Like so many men." I sighed, and Jane gave me a sharp glance, but made no comment. I went on asking questions.

"So if he lives alone, and Meg lives alone except for Jemima, there's no one to vouch for their whereabouts on the night — at any time."

I caught myself just in time, I thought, but nothing escapes Jane.

"On the night Lathrop's tea was doctored? Whole town knows she drank it the night before with no problem, then died of it early in the morning. Up to the police to find out where everyone was at the time."

I grinned in spite of the seriousness of the matter. "Jane, I don't know why Sherebury bothers with a police force at all. You know everything. Alan solemnly assured me that the time element was confidential."

Jane snorted. "One thing I don't know is why Richard Adam is lying. Went out of his way, Sunday, to sit next to me at coffee after church. Told me he was up early the morning Lathrop died, and saw nobody coming or going about the Hall."

I furrowed my brow. "Why did you ask him that?"

"I didn't."

I got it after a beat or two. "He volunteered the information. He told you because he knows you — um — have a finger on Sherebury's pulse."

She snorted again, with genuine amusement this time. "Finger in Sherebury's pies, you mean."

"Whatever. You're an information source. But why would he want you to spread the word that he didn't see anyone?"

"Only two reasons I can think of. He *did* see someone he didn't want to see. Or he didn't because he was there himself."

12

The more I thought about those conclusions, as I groped my way back to my darkened house, the less I liked either of them. Unfortunately, I couldn't fault their logic. That put me right back where I was before I'd gone to see Jane. I had hoped she might give me good reasons why neither Meg nor Richard had been involved. Instead she had added another plank to my shaky construction of fear and speculation. I put a CD on the player, stretched out on the couch with Emmy ensconced on my knees, and tested the wobbly structure a little further.

Richard was lying about what he had seen in those crucial minutes before Mrs. Lathrop had drunk poisoned tea. I had asked Jane if he could really have seen anything, and she had assured me that his cottage, on a little rise, actually looked down on the Brocklesby estate. In November, with most of the leaves off the trees, his view would have been clear. It was, of course, dark out, early of a November morning. But Wednesday, I recalled, had been a particularly lovely, clear day. If there had been a full moon that night . . . I shoved Emmy away, got up, and consulted the almanac. Thursday, November 11: Full moon, rising 2:30 A.M.

And Thursday — the sky hadn't begun to fill with clouds until the afternoon. I remembered that because they had matched my gloomy, confused state of mind so well.

So Richard could have seen anyone who had been abroad, on lawful or other occasions, in those dead hours before dawn, before Mrs. Lathrop brewed herself a dose of destruction. But had he, in fact, seen anything at all? Or had he left his cottage, dressed in dark clothes, perhaps, to slip more easily through the shadows of that bright moonlit night? Moon shadow is deceptive. Odd, humpy, terrifying shapes may be nothing more than knobby old trees, their patterns moving as if alive on the cold, silvery ground, while the forms that glide smoothly across the grass are shadows neither of clouds nor of trees, but of hunters: foxes, wolves — or men.

I shivered, picked up Emmy again, and turned off the music. *Symphonie fantastique* was not the sort of background my thoughts required. But if Berlioz's macabre strains had contributed an extra shudder or two, the deductions, shorn of their nightmarish trimmings, were sound enough. Richard could have seen anything, or nothing.

And I couldn't imagine how I was going to get him to tell me which it was.

They say one's subconscious sometimes works miracles. Go to bed with a problem, the theory goes, and your mind will work it out for you as you sleep. My mind must have been installed with some of the instructions missing, for in the morning it was functioning no more creatively than it had the night before. Even after more coffee than I usually allow myself, no sparkling insights swam to the surface, no lightbulbs went off.

My intuition hadn't deserted me, however. When the phone rang, I knew who it would be.

"Good morning, Alan. I sure am glad to hear from you!"

"One moment, please, Mrs. Martin." There was almost a giggle in the softly accented African voice, but she transferred the call before I could say anything.

"Dorothy, my dear."

"I swear, next time I'm going to wait until I hear your voice. I came *that* close to telling Betty Atieno I loved her."

Alan chuckled. "You do rush headlong,

don't you? One of the reasons I love you, actually. But this is serious, my love. You've heard?"

"About Claude? Yes, it was on the news last night. I didn't see it, but Jane told me. I don't know the details."

"What you'd expect. Claude and his bike were in the lake. Not together, however. And it's pretty apparent he didn't drown; there's a dirty great wound in the back of his head."

I must have made some sort of squeamish sound, because Alan stopped abruptly. Annoyed with myself, I kept my voice very level as I asked, "What about time of death? Any guesses?"

"You know how medical examiners are. Or perhaps you don't, but they never want to commit themselves. However, we can time it fairly well by other factors. It rained there last Friday, Derek Morrison tells me."

"Let's see, Friday. Yes, I went to Matins and then out for coffee with Margaret, and it was foggy and drizzly, then and for most of the day. Not hard rain, but steady."

"Yes. So the tire tracks and footprints by the lake had to have been made after that. We know they were, in fact, because our people inspected the area on Saturday and found nothing. Now. Saturday was quite warm and dry — you weren't there, but it was, according to Derek — much the same sort of weather that we had at Bramshill. And Sunday was dry as well, until about nine-thirty in the evening, when there was a bit of rain for about an hour. Not much, just enough to soften the ground. Then the temperature dipped sharply, and there was frost before midnight. The prints are good, clear ones, apparently made in damp ground, so they must have got there after the rain stopped on Sunday night, and before the frost set in. I might add, incidentally, that there are one or two blurred prints of a smallish foot in a woman's shoe, made at some time when the ground was much drier."

"Yes, well, I slipped. I wasn't looking where I was going; I was watching a great blue heron. I think it was a heron. Anyway, I didn't mess up anything, did I?"

"Not seriously. They'll have to come and take casts of your shoes for comparison, of course."

"They can take the shoes if they want them. I haven't cleaned them; they'd still have some of the relevant mud on them. So apparently Claude went into the water soon after that hour of rain on Sunday night. Who was at the Hall then?"

"No one, apparently. Sunday is the cook's day off; she says she spent it as usual with her married sister in Sherebury. The whole family went to the cinema in the evening and didn't get home until after ten, and Mrs. Hawes — that's the cook — stayed to help put the children to bed and have a nightcap, so she didn't get back to the Hall until nearly midnight. She says it was dark and apparently deserted when she got in, and she went straight to bed. She assumed Sir Mordred had gone up to London as he often does of a Sunday."

"And had he?"

"Not according to him. He says he pottered about in his workshop all afternoon and then went out to dinner. He had intended to go to the Old Bakehouse, in Maidstone —"

"Oh, I know that place! The Andersons took me there once. It has the most marvelous food!"

"Yes, well, it is also closed on Sundays, a fact Sir Mordred had apparently forgotten. So he says he had to drive about looking for a place to eat, and ended up at a pub, the Pig and Whistle just outside Hawkhurst."

"Somehow I can't imagine Sir Mordred in a pub. He's so prim."

"He didn't enjoy it much, or so he told

Derek. 'Chi-chi decor and food from the deep freeze' was the report. But he was late getting there to begin with and very late leaving. It's a popular place on a Sunday night, even if our little man doesn't think much of the food, so it was some time before he was served. And then he got lost on the way home. Derek said he was rather cagey about that. Probably had one or two over the limit and wouldn't, of course, admit it to the police. At any rate, he didn't get home until well after two in the morning."

"And in a terrible temper, I imagine, driving all over the countryside to end up with mediocre food, especially when he had his mouth set for Old Bakehouse fare. So. With the Hall and the estate deserted, anyone could have brought Claude to the lake and dumped him in. Alan, I've been finding out a thing or two."

I told him about Richard. "Are Jane and I jumping to conclusions?"

He laughed at that. "My dear, you and Jane are both Olympic-class contenders for the gold medal in the conclusion jump. It is a tribute to your powers of insight into the human mind that you are so often right."

"I hope I'm not right this time, though. I don't actually know Richard Adam, and he doesn't seem to like me, but Meg needs him.

But really, the two of them are the only suspects left, aren't they? With Thoreston out of the way — I presume he *is* out of the way?"

"Oh, yes, easily. He was arrested early Sunday afternoon in York, and his address since then has been one or another county jail. No, he's out of it, for Claude's murder, at any rate. And naturally Derek is having the cook's story checked, and Sir Mordred's, but short of homicidal mania there seems to be no reason why either of them should go around wiping out the Lathrop family."

"And that leaves Richard. And/or Meg." I thought I'd kept my voice neutral, but I couldn't fool Alan.

"You can't take it personally, you know, my dear. I've often had to put handcuffs on villains for whom I had a good deal of sympathy. If you're to keep poking about in criminal affairs, you're going to have to develop a certain detachment. Are you still there? Dorothy?"

I swallowed. "Yes, I'm still here. I just — you — when are you going to be home, Alan?"

I could actually hear him smile. "On Saturday, I think, as scheduled. And you're not to make any plans. You and I have a good deal to talk about."

For several minutes after I hung up the phone, I sat there, hearing his voice. "If you're going to keep poking about . . . a good deal to talk about . . . develop a certain detachment . . ." And he hadn't told me to be careful. For once, he hadn't warned me off.

Well. Well! If he was shifting around to my way of thinking, I was going to have to be very professional about this. Clearly I needed to find out more about Richard Adam, and the way to do that was to talk — very carefully — to Meg Cunningham.

This time I wasn't going to take any chances about getting into the Hall. I looked up the number and picked up the phone.

The voice that answered was female and dithery, one of the volunteers, I assumed. "Brocklesby Hall Museum of Miniatures. I'm sorry, the Museum is closed today because of an emergency."

"Wait! Don't hang up! I know the Museum is closed, but I'd like to speak to Mrs. Cunningham, please."

"She isn't here. Nobody's here."

Well, that wasn't quite accurate, was it? Plainly, the owner of the voice was there, and presumably there were police swarming all over the place. "This is Dorothy Martin. Who am I speaking to, please?"

"Clara Carter. I'm one of the maids, and

they said to say nobody's here from the Museum and you should try next week." She was losing patience.

"I see. May I speak to Richard Adam, please?"

"He can't come to the phone. The po— some people are talking to him."

That was interesting. "Then perhaps you can give me Mrs. Cunningham's home telephone number."

"I don't know if I'm supposed to —"

"At once, please, it's very important." I had assumed my schoolteacher voice and manner, and the young woman capitulated and read me a number.

"Who did you say this was, again? They'll want to know, because I'm not supposed to —"

I hung up gently and waited a moment before I punched in the new number.

"Meg, this is Dorothy Martin. I'm sorry to bother you at home, but I tried to reach you at the Hall and they said no one from the Museum had come in today."

"No, Sir Mordred told us to stay home. Oh, Dorothy, have you heard what's happened?"

"About Claude, yes. That's why I called, actually. I thought you might need someone to talk to." I kept my fingers crossed. "Are you free for a while, either now or this afternoon? May I come to see you?"

"Oh, yes, do come. Come now! Do you know where I live?"

The instructions were simple enough even for me to follow. I pulled up in front of Meg's house ten minutes later.

The place, a duplex built of shiny, ugly red brick, was almost painfully neat. Her next-door neighbor's front path was littered with children's toys; the flower garden consisted of gravel and weeds. Meg's path was swept and pristine; her two roses had been cut back for the winter and the annuals pulled up; her curtains hung white and straight.

She opened the door before I could ring the bell. There was no sparkle in the blue eyes today. Her face was pale with anxiety; there were purple shadows under her eyes. Nothing could dull her hair, but it seemed to have lost its bounce.

She made an effort to smile. "Come in. I've just put the kettle on; would you like some tea?"

"I'd love some, thanks."

She took my coat and hat, the latter a simple knitted affair (this was no time for frivolity), and established me in a front room as neat as the outside of the house. Here, though, there were touches of individuality. The furniture was cheap and ugly, the carpet — doubtless supplied with the house — was of a multicolored hideousness only English carpet makers seem able to produce. But a good painting hung on the wall, a couple of needlepoint cushions brightened the couch, and an inexpensive, plain blue rug covered a lot of the shrieking carpet. A pot of yellow chrysanthemums brightened the windowsill, between panels, not of the standard Nottingham lace, but of plain white cotton edged in blue-and-yellow braid.

"You've done a lot with this room, Meg," I said as she came in and deposited a tea tray on the one table. "I like that painting."

"Thanks. I wish I had more time to paint, but —"

"You don't mean it's your work!" I studied it more closely, with some awe. I can draw a cat that's almost recognizable, the two-circles-with-whiskers kind. Anyone who can render a flower bed full of daffodils and hya-cinths that actually look like flowers fills me with admiration. But this painting went be-yond mere skill. "I don't know a lot about art, Meg, but this seems like really fine work to me. It's well-balanced, the colors are clear and true, and I swear you can almost smell spring when you look at it."

She smiled. For a moment she was transformed, and my heart twisted. "How kind of you to say so, Dorothy. That's the effect I was trying for, bringing spring into the room."

"You're very talented. Even I can see that. But you said you don't paint much?"

"Not anymore." The smile had left her face; I almost wondered if I had imagined it. "I'm quite busy, you know, and I've no space here for supplies. I do try to teach Jemima some of the rudiments of drawing; it's something she can do without worrying about verbal communication. She could be rather good someday, actually."

She had already lost interest in the subject. Sitting, she poured tea into two cups, added milk and sugar, handed me one. Her own cup she left on the tea tray. "Dorothy," she said, resting her chin on her hands and looking at me with great intensity, "please tell me what's happening to Richard!"

13

A sip of tea bought me a couple of seconds' respite, enough time to decide that my only chance lay in telling Meg the truth, so far as I knew it. My suspicions, of course, I would keep to myself.

"I don't know what he's doing now, in any detail. I do know that he was talking to the police half an hour or so ago when I phoned the Hall to speak to you."

"You mean the police were talking to him."

"Probably." I took a deep breath and looked up to meet her gaze steadily. "I just hope he's answering their questions, and with the truth this time. He's been lying, you know, and that's a really bad idea. The police don't like it; they get very annoyed. Not only that, it makes their job harder, so they take longer to find the guilty — and exonerate the innocent." I waited for a moment. Meg picked up her teacup, stirred its contents, and put it down again.

"*Why* is he lying, Meg? I'm sure you know, if anyone does."

She stared at the chrysanthemums, reached over, pinched off a dead leaf.

"My dear, you have to make up your mind. Either you trust me, or you don't. If you don't, I'll go home and stop bothering you, but I'd rather we tried to help each other."

"Why should I trust you?" It wasn't a retort; she was asking a genuine question.

It wasn't an easy one to answer, either. It was my turn to fiddle with my teacup.

"The only answer I have to that, I guess, is that my intentions are good, and you have to trust someone. You can't go through life watching your back all the time. I can't make any rash promises about Richard; you know that. Quite frankly, at the moment I would guess he's at the top of the list of suspects. And, Meg, you think so, too, don't you?"

She didn't bother to deny it. Nor did she meet my eye. Her gaze was fixed on the plant, though I was sure she saw, not leaves and flowers, but something much darker.

"Don't you see, Meg, the truth can't hurt him. If he's guilty, the police will find that out. I have the greatest respect for the English police, and not just because I'm married to Alan. They really do get their man, nearly always. And they almost never send an innocent one to jail — but if Richard is innocent, they'll know it much sooner if they have all the facts at their command." And if I'd left a good deal out of that speech, at least what I'd said was honest.

"Yes, I see." She drained her teacup. Probably her mouth was as dry as mine. I sipped from my own cup and waited.

"Very well," she said suddenly. "You're right. I must trust someone. But I can't tell you anything, because I don't know what Richard is hiding.

"He's hiding something, though, you're quite right about that. He has been ever since Mrs. Lathrop was killed. He wouldn't even talk to me at first, except to keep insisting I leave town. Finally, on Sunday we saw each other in church, and I couldn't bear it any longer. I worked up my courage, and after coffee I went up to him and asked him to have dinner with Jemima and me. We ended by spending the rest of the day together, the three of us, but he took care never to be alone with me for a moment, so we couldn't really talk. Even after we put Jemima to bed, he insisted on watching some silly film on the telly. Dorothy, I'm so scared! He won't talk, and he hated the Lathrops so, Claude more than his mother, but both of them, really, because they were a threat to me and Jemima. And of course he

knows all about garden plants. What if he —
I don't really think he would, but what if —"

"Wait a minute, Meg, wait a minute! Go
back to Sunday. Richard was with you and
Jemima — starting when?"

She wiped a traitorous tear off her cheek
with an angry swipe of her hand. "What difference does it make? I told you he wouldn't
say anything, and I tried, I really did —"

"Just tell me. How long were you all together?"

She shook her head impatiently. "Oh, for
heaven's sake! He was in church, I told you
that. I saw him when we got there, a little before ten. Then we came here, to my house,
and stayed here all day."

"And he went home — when?"

"After that stupid film was over. I wasn't
watching the clock, but after midnight, I
know that much. And if it's our morals
you're concerned about —"

"Not at all." I had been holding my
breath; now I let it out in a great gust. "I'm
sure you can look after your own morals.
The point is, my dear, you and I need to
make sure Richard tells the police what you
just told me, and as soon as possible. Because if he was with the two of you all that
time on Sunday, he didn't put Claude
Lathrop in the lake!"

★ ★ ★

I called the police station from her house, and, after being passed up the polite but obstructive ladder, finally learned that Inspector Morrison was still out at the Hall. I asked them to tell him I was on my way with important information. Meg drove; I thought she'd make much faster progress than I, with my stupid foreigner's timidity.

"Do you have to pick Jemima up from school?"

"Not till after five. The school has quite a lot of working mothers, so they organize games and free playtime for the children after school. It's good for Jemima, the socializing, so I didn't want to cancel it today, even though I could have picked her up early."

"You worry about her a lot, don't you?"

"Too much, Richard says. He thinks I should let her live a more normal life, stop being so protective, and perhaps with Claude gone — oh, Dorothy, I can't believe I don't have to be afraid of him anymore! You're quite sure Richard's in the clear?"

"Quite sure. Richard couldn't have pushed him in the lake." Neither, thank God, could Meg. I grinned at her, giddy with relief. "I can't give you the details, but you can take it from me that there's absolutely no doubt. And I refuse to believe in two separate murderers, so that means he didn't kill Mrs. Lathrop, either."

And there was a fine, reckless piece of conclusion-jumping, I thought as we negotiated the double roundabout. I'd have to enter that one in Alan's Olympics. But I couldn't tell Meg that it was just possible Claude was murdered by one person and pushed in the lake later by another. For one thing, the fact that he was dead when he went in was confidential, and the police wanted it kept that way. For another, the only conspiracy I was prepared to consider was Meg-Richard, and they were now in the clear, at least for Claude's death. If there was any possibility of Richard's involvement in Mrs. Lathrop's murder — well, I simply couldn't mention it. I've never been much good at tearing the wings off butterflies.

This time I didn't have to bluster my way into the Hall. I was escorted by a deferential constable, Meg in tow. Inspector Morrison had established himself in Sir Mordred's office, which he had turned into an incident room. He rose as we came into the room.

"Mrs. Martin, how nice to see you. Please sit down. And this is?"

"Meg Cunningham, the curator and librarian of the museum here. Meg, this is

221

Detective Chief Inspector Morrison, one of the very best men on the force."

Inspector Morrison gestured her to a chair. "How do you do, Mrs. Cunningham. It is Mrs.?"

"I'm divorced, Chief Inspector. Mrs. or Ms., whichever you prefer."

He inclined his head. "I'm glad you came, Mrs. Cunningham. I was just getting around to sending someone to talk to you and now I won't have to. Mrs. Martin, you said you had some information for me?"

"Meg does. Tell him what you told me, my dear."

She recited her story of the events of Sunday, her eyes never leaving his face. Like the good policeman he is, he didn't let his expression change, but when she finished, he sat back in his chair looking bemused.

"And have you verification for any of these times, Mrs. Cunningham?"

"Well, there's Jemima. She was with us until she went to bed. I don't know if you accept the evidence of children, though — and she's deaf, of course, you'd have to have an interpreter —"

"We have expert signers on the force, and children often make very good witnesses. Is there anyone who can take up after the time when Jemima went to bed?"

Meg grimaced. "Mrs. Graham. She's my next-door neighbor, and a one-woman espionage patrol. She's always complaining when Richard spends more than five minutes at the house, and she watches like a hawk for him to go home. She'd love to catch him spending the night. As a matter of fact, she spoke to me Monday morning about it. 'Your gentleman friend stayed very late last night, didn't he? Watching the telly, were you?' She was quite rude when I told her we were."

Inspector Morrison sat up again and sighed. "Yes, well, we'll check, of course, but I've no doubt what we'll learn. Your Mr. Adam told us exactly the same story, you see. And so we sent him home."

She was on her feet and out the door before either of us could say another word. The constable taking notes made for the door, but the inspector said, "Sit down, Colin. She's gone to find him. And they're both out of it."

He looked at me and sighed again. "I suppose I should be grateful to have it all so nice and clear, but I'm not. You do realize, Mrs. Martin, that this takes us back to square one?"

"No other suspects at all?"

"Not for Claude's murder. It's wide open,

now. Everyone we might have considered was elsewhere Sunday night."

"Bob Finch?"

"He was under the firm surveillance of his mother, who's been keeping him at home. She's afraid he'll go on a world-class drinking bout, so she's keeping him tied to her apron strings. Vouched for by three neighbors who came in to keep Bob company."

"And Ada's word would have been good enough on its own. I'm sorry, Inspector. I seem to have put a monkey wrench in the works."

The inspector smiled, a little wearily. "It's not your fault. The works would have ground to a halt soon, in any case. You just speeded up the process a bit. We had a man on Adam, pending our talk with Mrs. Cunningham. Now we can call him off. For which, as I said, I should be grateful."

"Did Richard — Mr. Adam — say anything that was of any use at all? Other than the negative evidence, I mean?"

"Not he. He doesn't like us very much, and I must say the feeling is mutual. We'll need to talk to him again, of course. He's still lying about something, but I can't put my finger on what."

"Oh, I know what, I think. He saw something on the morning Mrs. Lathrop was killed, something he doesn't want to talk about."

"He's talked to you?"

"No. He doesn't like me, either. No, actually he talked to a friend of mine. Well, you know Jane Langland. She was the one who figured it out, really. He ran into her at church and went out of his way to tell her he saw nothing at all that morning. Which, of course, since he's innocent, means that he did."

Inspector Morrison didn't quite scratch his head, or let his eyes drift heavenward. He's a very polite man. Also an intelligent one.

"If Adam had been abroad that morning," he said after a moment, with precision, "he might have told us there was nothing to be seen, to try to discredit anyone who said they had seen *him*. But if we stick to the single-murderer theory, which is the most reasonable one at the moment, he was *not* out that morning poisoning Mrs. Lathrop's tea. Therefore, if he's lying when he says he saw no one, it means he did see someone. Is that your premise?"

"I must say, put that way, it has an awful lot more 'ifs' in it than I thought it had. But yes, that's the idea. And if it's the right idea, then I think he may be ready now to tell you the truth. If you'll excuse me, Inspector, I think I'll go and try to persuade him to do just that. If you have no objection?"

"Be my guest, Mrs. Martin. And the best of British luck to you."

Well, he could be excused for sounding just a little sour. But I didn't think I was going to need much luck, British or otherwise. Richard was not a stupid man or Meg wouldn't care so much about him.

And how was that for a fine conclusion jump?

I found Richard's cottage easily enough, and was invited in, though I must say I've received warmer welcomes. Meg and Richard seemed to have better things to do than talk to me. I could sympathize, but they'd have lots of time for that later. Just now there were important matters to clear up.

"I'm sorry to bother you. I do realize you have — um — things to talk about."

Meg giggled at that. Richard's face remained stony, but I ignored his displeasure and forged ahead. "Mr. Adam — or do you mind if I call you Richard?"

He shrugged. "Suit yourself."

Meg's eyes begged me to understand, but I ignored her, too.

"Richard, then, since you're easily young

enough to be my son. You've got to go tell the police what you saw on Thursday morning."

"I have told them," he said without an instant's pause. "I saw nothing. If they choose not to believe me, it's their affair."

"Oh, for Pete's sake, snap out of love's young dream for just a second and *think!* Meg was with you on Sunday night. That means you and she are both out of the running for Claude's murder. So, unless you can believe there's a second villain skulking around someplace, the person you saw going into the Hall on Thursday *couldn't* have been Meg!"

Richard's jaw, which had been set so tightly I could hear his teeth grinding, dropped, and Meg's did, too.

She turned on him. "You thought I — so that's why you — but how could you think —"

"Of course it couldn't — I never thought — but now that I know — what a fool I've been!"

They went on in that fashion for a few minutes. I was forgotten, so I stood patiently waiting until they had finished accusing and explaining and forgiving and doing a few other things along the way. When their incoherence had finally abated, I cleared my throat.

"All right, then. You saw someone you thought was Meg. That much is clear. You also thought she had a good motive to murder both the Lathrops, and you had no intention of giving her away. Meanwhile, *she*'s been scared to death *you* had something to do with the whole mess. Now that you've had the sheer good luck, both of you, to clear yourselves of Claude's murder, maybe we can make some sense out of what you saw, Richard. You're going to have to tell the police the whole story, of course, but I hope you'll tell me first. As a rehearsal. Or, darn it all, because I'm dying to know!"

Richard's face, like Meg's, was transformed when he smiled. For the first time, I could see the attraction.

"Very well, Mrs. Martin. I'm sorry I was so uncooperative. You've been doing your best to help us, I can see that now."

"Don't worry about it, and call me Dorothy. But please tell me. I'm dying by inches."

"Why don't we sit down?" suggested Meg. "And would anybody like some tea?"

"Look," I said desperately, "I'll treat you both to lunch in a few minutes, and we can have all the tea, or any other beverage, that anyone wants. But can we settle this business first?"

Richard and Meg sat on the couch. If they had been ten years younger they would have held hands. At almost thirty, English reserve had set in, and they were careful not to touch. It didn't matter; the sparks between them flared as brightly as if they'd been intertwined.

Richard cleared his throat. "First of all, I need to apologize to Meg for being an ass. I ought to have known she could never be mixed up in something like murder. But I wasn't thinking very clearly.

"I was up early that morning, as usual. In summer, of course, I'm at work soon after dawn, and it takes me a while, in the autumn, to slow down from the summer rhythm. I've always liked being awake in the early morning, anyway. There's a stillness, with only animals abroad . . . it's peaceful, refreshing."

Meg did touch his hand then, gently. He said nothing, didn't even look at her, but he gripped her fingers.

"It was a little before six. I was making tea and planning out my day. That's why I was looking out of the window. It was bright as day, or nearly, with a full moon and no clouds. I was looking at the terrace garden and hoping the earth would be warm enough to dig, because the bulbs needed to be separated and new ones planted.

"When I first saw the movement, I didn't pay particular attention. It was just in the corner of my field of vision, and if I thought anything at all I suppose I thought it was a dog, or a fox. You know how tricky moonlight can be."

I nodded. Exactly my own thoughts, if more prosaically expressed.

"But I kept looking out the window, not really noticing much. I was thinking about my work. And then I saw it, unmistakably."

"Saw *what?*" said Meg and I in unison.

"A woman. On a bicycle."

"Where?" I said.

"She was going along the main road, just where the drive comes out. It was pretty early for any traffic on that road, but I wouldn't have thought anything about it, particularly, except that she was wobbling a good deal. It didn't look as though she was used to a bike. And then she stopped and got off and walked the bike, as if she was going to turn up the drive. I watched closely, then, to see if she did, because she had no business there. I'm not hired as a watchman or guard, you understand, but I try to keep an eye on things. I couldn't see anything, though; the shadows were too long in the drive. I kept watching, but I didn't see her go on past on the road, either. And just then the kettle came to the boil and started screaming, so I made my tea, and when I looked again, there was nothing to see."

"How did you know it was a woman?"

"She was wearing a skirt. And a scarf. And — oh, it was everything about her. The awkward way she handled the bike, the way she walked."

"You could see all that from here?"

"Look for yourself. The kitchen window."

I looked. The kitchen window was larger than those in the rest of the cottage. I thought Richard had probably enlarged it to take advantage of the view. Brocklesby Hall, sitting in a little valley, was spread out in all its gaudy grandeur for Richard to see while he ate his breakfast. Even on a gray, cloudy day the window commanded miles of countryside. I could easily believe that on a moonlit night he could pick out details on the road by the entrance to the drive.

I came back and sat opposite the two of them. They hadn't moved closer, they weren't touching anymore, but the electricity between them was palpable. I wasn't needed, and they certainly didn't want to share lunch with me. I doubted they would remember to eat at all. It was time I was out of there.

There was one more thing I had to clear up first, though.

"Why were you so sure it was Meg?"

"I wasn't! It never occurred to me that it was anyone I knew, at the time. A woman, and not young, was the only impression I got. It was only afterward, when I knew about Mrs. Lathrop, that I began to think it was odd, someone being near the house just about the time when the tea could have been poisoned, and to wonder who the woman could have been. And then I could only think of Meg, and I thought I must have been mistaken about the woman's age, with the moonlight and all, and — well, I was an ass, as I said."

"Fear can obscure anyone's mental processes. Yes, you were stupid, but we all are, now and then."

"But, Mrs. Martin — Dorothy. I'm still wondering. It wasn't Meg. It wasn't Mrs. Hawes; she was in the house already. And there's no other woman with a key to get into the Hall.

"So — who was it?"

14

That was the question of the day, and, in fact, of the next several days. Inspector Morrison, when I walked back to the Hall to report, was, of course, furious with Richard.

"Five days later, he tells us! Five days!" He clenched his jaw. "Do you realize how much harder it is going to be to trace an unknown female after five days? It is entirely possible that Mr. Richard Adam may be charged with obstruction of justice, and I, for one, would be delighted to see him convicted!"

That was just temper, of course. The inspector had no time to waste on such side issues, much as he might have liked to. He set in motion the whole vast machinery of "routine," instituting a far-flung network of inquiries, organizing his small, always too small complement of men and women to do what had to be done. Nobody had much hope, after all this time, that anyone would remember a woman, not young, not a very good cyclist. But it all had to be tried, the questions had to be asked, however useless they might prove to be.

I had to look for a lift into town, since Meg had forgotten I existed. Not that I could blame her. She and Richard could both work at the Hall now and live in Richard's idyllic cottage, happily ever after, presumably. On a practical level, I thought he'd be good with Jemima, and that, after all, was one of the really important things.

Inspector Morrison had also forgotten about me, in the flurry of issuing orders, so I wandered out to the parking lot to see if any of the police were bound for town. On the way I ran into Sir Mordred, coming out of the workshop. He looked awful. His face was white, his hands were shaking, his breathing was labored.

"Sir Mordred, are you all right? You don't look a bit well. Is there anything I can do for you?"

He looked at me without recognition for a moment, and then ran a handkerchief across his face.

"Mrs. Martin. Thank you, no. I shall be quite all right. These past few days have been frightful, and I'm a bit tired, that's all."

"I'm sure you should have a doctor. Is there someone I could call?"

"No! I don't believe in doctors. I shall be quite all right. Please don't bother!"

He tottered off to the house, leaving me shaking my head in the parking lot.

Eventually, one of the policemen took me back to Meg's house, where I picked up my car, went home, and put in a call to Alan. I was bursting with conversation.

It was one of those days when he was heavily burdened with meetings, so it wasn't till after dinner that he was able to call me back. By that time he had heard the latest developments from Morrison, which relegated most of what I had to say to the category of old news.

"I hear you've been making my DCI's job harder for him," was his greeting.

"Thanks a lot! I saved him hours of chasing up blind alleys, is what I did!"

Alan gave the comfortable chuckle I so love. "You did, indeed. So I informed him. He said he'll remember to thank you later."

"Smart aleck. At least I got Richard to talk, and that puts the poor inspector one or two steps off square one."

"Only one or two, I'm afraid. Until we trace the mysterious lady, Derek's absolutely in the dark. And, of course, tracing her is going to be much harder than it would have been several days ago."

"Yes. Still, it shouldn't be impossible.

Farmers would have been awake at that hour, and an old lady abroad on a bicycle before 6 A.M. would stick in the mind, wouldn't you think?"

"Perhaps. It would be useful if we had any idea at all of whom we were looking for."

"Another illusion shattered! I thought you went at these things like scientists, trying to gather facts, not prove a theory."

He heaved an exaggerated sigh.

"You do read the wrong sort of books, my dear. I shall have to educate you properly. We try to be unprejudiced in our approach, of course, but we cannot gather all the facts in the world. Even scientists set limits to their experiments, so that it's clear what data they are trying to collect.

"Derek's people will be asking everyone they can find whether they saw anyone at all on that road, or any nearby road, at any time before dawn that morning. They'll check out bicycles in the neighborhood. They'll try to trace the woman's movements, where she came from, where she went after she left the Hall. If, indeed, she ever went to the Hall. It's the slimmest possible lead, but as it's the only one we have, we have to follow it up. But hunting an unknown is worse than the proverbial needle in the haystack. It would be extremely helpful to know we were looking for a bright blue knitting needle, size thirteen."

"Well, then, I'll nose around and see if anyone has any ideas about stray knitting needles wandering in the vicinity of the Hall."

"Do that. Who knows, it might just help. Now that you've managed to destroy Derek's case, it would be useful if you could build up another one."

Well, a little sarcasm wouldn't hurt me. Once again he hadn't told me to go peddle my papers, and unless it was an accidental oversight, it was a very good sign.

Next morning, a cold, rainy morning, I poured a third cup of coffee, pulled out a small notebook and a pencil, and tried to think. The weather was not conducive to thought. The rain dripping steadily from the eaves had a soporific effect; so did the cats, sleeping heavily one on either side of me as I sat on the couch.

I shook myself awake and started to make random notes. The first was a list of all the older women I could think of who were in any way connected with the Hall.

It was a very short list:

Mrs. Hawes, the cook
What's-her-name, the new woman who

dealt with school groups
Tearoom volunteers

Totally unproductive, I thought in disgust. The police would be checking out all those people. It was silly even to mention Mrs. Hawes; she was in the house that night, not wobbling around the countryside on a bicycle. I knew nothing about the tearoom volunteers except that they made terrible sandwiches and worse tea, and the police would be much more efficient than I at getting their names and verifying their whereabouts. And it would turn out that they had all been in their blameless beds on the night of November whatever-it-was, and their feathers would get ruffled at the very idea of being questioned, and some of them would quit in disgust, and where would Sir Mordred be then, poor thing?

I shook my head and uttered an exasperated noise. Samantha uncurled her lean, elegant body, opened one blue eye, stuck her front claws gently into my hip to reprimand me for disturbing a cat's rest, and went back to sleep, one paw over her eyes.

"Well, pardon me, Your Majesty!" Sam ignored me, having made her point. Emmy chirped irritably and rolled into a ridiculous position on her back, all four paws in the air.

238

I went back to my sorry list.

There was exactly one item that was worthy of a follow-up, and it wasn't even a name. I searched my memory of that day — surely it was more than a week ago! — when I had arrived at the Hall to find it swarming with schoolchildren. I could call up the woman's appearance: calm, authoritative, short graying hair, glasses, ordinary sort of figure clad in a brown tweed suit. For the life of me, though, I couldn't remember her name. Oh, to be thirty again, with a memory!

I sighed loudly and got up. At my age and weight that is not as simple as it sounds, especially from a squashy couch; both cats were seriously annoyed by the amount of shoving and grunting I had to do, and said so. I went to the phone.

"Brocklesby Hall Museum of Miniatures."

The voice this time was crisp and professional.

"Yes, may I speak to Mrs. Cunningham, please?"

"I'll connect you."

Meg's voice was bright and eager. "This is Mrs. Cunningham."

"Hi, Meg, Dorothy Martin. I gather the Museum is open today."

The voice changed only a little. She

wasn't displeased to hear from me; I just wasn't the one she was hoping was calling. "Good morning, Dorothy. We're not actually open, not to the public. The police won't let us, yet. But the staff are all in and working like mad."

"Well, I won't bother you. I'm sure you must be very busy. I just wondered if you and Richard would like to have that lunch we never got around to yesterday. He can't have an awful lot to do on a day like this, and surely you can leave your duties for a little while. I'd very much like to treat the two of you to a celebration."

"That's kind of you. I'd like that, and I'm sure Richard would, too. He's not working today, of course, it's far too wet, but I'll ring him. Would you like us to pick you up, or shall we meet somewhere?"

"I thought I'd pick you up. I'd like to make sure Sir Mordred is feeling all right. He was looking very ill yesterday."

"I think he's fine today, but come fetch us if you like. There's a pub not far from here that does excellent bar food, if that's okay with you?"

"Perfect. Around twelve-thirty?"

The rain made me extra cautious about my driving, and my Milquetoast style was not appreciated by others on the road, but I got to the Hall without incident and exactly on time. I had to ring the bell; the door was locked, but not guarded. Presumably Inspector Morrison had found more productive work for his men.

Meg answered the door herself.

"Ready to go?" I asked.

"Ready. What a marvelous hat!"

"I'm glad you like it," I said demurely. I had taken an old orange knit cap and dressed it up with feathers given to me by a dear friend, including one rakish pheasant feather. "At least the rain can't hurt it much. Is Richard coming?"

"I am." He appeared behind Meg. "I'm in working clothes; I hope you don't mind." He eyed my hat doubtfully.

"Oh, don't let the hat bother you. I wear them everywhere except the bathtub. Got into the habit when I was young and somehow never got out of it. You look fine. Um — would one of you like to drive, since I don't know where we're going?"

They exchanged amused looks, and Meg led the way to her car.

It wasn't until we had ordered and settled ourselves that I brought up my agenda.

"Meg, I saw the new education director the other day, but I can't remember her name."

"Butler. Dulcie Butler."

"Oh, my, she didn't look at all like a Dulcie. Very efficient woman, more of an Edith or a Caroline, or something of that sort."

"I suppose," said Meg with a smile, "that she didn't have gray hair and a commanding personality when she was christened."

"Maybe not gray hair," I said doubtfully. "I'll bet she's always been the commanding type; that kind are born, not made. I stand in awe of anyone who can make that many children behave. I used to be a teacher, and I could handle my own class well enough, but not hordes of somebody else's kids."

"She's very good," agreed Meg. "There's a lot more to the job than supervising the school tours, of course, and she's barely had a chance to begin, what with all the upsets, but she's going to make a real difference. I think, when the current crisis has been sorted out, the Museum is going to be really well run. It'll make a big difference to have a full staff. I'm glad Sir Mordred is finally getting around to seeing to it."

"Has he had any luck finding a new accountant?"

"Not so far, but he's looking. I think he's close to hiring a new assistant director, as well. It'll be a happy day for me when I can get back to doing what I'm supposed to be doing, looking after the collection."

"How about a housekeeper?"

"That'll come after he has the Museum re-staffed. I know he needs one badly, but he cares more about the Museum than he does about the Hall, or about his own comfort, for that matter."

Richard had been silent, but he spoke up at that point. "I intend to ask him for a second undergardener. I can't go on trying to hold together a place this big without more help. I'd like to have Finch full-time, but I don't think he'll agree to that."

"You don't think Sir Mordred will —"

"Sorry. I meant I don't think Finch will agree to come. He likes his independence. Sir M. wouldn't mind. He's always said Bob was a good man, and he thinks there was some mistake about the thefts. It's my opinion there've been no real thefts, just what you might call natural attrition."

"I hope you're right, I must say." I took a swig of my half-pint. "About the thefts, I mean. And you might be surprised what Bob would agree to. He's in a bad way right now. He's lost a couple of jobs because of all the uproar at the Hall. Grossly unfair, but what can anyone do?"

Richard finished his beer and growled.

"Pack of idiots. If they can't see Finch is honest, they deserve to have their gardens go to couch grass."

"Indeed." I drained my own glass, and our food arrived. Richard had another beer; Meg and I, mindful of the drinking-and-driving laws, switched to mineral water.

"So what do the two of you think about the latest developments?" I asked when we had taken the edge off our hunger. "Have you had any thoughts about the mysterious woman?"

Both of them shook their heads.

"We've thought and thought," said Meg. "Richard's tried to remember a bit more of what she looked like, but of course he couldn't see details, and it's nearly a week ago, now. He can't even say how tall or fat she was, because of the angle, and the moonlight. He's pretty sure she wasn't young."

"She moved a bit stiffly, like someone with a touch of arthritis," Richard elaborated.

"Like me," I said ruefully.

"Well —"

"It's all right. I'm not embarrassed about getting old and creaky. It happens to the best of us, if we're lucky. I'm just old on the outside, though, not on the inside." I looked to see if they knew what I meant. They were too young to know from experience that a person's age doesn't have much to do with what the calendar says.

Meg looked polite, but Richard smiled, that warm smile that so changed his solemn countenance. "I know. My mother is like that. Nearly sixty, but she says she's younger than I am, and she acts it, too!"

"Good for her. She doesn't live around here, does she?"

He surprised me by roaring with laughter. "No, and she'd not be bicycling about the countryside doing in housekeepers if she did! But that's the sort of person we're looking for, I'd bet."

Despite my resolution not to get into an exhaustive examination of all the possible women connected with the Hall, we ended up doing just that. Meg came up with more names than Richard did. He had little to do with the Museum staff, and he was sure neither of the maids at the Hall fit his mental picture. But Meg's names weren't much help, and she said she'd already given them to the police.

"There's really only Mrs. Butler. Oh, I knew why you were asking, Dorothy. But I'm sure it wasn't her. She's a nice woman, and anyway, why would she murder two people she scarcely knew?"

"Does she have a key to the Hall?"

"Yes." Her blue eyes flashed. "She has to," she added defensively, "for special events and that sort of thing."

"Then she has to be considered as a possibility. I agree that she isn't likely, but I'd like to talk to her, anyway. Is she in today?"

Meg, rather unwillingly, said that Mrs. Butler was indeed working today, and added that she had better get back to work herself. She wasn't very happy with me, I could see. Neither was Richard. Well, they couldn't have everything. I'd gotten them out from under suspicion, but that meant other people had to be suspected. We drove back to the Hall in an uncomfortable silence.

When we arrived at the parking lot, I stopped them for a moment before they went their separate ways.

"I forgot to say, by the way, that I'm very happy for you both. Don't let what's happened spoil your happiness. You deserve it."

Their acknowledging smiles were a trifle stiff, and very much alike.

"Now. Where would I be likely to find Sir Mordred?"

"I thought you wanted to talk to Mrs. Butler." Meg still sounded annoyed.

"I do, but later. Just now I'd like to make

sure Sir Mordred is well."

"He's probably in his workshop, making furniture." Meg sighed with the old grievance and shook her head. "He insists on stocking the rooms with reproductions, no matter what I say. And Mrs. Butler is on his side; she says the children appreciate the houses more if they're complete, which I suppose is true. Or if he's not there, you might try his rooms. He's been on the telephone a lot, trying to settle the staffing problems."

"I'll try the workshop first. I'm sure I can find it, whereas his private rooms . . ." I made a face, inviting a laugh, and got it, though a grudging one.

"I'll lead you through the maze, if necessary."

"Thank you, my dear. And give me some bread crumbs, so I can find my way out."

She disappeared into the Hall and Richard down the drive, and I squelched through the parking lot, glad I'd remembered my wellies. They were heavy with mud by the time I reached the corner of the workshop; I stepped off the path to wipe them in the soft grass that surrounded the building.

I didn't mean to startle anyone. It was just that the grass muffled my footsteps. I paused in the doorway and spoke. "Anyone home?"

In the shadows by the far corner of the workbench a figure whirled, hand to mouth. Before I could say another word it sagged against the bench and started to slither to the floor.

15

With a lunge that my joints and muscles would regret later, I managed to reach him before he hit the floor, and softened his fall a little. It was the least I could do, seeing as how I had caused his collapse.

He was out cold for a few moments, only a few, thank goodness. I aged a good deal in those moments, caught in an impossible predicament: I could neither do anything useful nor go for help. It was with enormous relief that I saw his eyelids flutter, but he wasn't quite functional for another five endless minutes. I helped him to a chair and hovered anxiously.

"Sir Mordred, I am most terribly sorry! I didn't mean to sneak up on you like that. Will you be all right alone for a little while? Because I need to get help. There's no phone out here, is there?"

"No — phone," he said vaguely. "No — help."

I remembered his phobia about doctors. Well, I intended to get a doctor, but I'd only upset him if I said so.

"All right, but I'll just run into the house and get some tea. You need to get warm. Here, I'll tuck this around you." I stripped off my coat and laid it over him like a blanket. "Now don't you move; I'll be right back."

I tried to run between the raindrops, but I was pretty wet anyway by the time I made it to the front door and rang the bell. If it hadn't been for the deep portico over the door I would have gotten much wetter; they took their time about answering the bell. Growing more and more frantic, I finally put my finger on the bell push and left it there. When the door finally opened it was with an angry jerk.

"The sign plainly says that we're not open. What do you think —"

"Mrs. Butler, where's Richard?"

"What do you mean, where's Richard? Who are you? How do you know me?"

"My name is Dorothy Martin, and I need Richard Adam immediately!" I, too, can be commanding when I need to be. "Sir Mordred is ill and needs help at once. Please find Richard and tell him to go to the workshop with blankets, while I get some tea." I strode off in what I hoped was the direction of the kitchen, leaving the suddenly galvanized woman to run like a rabbit down another corridor.

Fortunately, lunch was not long past. When I got in the general vicinity I could follow my nose down to the kitchen. It was deserted (I assumed Mrs. Hawes was resting from her noontime labors), so I put the kettle on the hottest burner of the Aga and began to rummage for tea and a pot.

"And what," said a loud voice behind me, "do you think you're doing, poking about in my cupboards?"

She stood in a doorway, massive arms crossed, the bosom of her white apron heaving with disapproval.

"I'm sorry, Mrs. Hawes." Now that Richard was presumably dealing with the emergency, I could afford manners again. "I'm trying to make tea for Sir Mordred. He had some sort of fainting spell in the workshop, and I thought he needed something hot."

"Hmmph!" She didn't seem overly impressed, but she moved forward, quickly for a woman her size, and began laying out a tray with the necessities. "And who might you be?"

"My name is Dorothy Martin. We did meet, when my husband and I had tea in the kitchen that terribly stormy day."

"Oh." Either she didn't remember, or her memory was not pleasant. I didn't pursue it.

"Does Sir Mordred have a heart condition, or something like that?" I ventured while we waited for the kettle to boil. "I did startle him today, I admit, and that's probably what made him faint, but I've seen him looking pretty pale and shaky on several occasions now. Do you know what doctor we should call?"

She sniffed and filled the teapot with boiling water. "Won't see a doctor. One of them Scientific Christians, or whatever they are. I've got no patience with that sort of nonsense. What have we got the National Health for, is what I say. Drop down dead one of these days, I tell him, and then where'll we all be? But he don't care for nothing but them toys of his."

She thumped the teapot down on the tray. "Here's the tea. I hope you don't expect me to carry it out to him. I got the rheumatics something cruel, and I'm not traipsing out there on a day like this. Not to mention I need my rest. Doing the work of five people in this great barracks of a house, and at my age!" She thrust the heavy tray into my arms and clumped back toward the door into her quarters, breathing heavily as she went and slamming the door behind her with a loud thump.

I might have to rethink my opinion of

Mrs. Hawes as a murder suspect.

Meanwhile, however, there was Sir Mordred. I put a few more cups on the tray and hurried back through the long hallways to the front entrance hall, where I filched someone's coat off the rack and squished my way to the workshop, tray in hand.

The lord of the manor was ensconced on a chaise longue that someone, probably Richard, had brought from some garden storage. It was the folding kind, and didn't look particularly comfortable, but it was well padded with blankets, and Sir Mordred seemed to be doing all right. His color was back, and so was his temper.

"Doctors! Pack of idiots!" he was shouting to the little group hovering around his chair, Richard and Meg and Mrs. Butler. His voice rose to a higher and higher squeak. "Nincompoops! They let my mother die, couldn't decide whether she had the flu or pneumonia. It turned out to be TB. She could have been cured, if they'd had the sense God gave a newt, but not by the time they — what do *you* want?"

"I brought you some tea, Sir Mordred. It's chilly out here, and I thought you —"

"I don't want it." He turned his shoulder away from me. "I don't want anything. I have work to do."

"But you might as well have some tea, now that it's here," said Meg gently. "That can't hurt anything."

"Killed Mrs. Lathrop, didn't it?" He eyed the tray with suspicion.

"That was her herbal tea, Sir Mordred," I said, trying to be patient. "This is real tea, good Darjeeling, and if you don't want any, I'll have a cup myself." I suited the action to the word. "Would anyone else like one? It's awfully cold out here."

I poured, we drank, and when, after a moment or two, none of us showed signs of expiring, Sir Mordred condescended to accept a cup. "I'm sure it's very kind of you all," he said with a grudging nod, "but I don't like fusses. Someone's always fussing about my health. I'm healthy as a horse. You simply startled me, Mrs. Martin. My nerves are on edge, and whose wouldn't be, with what we've been through here? I'm obliged for the tea, but I must get on with my work."

"Can't we at least turn on some heat?" I begged. "Surely you can't do delicate work out here in the cold. I'd think your fingers would refuse to move."

"Oh, very well, there's an electric fire next to the workbench. I suppose the room may be a bit chilly, though I'm roasting in these blankets."

Americans and Englishmen are born with different internal thermostats, I'm convinced. My teeth were chattering. Richard found the electric heater before I did and turned it on, picking up a cloth from the floor as he did so.

"Where do you want this?"

"Put it on the bench. I don't like mess. I dropped it, I suppose, when I — um — became dizzy. I was cleaning my tools."

"A bit rusty," commented Richard, looking at the rag.

"Yes, it's the damp. I do my best, but metal *will* rust. I daren't put too much oil on them; a stain is so hard to get out of a tiny piece of wood."

Eventually he shooed us all out, insisting he felt perfectly fit. I was the last to leave, staying to retrieve my rumpled coat and apologize once more.

"No harm done, Mrs. — er — Martin," he said grudgingly. "But it has cost me a great deal of time, so if you don't mind . . ."

I couldn't think of any excuse to remain, in view of his obvious preference for my absence. I left him fanatically polishing the jaws of a vise and tramped back to the house to talk to Mrs. Butler.

I let myself in, someone having left the door unlocked, and finally tracked the woman down in the library. She was almost hidden behind a stack of books and pamphlets. Meg was elsewhere: with Richard, I speculated with a mental grin. I sat down beside the education director, who did not so much as look up.

"Mrs. Butler, thanks so much for your help. I was really in a state, and I'm afraid I wasn't very polite."

"Not at all," she murmured coolly. I wasn't sure whether she was uttering the standard English version of "forget it," or agreeing with my own description of my behavior. I tried again.

"I was really worried about Sir Mordred, you see. Does he often collapse like this?"

"I'm sure I've no idea. I've been employed here only a few days."

I seized on that. "Yes, Meg says you've done a marvelous job in the little time you've had. I suppose all the crises have meant you've had to put in a lot of extra time, coming back at night and that kind of thing."

I was watching her carefully. She turned a page, picked up her pencil, made a careful note, and looked up at me.

"I shouldn't dream of coming back at night. I live quite some distance away, beyond the university. I have been hired to do a job, Mrs. Martin, not to worry about my employer's health or ruin my own with night work. I am kept extremely busy during normal working hours," she added pointedly.

It seemed that no one wanted my company today. I plodded away; I doubt Mrs. Butler even noticed that I had left.

There was one more thing I wanted to do before I left the Hall, if I could get by with it. I wanted to have a look at Mrs. Lathrop's rooms.

Now was as good a time as any. Mrs. Hawes was probably down for another half-hour's nap, at least. I didn't know where the maids were, but if they were working hard, in the absence of any sort of supervision, they were more than mortal. If Meg and Richard were together, they wouldn't notice a herd of thundering busybodies, let alone just one who was trying to be inconspicuous. Sir Mordred was safely out of the way, and I had seen no police around at all.

Fine. I could snoop unobserved. If, of course, I could find the rooms in a house with fifty bedrooms. Slipping out of my boots — no point in leaving a trail of muddy footprints — I tiptoed up the main staircase, trying not to look the leering cupids in the eye.

It took me a while to find the rooms, but meantime I learned quite a lot about Brocklesby Hall. Most of it was obviously not in use. Many rooms, completely unheated, were filled with ghostly humps of furniture, shrouded in big once-white dust sheets. Cobwebs festooned the corners, and when I opened doors, there were often rustlings that I preferred not to speculate about. On the whole I hoped they were mice; the alternatives were even less appetizing.

Sir Mordred's miserliness was strongly in evidence on the upper floors of his fantastic mansion. Many of the light fixtures were without bulbs, so I did a good deal of stumbling in dark corners, especially where hallways indulged in entirely unnecessary three-steps-down-and-two-up routines. If anyone had been trying to track my progress, he would have had no trouble; with all my barging into things I was about as quiet as a rampaging she-grizzly. But no one interrupted me, and in due time I found the right rooms.

I could tell, not only because they were the first I saw that showed any sign of occupation, but because of the black dress draped pathetically across a chair. Evidently the rooms had been kept as Mrs. Lathrop left them that last night. I shivered slightly, and not just from the cold.

The rooms were large: sitting room, bedroom, bathroom. (Evidently, someone since the first Brocklesby had seen fit to modernize the sanitary facilities.) With a little love they could have been made pleasant and comfortable, but as they were I found them infinitely depressing. Heavy, dark paneling; heavy, dark furniture; even a heavy staleness to the air, which was only marginally warmer than in the disused rooms.

Mrs. Lathrop had made little effort to personalize her surroundings. There were no photographs, no knickknacks, nothing feminine lying around. Without the dress on the chair, they might have been a man's rooms.

There were a few touches. In the sitting room one small vase held some chrysanthemums. They were long dead, and the rank water contributed to the unpleasant atmosphere of the room, but the vase was beautiful, also valuable, if I was any judge. Certainly antique Chinese, very possibly Ming. An expensive, though very ugly, jewel box held a few pieces that looked to my inexperienced eye as though they were worth a good deal: a large, rather dirty diamond brooch, some massive gold earrings, one or two rings heavily laden with stones. I remembered that Jane had said Mrs. Lathrop's mother had been "gentry," and wondered if the small collection of treasures was inherited.

The huge mahogany wardrobe held two more black dresses cut along the same lines as the one on the chair, a couple of sensible suits in depressing tweeds, and one appalling black taffeta evening dress. What a shame! The fabrics were good, the tailoring impeccable, but the garments had been made without any sense of style or flair. Even the Mrs. Lathrops of this world look better if they're properly dressed, and if she could afford to have her clothes custom-made, surely she could have had them made attractively, as well?

An image sprang up in my mind of Mrs. Lathrop, icily edging past Ada Finch in the King's Head. Well, maybe, after all, it wouldn't have mattered much what she wore.

Suddenly revolted, I realized I couldn't bear to go through her dresser drawers. Even if I had known what I was looking for, who was I to pry into the most personal belongings of a dead woman? She would have hated my seeing her clothes and the way she lived, and the heavy stuffiness, or my sense of guilt, was giving me a headache.

Thankfully, I closed the door behind me, groped my way back to the public area of Brocklesby Hall, and slipped out the front door. No one saw me leave.

I drove home with the car windows open. I got rained on, but the fresh air smelled wonderful.

When I got home, the telephone was off the hook, a sure sign someone had been trying to call me. Samantha doesn't like the sound of the phone ringing, so she knocks off the receiver and then tells it how annoyed she is. Most of my friends have by now gotten used to hearing unearthly yowls at the other end of the line. I replaced the receiver and thought about scolding Sam, but there was little point. Even on the doubtful chance that she would understand why she was being scolded, it would make not the slightest difference in her behavior. Some cats can sometimes be taught. Not Sam; her goal in life is to get her people properly trained.

I made a cup of tea and sat down, dissatisfied, with my morning's list in front of me. It looked even less helpful now than it had then. Mrs. Butler? She'd denied working late any night. My questions had produced no reaction but mild irritation, and that only, it seemed, because they'd interrupted her work. I'd done nothing either to confirm her as a likely suspect or to eliminate her from contention. Her name stayed, but with a very large question mark beside it.

I sighed and considered Mrs. Hawes. She was an unpleasant woman, with an abrasive personality. She, of all people, would have had a splendid opportunity to doctor Mrs. Lathrop's herbal tea. But she would have had no reason to be abroad on a bicycle before dawn. Scratch Mrs. Hawes. I was convinced the bicycle woman held the key to Mrs. Lathrop's murder.

Was that a stupid conviction? Was it just as likely that the woman was a blameless passerby who would turn out to have been on her way to market with turnips in the bicycle's carrier baskets? It was entirely possible; Thursday was one of Sherebury's market days. And the fact of the market traffic, I realized with a groan, was going to make the job of the police much harder. Anyone could have been out on a bicycle for legitimate reasons.

But if our particular woman on a bicycle was irrelevant, we had reached a dead end. I would cling to my bicycle woman. A slim hope is better than none.

I had reached that stage, and had let my tea get cold, when the phone rang. I beat Sam to it by a whisker.

"Ah, you're home, my dear. Samantha answered last time. We had quite a lengthy conversation, if you can call it conversation when one party does all the talking."

"Or screaming. I hope nobody was close to the phone on your end."

"As a matter of fact, Betty placed the call for me. She is now convinced my home is inhabited by banshees, or whatever the Kenyan equivalent may be. What have you been up to, gadding about and letting cats answer the phone?"

"Only one cat," I pointed out. "Emmy never pays the slightest attention. I suppose we really should get an answering machine. I've been chasing wild geese, to answer your question. And running up blind alleys and barking up wrong trees."

"Sounds like quite a lot of exercise."

"Not to mention going around in circles. Has your day been any more productive than mine?"

"I'm beginning to get a much fuller picture of operations here, and frankly, they're quite exciting. I want to talk about the whole thing in detail when I get home, but I really called because Derek told me some interesting things a couple of hours ago."

"Oh? They haven't traced the bicycle woman, have they?"

"Unfortunately, not yet. They've eliminated a number of possible sources of information, speaking of those blind alleys of yours, but they're still trying. However, they've also been looking into the recent movements of Claude."

"And?"

"It seems that Claude had managed to land himself in important trouble in London. He was in serious debt to some very nasty lads indeed. Gambling and drugs, apparently, although our sources are somewhat cagey about that. However, they all said that he was quite literally a marked man unless he came up with a fair sum of money in a week or so."

"Good heavens! So you think he was killed by gangsters, and it didn't have anything to do with Brocklesby Hall, after all? But then why was he pushed into the lake, and — ?"

"Hold hard! There you go again! No, his deadline was the end of this week, and the wide boys are odd about sticking to that kind of agreement. They'll usually give a man exactly as much rope as they say they will. No, the interesting thing is what Claude was saying to his mates."

"I give up."

"He told them he wasn't worried. He was

going to get the money from his mum."

"But, Alan! What kind of money are we talking about?"

"Somewhere around ten thousand pounds."

"Alan, that's preposterous! Where on earth would Mrs. Lathrop come up with that kind of money?"

"Where, indeed?"

16

We tossed it around for a few minutes, but neither of us had any inspiration. I decided not to mention the jewelry I had seen. Certainly the police had seen it, too, and I didn't want to have to explain how I knew about it. I was sure, anyway, that it wasn't worth anything like ten thousand, even at full value, let alone from a pawnshop or secondhand jeweler's.

I did tell Alan about my unfruitful day at the Hall, though. He tried to be comforting.

"Now you know what ordinary police work is like, love. Day after day of slogging routine, questioning everyone, learning absolutely nothing."

"And, incidentally, making enemies. Mrs. Butler thinks I'm the world's worst nuisance, and I imagine Mrs. Hawes will lock up the spoons the next time she sees me coming."

"That comes with the territory, as well. Darling, things are going quite smoothly here, and I may be able to get home a day early, on Friday afternoon. Would that disrupt your schedule?"

I told my husband what I thought of the idea of seeing him a day — and a night — sooner, and one way and another, we took quite a long time to say good-bye.

That night my subconscious lived up to its reputation. Maybe it needs to be happy to function. At any rate, I awoke in the chill gray morning with a brilliant idea.

"The miniatures!" I said to a surprised pair of cats, who viewed me with deep suspicion. The missing miniatures. What if they really had been stolen, and by Mrs. Lathrop? I knew nothing about her, really, except the sketchy background Jane had given me. Her son moved in very shady circles in London. What if Mum had decided she needed some extra money, either to support the appalling Claude or for purposes of her own? She had a few possessions that someone in her position wouldn't normally be expected to have; she must have had money from some unknown, and very possibly illicit, source. It would have been easy for her to steal the miniatures, and Claude could have fenced them for her, probably for only a small fraction of their real value, but that was the usual disadvantage of theft as a source of income.

Then who had murdered her, and why? I poured a second cup of coffee and considered that problem.

Mr. Thoreston. I had forgotten about Mr. Thoreston as soon as it had been established that he could not have killed Claude. Now. Suppose that somehow Mrs. Lathrop had found out about the irregularities in the Museum's books. Never mind how. A dedicated snoop can find out anything, given the desire and the opportunity. The housekeeper certainly had the opportunity, and maybe some peculiar behavior on Thoreston's part had given her the desire. Anyway, assume she got the goods on him. As I saw it, she might have had two possible reactions. One, a proposal that the two of them, thieves both, might work together for bigger and better gains.

Or, two, righteous indignation and a threat to tell Sir Mordred and the authorities immediately.

On the whole, I thought the latter more probable. I couldn't see Mrs. Lathrop putting herself in someone else's power, as she would have done if she had told Thoreston that she, too, was robbing Sir Mordred. Nor had I seen any evidence of a sense of humor that would have reveled in the coincidence of two thieves in the same ultrarespectable establishment. No, I thought she would have climbed on her high horse and told Thoreston the jig was up. And he, of course —

My train of thought came to a screeching halt and nearly jumped the track. Alan and I had already been over this ground once, hadn't we? And I had quite firmly decided that Thoreston wouldn't have committed that particular murder, involving careful planning and a knowledge of plants. It further involved a period of waiting, until Mrs. Lathrop felt ill and needed her herbal tea, and how could Thoreston have known when that might be? He couldn't afford to wait; Mrs. Lathrop might spill the beans at any time.

I got back to my original thought that Mrs. Lathrop had stolen the miniatures. The Thoreston theory made those thefts basically irrelevant, and surely they couldn't be. That would make entirely too many different kinds of crime going on in one place, and although I could believe almost anything of a nightmare house like Brocklesby Hall, I couldn't believe in embezzlement and theft and murder, all unconnected.

Very well, then. Lathrop had taken the miniatures. Suppose Thoreston had discovered her, instead of the other way around. Again, I wasn't sure how. Just seeing her removing pieces from a display wouldn't be enough. She could have thought of a convincing, legitimate reason to be handling the things.

Let that go for the moment. He had discovered her secret. He had threatened her . . .

The train lost its steam completely and sat there refusing to move. The thought of little John Thoreston threatening the formidable Lathrop was ludicrous.

"And it seemed like such a good idea," I said mournfully to Emmy, who happened to be lying on the floor next to the Aga. "The trouble is, it doesn't seem to go anywhere. I still think Mrs. Lathrop stole the miniatures, but it doesn't lead me any closer to who murdered her and Claude."

Emmy yawned, resettled her warm gray bulk, and firmly closed both eyes.

Maybe she was right and my idea wasn't even worth considering, but it was the only one I had and I wanted to follow up on it. The question was, how? That took another cup of coffee.

The first, obvious step would be to examine Mrs. Lathrop's bank records to see if there were large, unexplained deposits. Unfortunately, there was no way I could do that. The English have a strong sense of privacy, especially when it comes to money, and bank managers are very sticky about protecting their depositors, even when they happen to be dead. The police have a hard enough time getting into people's bank accounts. A private citizen, and a foreigner at that, wouldn't stand a chance.

I could always suggest to Alan that the police look into Mrs. Lathrop's finances, but they were probably already doing that, since the money question had arisen with the revelations about Claude's problems. I could also, of course, tell my loving spouse about the few expensive little trinkets I had seen in Mrs. Lathrop's rooms. If it turned out that they were recently purchased, that would strengthen police interest in following the money. It would also strengthen police interest, particularly Alan's interest, in my activities at Brocklesby Hall, many of which were dubious and some of which — like searching Mrs. Lathrop's rooms — were probably illegal.

I have never been one for sawing off my own branch. Time enough to tell Alan, if and when the information proved to be relevant. I could find out easily enough if the jewelry and vase were family heirlooms just by talking to people.

Jane was just returning from walking the dogs when I arrived at her backdoor. There was considerable confusion of snuffling and licking and treat-giving before we could settle down at her kitchen table.

"Coffee?"

"Heavens, Jane, I've had three cups already; I'm bouncing off the walls. You go ahead."

Jane's kitchen, large and cheerful, was a haven on a cold, gray day. The dogs, tired and content, wandered off to their beds in the back hall, leaving quiet in their wake. The teakettle hummed. Jane bustled about making coffee.

"Jane, it's a shame I only seem to find time for a visit when I need something. Someday I'm going to come over here for no reason at all, just to talk."

Jane sat down with her coffee. "Right. Be bored to tears, you would."

"What a thing to say!"

"You like action," she pointed out. "Have to have something going on. What now?"

I didn't argue; she was too nearly right. "The same thing, really. I'm still gnawing away at the Brocklesby Hall murders, and I'm not getting anywhere."

"Neither are the police."

"I know. That's one reason I keep on, even with Bob Finch pretty well out of danger."

"Still not working at all, you know. And back to the drink, or so I hear. Until someone is arrested, still be under suspicion. People are a pack of fools."

"A lot of them are. And Bob deserves better. So what I need from you now is some information about Mrs. Lathrop."

Jane shrugged. "Already told you all I know."

"No, I know you gave me general background, but this is something specific. Did she inherit any money from her mother? Or family treasures, jewelry or that sort of thing?"

I knew the answer before Jane opened her mouth. She was looking at me with elaborate patience.

"Told you her father went through all the money. Wasn't much to begin with, certainly no 'family treasure.' " The tone she used for the last phrase relegated it to the realm of sensational fiction.

"All right, all right, so I get carried away sometimes. But the fact is, Jane, that Emma Lathrop died with a modest collection of jewels and at least one fine piece of porcelain."

"Couldn't have." This time her tone was flat and unequivocal.

"She did, though. I've seen them. And if you tell Alan, I'll —" I met her gaze and sighed. "— I'll be upset. I know I had no business going into her rooms, so you don't have to bawl me out. Goodness only knows what Alan will say when he finds out, and yes, I will tell him. Eventually. Anyway, I did go poking around and I did see a few pieces of good jewelry and a small Ming vase."

Jane looked at me sharply. "Sure?"

"I'm no expert, but I'm pretty sure I can tell gold and diamonds from costume jewelry, and I can identify some kinds of porcelain. I'm reasonably sure. So if you say she didn't inherit anything like that, where did she get them?"

The silence in Jane's kitchen lengthened. I could hear a dog's muffled snores and the tick of the clock on the wall.

"Gifts?" said Jane at last.

"From whom? Did her husbands have money?"

"Butlers," said Jane with a snort. "Sir Mordred, then?"

It was my turn to snort. "Every cent of Sir Mordred's money goes to his ruling passion, and I'd bet my last dollar he never gave the Lathrop the time of day if he could help it, let alone expensive presents."

More silence.

"So you think she stole them."

"I think she stole a bunch of miniatures to pay for them," I corrected. "The ones Sir Mordred kept saying had gone missing, and blamed Bob for."

"Hmmm." Her lower lip protruded as she considered. "So what does that have to do with her getting herself killed?"

"That's the trouble, you see. I've tried and tried to tie the two things together, and I can't. And it's driving me crazy, because there has to be some connection between all the things that've been happening. Thoreston's embezzlement, and the miniature thefts, and the murders, and Claude's money problems —"

"And the mysterious cyclist, don't forget her."

"Oh, good grief, I had! And Jane, I just realized I probably shouldn't have mentioned Claude. Alan told me some things, but I can't talk about them."

"Didn't hear a thing," said Jane.

"But what's the connection?" I went on. "What are we all missing? What's the common thread?"

"Brocklesby Hall," said Jane promptly.

"Well, yes, of course, that's where they all happened, but —"

"More than that. Key is there. Don't

know what it is. But the Hall's at the center of it, mark my words."

Jane doesn't often go in for prognostication, so I did mark her words as I went back home. I couldn't, however, see how a house, however large and ugly, could be an important element in several disparate crimes.

Except, of course, as a background. Maybe what Jane meant was that the unlovely atmosphere of the Hall acted as a catalyst, encouraged violence. Well, I didn't like the place, either, but I didn't have Jane's obsession about it.

And a good thing, too, because I was going to have to go back out there again. I was doggedly determined to solve the puzzle of Mrs. Lathrop's unexpected wealth, even if it ended up being totally irrelevant. And the place to begin doing that was in Meg's records of Sir Mordred's collection. It was time to take the question of the missing miniatures out of obscurity and expose it to the light. I reached for the telephone.

It was obvious from Meg's response that I was becoming a nuisance. She was reasonably cordial, but less than enthusiastic about a visit from me. Yes, the Museum was open today, and they were flooded with visitors. Yes, she was extremely busy. If I really wanted to study her accession cards, she supposed I might do so, but she would not be able to give me much help with deciphering them; she and a helper were busy entering data on the computer.

I didn't blame her. Now that both she and Richard were cleared of suspicion, and the Museum staff was back to something approaching normal strength, she could resume her neglected work, and was anxious to do so without the interference of a busybody, however well-meaning. "I promise I won't get in your way," I said. "I don't suppose I'll need any help. I knew my way around libraries before you were born, and long before there were computers. I'll be there soon."

At least the parking lot wasn't a sea of mud today, though it hadn't completely dried out from yesterday's rains. I resisted the temptation to look in on Sir Mordred, though there was a light in the workshop. I'd nearly killed the poor man the last time I'd dropped in unexpectedly.

Meg was indeed busy, sitting at her desk with cards spread out in front of her, gazing intently at the computer screen. An extra chair had been pulled up and a young woman who looked familiar was reading the cards aloud.

"Hello, Dorothy," said Meg, sounding tired. "Do you remember Susan Eggers? I've commandeered her again from the ranks of the guides. She's been helping me quite a lot, actually."

"She let me in the day of my very first visit, but we haven't actually been introduced."

We shook hands, young Susan eyeing my pheasant-feathered hat but politely saying nothing, and I got right to the point. "Now, Meg, I meant it when I said I didn't want to bother you. Just point me in the direction of the files and I'll cope. I simply want to familiarize myself with your cataloguing system before I try to figure out some things."

Meg sighed. "I'm afraid you'll find a great many of the cards missing. We're using them, entering data, and it's slow going. I can spare Susan for a minute or two to orient you; that'll help some. The principles are the same as those used in book collections, of course, but we need a great deal more information about each artifact. Here, Susan, we've finished with these cards; you can use them."

Susan took me to a reading table and picked out a few cards to show me.

"It's quite a complex problem, you see," she said in that kind, indulgent voice polite young people often use to their doddering elders, "because a large dolls' house may contain literally thousands of separate objects, and some system must be used to list them all, with at least a sketchy description, and yet identify them as belonging to a particular house."

"Yes, I wondered about that. And of course you must list provenance, and age, and condition — a good many things that aren't necessary with a book. Surely you don't attempt a description of every tiny cooking pot and piece of china?"

She looked at me with increased respect. "Not usually, no. Look, this card will show you. It's the master card for one of the Nuremberg houses. This is the probable date of the house, 1647. This is the provenance, insofar as it can be traced. There are some gaps, regrettable, but only natural in an artifact which is over three hundred years old."

"And which, I suspect, was not considered to be valuable by some of its owners over the years."

"Indeed. The oldest houses were probably intended, originally, to be collections of arts and crafts, but they were often treated by later generations as children's toys, which meant that many objects were lost and records weren't kept properly." Her voice, I was pleased to note, had lost its condescending tone. She continued her explanation.

"Here we would list the makers of the house by name if they were known; as it is, we've been able only to determine that the work of many different Nuremberg guilds is represented. Then there is a general description of the house itself, the shell, by dimensions —"

"It's surely very large," I interrupted, peering at the card through the bottom of my bifocals.

"The dimensions are given in centimeters," Susan said, smiling. "It does make everything sound huge, doesn't it? And it's rather awkward for the newer English and American rooms, which are usually in one-twelfth or one-twenty-fourth scale. An inch or a half-inch to the foot doesn't make a lot of sense translated into metric.

"Anyway, then the card is cross-referenced to separate cards for each room. Here's the master bedroom card for the '47 Nuremberg house, you see. It's actually several cards, because all the furniture must be listed and briefly described, including any damage."

"What about something like a kitchen,

though, with dozens of dishes and knives and forks and pots?"

"Then there are sub-cards yet again, with the sets listed and described. If a set of objects is particularly valuable, it will be described in some detail. Wait, I know it's here somewhere — ah, yes. This is the dining room card for a lovely little house that belonged to Marie Antoinette. There's an extremely valuable tea set in that room, and it would be described on a separate card, right down to the —"

She paused, frowning at the card in her hand. "Hmm. That's odd."

"What?"

"The card shows that the dining table in this room has a deep scratch on the bottom, and that the upholstery on the chairs is shattered."

"Shattered? How can upholstery shatter?"

"It's a term used for a certain kind of fraying that sometimes happens to old silk. But the thing is, I looked at this house last week, when I was helping Meg with inventory. I'm quite sure there was nothing wrong with the dining room furniture. Look, here in the 'new remarks' section, I've penciled in 'ND.' For 'No Damage.'"

My heart was starting to beat faster. "And

you didn't check the old damage report?"

"No, I was working fast, basically just checking them to make sure they were still there. A few things have been stolen, you know."

"Is there any chance that the card is in error?"

"I think we should ask Meg."

"There's always a chance," Meg said to Susan, when questioned. "I didn't provide the information for the cards; Sir Mordred did. I simply entered it in coherent fashion. But it's easy enough for you to check it again."

"Susan, may I come along?" This could be important.

"Sure. Follow me."

She knew her way through the maze, of course. We went directly to a room I hadn't seen before, where (according to a sign by the door) most of the French dollhouses were displayed. Susan led me to a large, elaborate house in the corner.

I was distracted in spite of my other concerns by the elaborate details. Ormolu chandeliers, carved paneling, intricately woven rugs on parquet floors, tapestries —

"Look! That must be the famous tea set!"

"It is, as a matter of fact. But look here at the table." She turned it upside down.

"There's no —" She stopped and looked more closely. "There is, though. Right there." She pointed with her fingernail.

The scratch was long and deep, though old enough to have darkened considerably over the years. "Susan, I don't see how you could have missed this. It's pretty obvious."

"So is this." Her voice was deeply puzzled as she handed me a tiny chair. The upholstery of the seat was in shreds.

We looked at each other.

"Mrs. Martin, I don't understand what's going on here, but I'm sure of one thing. This is not the dining room furniture I saw in this house last week!"

17

"Come on!" Susan seized me by the arm and pulled me out of the room.

"Wait a minute. Where are we going?"

"Back to the library to get more cards. Something very odd is happening here."

The cards Susan had checked the week before were the ones Meg was methodically entering in her data base. Susan seized them over the curator's protests.

"Look! There are a lot of them. See, in this section it says 'ND' in my writing, but here the card says there's a nick in one leg. And there's a discrepancy here — and here —"

She thumbed through the cards rapidly, discarding some, but keeping a large handful.

"Do you want to come with me? I'm going to check the rest!"

We made a whirlwind tour of the Museum, checking individual pieces here and there. Susan's puzzlement, and mine, grew by the moment. Almost every piece she checked showed perfect work where it should be damaged, matching her recent notations rather than the typed description on the card. Every now and then, though, whole sets of pieces that she had noted as undamaged were noticeably marred, like the French dining room set.

"Is that everything?" I finally said, panting in her wake.

"No. Not by any means. But it's a representative sampling, and I haven't the slightest idea what it means."

"Well, then, do you suppose we could sit down and think about it?"

She looked at me and blinked. "I'm sorry. I have rather dragged you about, haven't I?"

"Don't worry about it. It's just my knees. They don't like stairs, or hard floors, and they get worse as cold weather sets in."

"Of course. Let's go back to the library, then, and try to sort this out."

There were a couple of deep leather chairs in the library, by the fireplace. I sank gratefully into one of them. I would have to be hauled out of it later, but never mind. The fireplace, like so many in modern England, was sealed up and equipped with an electric heater, but at least it provided warmth, if not atmosphere. Meg took the other easy chair, Susan pulled up a library-issue oak one, and we contemplated our puzzle.

"You're quite sure you're right," said Meg. It wasn't really a question.

"Quite sure," replied Susan firmly. "They're absolutely first-class reproductions. But they're reproductions. You can look for yourself."

"I certainly shall, but for the moment I'll take your word for it. You know something about antiques, as I recall."

"Rather a lot, actually. That's one reason I wanted to work here. I'm reading for a degree in fine arts, and I want to deal in antiques when I leave the university. I haven't had the chance to learn much about antique dolls' houses, and they've always fascinated me. So . . ."

"So. So someone has been systematically replacing our furnishings with reproductions. Expertly made reproductions."

We all, of course, had the same idea. I let Meg voice it.

"Sir Mordred makes some of the finest miniature furniture in the world. But why would he make copies of his own possessions?"

I glanced around me, rather melodramatically, perhaps, before I spoke, with lowered voice. "I had an idea, this morning. I thought perhaps Mrs. Lathrop was stealing miniatures and trying to put the blame on

Bob Finch. That's really why I came here, to see if I couldn't find some gaps in the collection. I certainly didn't expect to find substitutions. I don't understand it at all."

"But why did you think of Mrs. Lathrop, of all people?"

Oh, dear. "Well — if I must admit it — I looked in her rooms yesterday."

Meg looked shocked.

"All right, I know I shouldn't have, but I thought I might see something significant, something the police might have missed. And I think I did. I don't know if the police took any notice, but she has — had — some perfectly hideous jewelry that looked as if it was worth a lot. And there's a vase that I'm almost sure is Ming. So I got to wondering where a housekeeper would get that kind of money, and I remembered that Sir Mordred had claimed some miniatures were missing, and . . ."

I spread my hands. "It seemed to hang together. Now I don't know what to think. I have no trouble with the idea of Mrs. Lathrop stealing things. She struck me as the kind of woman with a strong sense of respectability, but no particular morality. But I can't imagine her convincing Sir Mordred to replace the things she stole, even if he was scared to death of her."

"No," said Meg. "Definitely not. He loves his collection as I love my daughter. He would never agree to part with any of it, much less connive at its disappearance."

"Is there anyone else in the country who makes such fine miniature furniture? Do you know?"

Meg shrugged. "A couple of people are nearly as good. But they know the value of their work, and I shouldn't imagine a thief would end up with much profit at the end of the day. Besides, they're very reputable men. They wouldn't copy a piece without the permission of its owner."

"But it's such a very odd thing for a thief to do," said Susan, leaning forward intently. "Never mind how they did it. *Why* would anyone steal something and then put it back?"

"And how, and when?" I added. "If it was Mrs. Lathrop, it obviously had to be before last Thursday, when she died. And since then the place has been swarming with police most of the time."

"What about the bag of miniatures they thought the undergardener was trying to steal?" put in Susan. "What does that have to do with it all?"

"Nothing, I think. I'm reasonably sure that whoever is responsible for everything that's going on here planted that bag on purpose to incriminate poor Bob Finch. The fact that it didn't, or not for very long, is a tribute to the intelligence of the police. But it doesn't get us anywhere at the moment."

"You don't suppose Claude . . ." said Meg.

"My dear child, one is traditionally not supposed to speak ill of the dead, but can you see Claude ever putting back anything he had stolen?"

"I can't see any of it," she said with a groan. "My brain has stopped working. The only explanation I can come up with is that Sir Mordred made copies of his own prized possessions, sold the originals, and then somehow got some of them back. That's entirely plausible. He does very fine work, and very fast. The trouble is, it's totally insane. Even if you can imagine him doing it, which I can't, there's no benefit for him."

"And what benefit would he derive from killing?"

Meg and Susan were silent.

"I don't know about you, but with all the side issues that keep coming up, I keep losing track of the primary fact that two people are dead. Not very pleasant people, perhaps, but dead before their time and by the hand of violence. That's the important issue here. Would Sir Mordred be capable of murder?"

"I think he would," said Meg slowly. "I think he'd do anything he thought necessary to protect his collection. I'm afraid he's not really a very nice little man, in many ways. Yes, I think he could kill, if he thought there were good reason. But . . ."

"But there wasn't any reason. And he wasn't here, on either occasion."

I stood, after considerable maneuvering.

"Meg, I give up. I'm going home."

Meg stood, too. "Oh, Dorothy, go home and rest your knees, but *don't* give up. We've got to have this settled, or go mad, and the police aren't doing a bl—ooming thing. You're our only hope." To my astonishment, she flung her arms around me in a warm hug.

I grinned back. "Oh, it was just a figure of speech. A confirmed meddler never gives up, especially an American one. I come of tough midwestern stock. Never say die, that's us."

I was to remember that little speech.

I put in the usual call to Alan and had some lunch during the usual wait for him to call back. I don't know what was in the sandwich; I was eating for sustenance, not for pleasure. My mind was working as fast as one of those little wheels in a hamster's cage, and to as little purpose.

When the phone rang, I wasted no time on polite chitchat. "Alan, I need you to find out something for me, if you can."

"If I can." He sounded cautious.

"Well, I know it isn't easy, even for the police, but has anyone been looking into Mrs. Lathrop's financial position?"

"Ah. Derek is working on it. He hasn't reported anything to me, but you do understand he is fully in charge of this case? He does not report to me on a regular basis, only when I ring him and ask, and I wouldn't do even that if I weren't personally concerned."

"Yes, of course, I know all that, but I'd appreciate it if you'd let me know when he finds out anything. Some very peculiar things have been going on at the Museum."

"More peculiar than murder?" His tone was dry.

"In a way." I told him about the substitutions, and more puzzling still, the replacements of some of the miniatures.

"I see. Most unusual. Have you any theories?"

I tried to hear a note of sarcasm, but he

sounded genuinely interested in my opinion.

"I did think maybe Mrs. Lathrop was stealing from the Museum. It would have explained — would have explained the money Claude thought he was going to get from her."

"And?"

I chose to misunderstand.

"And I decided I'm wrong. She wouldn't have substituted copies, and she's been in no position recently to put anything back."

"True." He waited, but I had said all I intended to say until he got back and I could talk to him in person.

"Very well, I'll keep you informed. There is just one thing Derek has learned that might interest you."

"Tell, tell!"

"The mysterious woman has been traced."

"Alan, that *is* news! Who is she?"

"Not traced that far. But she's from Sherebury, apparently. She was seen getting off the first train from London on the Thursday morning, the 5:33. The station-master noticed, because it's very uncommon for anyone at all to arrive so early, or even for the train to stop. It's really the train for Hastings, and stops at Sherebury only by request. In any event, he noticed the lady. She had no luggage, just a handbag, and she made directly for the car park. He quite distinctly saw her unlock a bicycle that was in the stall, and ride off."

"So she was a local who had gone to London the day before —"

"At some time before. The stationmaster doesn't recall seeing her leave the bike there, and didn't notice it, especially, on the Wednesday. There are usually quite a number of bicycles coming and going."

"— at some time before, and left the bike to provide her transportation home. But who is she? And where does she live? And why was she stopping on the road near Brocklesby Hall? And what did she have against Emma Lathrop? And —"

"We're working on it, love. And you're making some unwarranted assumptions, you know. There is no proof at all that she had anything to do with the murder of Mrs. Lathrop, and nothing even to connect her with Claude's."

"I know. I simply refuse to accept too many coincidences. She'll turn out to have something to do with it, even if she isn't the murderer. But I wish I had even the faintest clue who she was!"

"You don't wish it as much as Derek does."

"I'm sure. Alan, when do you expect to be home tomorrow?"

"Mid-afternoon. Would you like me to ring you just before I leave here?"

"No, as long as it isn't a question of having a meal ready or not, it doesn't matter. But the sooner the better!"

"I agree."

I spent the rest of the day cleaning house. I'd really been neglecting my duties, and it showed. But all the time I was dusting, and scrubbing, and vacuuming (to the cats' distress), I was thinking.

Why would a person steal something and then put it back?

Because the thief didn't want anyone to find out it was stolen in the first place.

Did that make sense? Embezzlers did that, or always said they were going to do that. They were "borrowing" the money, not stealing it, and their goal was to get the funds back in the account before their little withdrawals were noticed. I had fleeting thoughts once more of little Mr. Thoreston, and dismissed them. He had "borrowed" money, not miniatures. Even if, for some silly reason, he had also pilfered from the dollhouses, he had been missing from Shierebury since last Thursday and had had no chance to replace anything.

But the embezzling thought had raised the ghost of an idea, somewhere deep in my brain. I teased at it, but it remained stubbornly elusive until I finally gave it up and devoted my whole energy to scrubbing the bathtub. Then, of course, it popped to the surface obligingly.

Embezzlers put the money back, sometimes, when they no longer have need of it. The temporary crisis has passed, the thief has been able to sell something or otherwise realize some cash, and he or she replaces what was stolen.

Suppose somebody stole the miniatures, sold them, and then bought them back when the need for money had abated?

I tested that theory while I cleaned out the fireplace and laid a fresh fire ready to light when Alan came home the next day. It seemed to hold together, as far as it went. It would explain why most of the substitutions were still in place. Those were pieces that the thief was having trouble getting back, or couldn't yet afford to buy, or simply had not yet gotten around to dealing with.

It would even explain the nature of the pieces that *had* been swapped back. They were all in sets: dining room, bedroom, living room. A table and chairs, or a matching bed, dresser, and wardrobe, or a velvet couch and two chairs. Couldn't it be that these had been sold to collectors who were furnishing a dollhouse of their own, and who would actually prefer new work to antiques? Who would be happy to buy Sir Mordred's exquisite work, or take it in exchange for the old, somewhat battered pieces?

I crumpled some newspaper to put in the grate, and both cats jumped on it. There was a fierce struggle for possession, in the midst of which I got a scratch on my hand. "Bad cats! Stop it!" I slapped the floor with a newspaper, scattering my erring companions, and dabbed at my bleeding hand with a tissue. It slowed down to an ooze after a while, and I finished the job, collecting thoughts that had scattered like the cats.

Sir Mordred. It all came down to Sir Mordred. He could have taken his antique pieces. It would not even have been stealing; they belonged to him. He could certainly have planted them to implicate poor Bob. He could have sold them, and he could, in some cases, have retrieved them. He was virtually the only one who could, easily, have made the tiny copies. But why would he have gone to all that trouble? If he needed money, why not just sell some of the collection?

Because he didn't want anyone to know what was going on. I'd been right the first time. Because he hoped to put the objects back before anyone noticed. Because — it was coming — because there was something shameful or dishonest about the use to which he was putting the money.

The idea made me slightly dizzy. Respectable little Sir M.? Knighted for his service to his country's arts? What dark secret could he have? My head spun.

Or perhaps it was spinning because I was hungry. It was after eight and I'd had no dinner. Neither had the cats. I remedied both situations and sat at the table, musing as I ate.

I think best on paper. I pulled a pencil and pad toward me and began a list of dubious activities that require quite a bit of money.

Gambling
Drugs
Bribery
Gang connections
Prostitution

The mind boggled at that last in connection with anyone as prissy as Sir Mordred. It boggled at all of them, to tell the truth. Gambling is an obsession, and people seldom nurse two obsessions at once; Sir Mordred's was miniatures. I had never seen any sign of his taking drugs, and as for gangs, the very idea was ludicrous. Bribery? Whom would he bribe, and why?

How about art theft? Was he stealing some of his dollhouses, or buying them from an unscrupulous dealer? Maybe, but why, then, would he at the same time be selling some of their furnishings?

I gave it up. I was tired. Morning would do for more thinking, and in the afternoon — calloo, callay! — I could talk it all over with my husband the chief constable, who knew a thing or two about crime. Meanwhile the night was cold and my blankets warm. I was going to bed.

With a book, of course. I hadn't bought any new books lately, so I perused my mystery shelves for old favorites and pulled down Agatha Christie's *Cat Among the Pigeons*. There is nothing so soothing as reading an excellent mystery for the fifteenth time. I pulled the covers up to my chin, settled myself comfortably between two warm cats, and began the story of intrigue, kidnapping, blackmail, and triple murder in a girls' school, falling asleep just as the mistress of French was hit on the head . . .

18

I had planned to do more thinking in the morning, but by morning I didn't have to. Really, I was going to have to stop insulting the theory of subconscious problem-solving, because I woke, not only with the beginnings of a bad cold, but with all the details of a brilliant solution lined up in my somewhat stuffy head.

Well, all the details but one. I still couldn't figure out *why*. Why the whole thing got started, that is. But I knew who the murderer was, and why the victims were killed, and why the miniatures were stolen and put back, and who the mysterious woman on the bicycle was, and how it all happened.

Of course, I had no proof. And I really wanted to have the whole thing neatly laid out for Alan when he came home. That didn't leave me any too much time. I had to make some fast plans.

Plans, however, don't come to order, and I don't think very clearly when I feel awful. How was I going to get proof? My murderer had been very careful. I would get nowhere by flinging accusations all over the place; they would simply be denied, and the murderer would be warned. I sniffled and reached in my pocket for a tissue.

I had put on the same slacks I'd worn the day before, and there in my pocket was the rusty-looking, blood-stained tissue I'd used to mop up my hand after Sam scratched it. I was about to throw it away when I looked at it again and yet another lightbulb went off. Good grief, whatever I was going to do, I'd better do it soon or the best piece of evidence would be gone — if it wasn't already.

If it were done when 'tis done, then 'twere well it were done quickly . . . I shivered, brushing away the uncomfortable analogy.

This was going to be tricky. If I went out willy-nilly and put myself in danger, Alan would have some very pointed remarks to make, just when he seemed to be accepting the idea of my involvement in matters criminal. I'd better be sure of my ground before I did anything. It might even be better to wait until Alan got back, and we could plan out something together.

But how was I going to keep that evidence from being destroyed? I couldn't very well just go and steal it, partly because it would be much more useful to the police in situ, partly because, if I were caught — that didn't bear thinking about.

Get hold of yourself, Dorothy. It's the police who need that piece of evidence. It will be important to their case. Stop playing Nancy Drew and turn this over to the people who can do something about it properly.

I called the police station and asked to speak to Inspector Morrison.

"I'm sorry, madam, Chief Inspector Morrison is not in the building. May I give him a message?"

"Is there someone else working on the Brocklesby Hall murders I could talk to?"

"Concerning what, madam?"

"I have some information that may be useful."

"I see. I will be happy to let someone know, when they return, if you will tell me your name and the nature of your information."

I sat silent for a moment, fuming. My name? Risk involving Alan without his knowledge? And did I want to tell just anyone the nature of my information? Most of Belleshire's police force, under Alan's administration, were extremely competent, but there might be one blabbermouth in the outfit who could spoil everything.

"Are you still there, madam?"

"Yes. Thank you, but I'll call back later."

I replaced the receiver, picked it up again, and called Alan.

"I'm sorry, Mrs. Martin," said Betty's soft, melodic voice. "He has meetings scheduled for nearly the whole morning, right up until he leaves. Shall I interrupt him?"

"No . . . no. But when he does surface, tell him I need to talk to him before he leaves for home. I may not be reachable; it depends on when he calls. If I'm not, tell him not to worry."

After I'd hung up I realized that telling someone not to worry was exactly like telling children not to put beans in their ears. Too late now.

It might also be too late, now or soon, to save the vital clue. What to do, what to do, without the police help that wasn't going to be forthcoming for a while?

Aha! I picked up the phone again, looked up a number, and waited while Richard Adam's phone rang and rang.

Was I doomed to frustration at every turn? Was there nothing I could do? Richard could have put the evidence in a safe place for me, probably without incurring any suspicion. I'd simply have to find him, but there was one thing more to check, meanwhile.

The phone call was successful, this time. I tried Sotheby's first, and was shunted around from one expert to another before finding the right one.

"Yes, madam, we frequently have dolls' houses and their furnishings offered for sale. We had quite a nice lot in just recently, as a matter of fact — let me just check." Various subdued noises for a while, and then the woman came back on the line. "I'm very sorry. That lot seems to have been removed from the catalog."

"Oh, dear. Were those from Sir Mordred Brocklesby's collection, by any chance? I particularly wanted to see them; we seldom see anything of that quality in America."

"What a pity! They were, as a matter of fact. But items from his collection do turn up from time to time. Would you like me to send you a catalog when we next have some in?"

"No, I'm going home soon, so I'll have to get back in touch with you. Thank you very much."

The people at Christie's said much the same thing. Confirmation of my theories, useful, but incomplete without more proof.

I tried Richard Adam again, with no success. I was sitting with my hand on the phone, debating, when it rang and startled me. I picked it up, eagerly.

"Alan?"

" 'Ullo. Is this Mrs. Martin? Dorothy Martin?"

"Yes, I —"

"This 'ere's Ada Finch."

"Ada! I haven't talked to you in a long time. How nice to hear from you."

"I wouldn't bother you at 'ome, madam," she said, oddly formal on the telephone, "only as 'ow that Bob, 'ee's took off, an' I thought you might've seen 'im. 'Ee ain't fit to be drivin', nor yet walkin', if it comes to that, an' 'oo knows where 'ee might fetch up! 'Ee ain't been round your 'ouse, 'as 'e?"

"No, Ada, I haven't seen him. He's drinking, then?"

"Like to drown hisself." She sounded despondent. "If you see 'im, I'd be obliged if you'd send 'im 'ome. 'Ee has the devil's own luck when 'ee's right pissed, but 'is luck 'as to run out sometime."

"Ada, I'm sure he'll be fine. The Lord takes care of fools and drunkards, you know."

Ada muttered something that sounded like "one too many times."

"I'll keep my eyes open, I promise, but try not to worry. I'll call — er — ring you up if I see him."

Well, that made my mind up for me. Bob could very well be out at the Hall, but if he wasn't, he was busy getting into trouble somewhere else. If he was driving, it was only a matter of time before the police stopped him, and he'd lose his license for a long time — and with it his livelihood. And on the whole, that was the least serious thing that could happen.

Bob needed to be found, and this mess needed to be cleared up. I was going out to the Hall. I'd be careful, but I couldn't just sit around and do nothing, with critical issues at stake. I really will be careful, Alan, I promised him in earnest thought waves.

I donned the chrysanthemum hat for moral support, stuffed a wad of tissues in my purse to deal with my cold, and climbed in the car.

It was actually easier than I had feared. When I got to the parking lot at Brocklesby Hall, Richard was working in one of the gardens, digging and mulching and obviously preparing it for winter. Winter seemed rather far away; the day was gray, but warmish, and many of the plants were still growing with apparent vigor.

"That looks like warm work," I commented, approaching him.

"It is that, but this is a good day for it. I

like your hat." He grinned at it and went on with his work.

"Richard, I don't want to bother you, but Bob Finch hasn't been around, has he?"

The gardener rested on his shovel. "Haven't seen him. I could use him, today, but he hasn't turned up."

"That's bad. His mother called me, very upset, though she tried not to show it. He's on a real bender, and she thinks he might be driving. I'd hoped he might have ended up out here."

"Not today. I'll watch for him. I could always bed him down at my cottage, give him a place to sleep it off. He's a good man, Finch, if he does have a weakness." He picked up his shovel and levered a clump of irises out of the ground.

"I'm glad you think so. He needs a friend right now, and until these crimes are cleared up, he doesn't have many. So I'm doing my best, and there are some other things I need to know, but I can see you're busy. Can you talk and work at the same time?"

"Why not?"

"Well, most men I know can't. What I want to know" — I lowered my voice and looked around — "what I want to know is, what was the bicycle woman wearing?"

"A skirt, I told you. That's how I knew at

first she was a woman."

"And a scarf. I know. But what about details? Was the skirt light, dark, long, short? What kind of coat did she have? Et cetera."

"The police asked me all those questions."

"I'm sure they did. But I need to know, and I can't ask the police right now." I fumbled for a tissue and blew my nose.

He looked at me appraisingly (and stopped work again as he did so).

"It was dark, you know. A moonlit night. And she was down by the front gate. I couldn't make out details. She was wearing something dark with a skirt. I could see her legs, quite distinctly, because they were pale. The skirt couldn't have been all that long or I wouldn't have seen her legs at all from this angle. It certainly wasn't a mini; I'd have noticed that."

"I'll bet you would."

His eyes glinted at me, but he didn't smile. "Her scarf was light, and I think patterned. Colors get washed out in the moonlight, you know. I'm sorry I can't tell you more."

"How about shoes?"

He considered. "Not high heels. She didn't walk that way. I can't remember anything else."

He began to dig again, oblivious, manlike, to the fact that he had stopped.

It wasn't a lot to go on, but I supposed I couldn't have hoped for more. Even if I could find what I was looking for, though, it wouldn't provide definitive proof, not with a vague description like that. I had to go ahead with the other thing.

"Richard, there's one more thing I wish you'd do for me."

"And what would that be?"

A noncommittal soul, this man Meg was so devoted to. Not given to rash promises. "I want to take a look at some of the tools in Sir Mordred's workshop. The ones he was cleaning so assiduously the other day."

He rested on his shovel and studied me closely. "I'm sure he would be happy to show you his tools. He's proud of his workshop."

"I don't want to ask him."

"I see."

I had the feeling he did, and in any case, I didn't intend to explain further. "What I hoped you could do was take them to your cottage. Just for a little while. You could say — you could say you had something that would clean them properly, get rid of the rust."

He considered that for a long time, or

what felt like a long time. "Very well," he said finally. "I'll see if I can manage to take them away. It may be some time before he'll leave and let me get at them, you know."

"He's working in his workshop now?"

"So far as I know. He usually is."

"Richard, I don't want to say too much, but I think it might be important to examine those tools as soon as possible. When does he have his lunch?"

"Sometimes not at all, when he's working. He's fussy about his work, forgets to take his meals."

"Well, then, could Meg think of some excuse to get him out of the way for a while? It could be important," I repeated.

His face set. "I'll not involve Meg." It was an ultimatum, but he continued to fix his eyes on mine.

"Is it a police matter?" he asked.

"It may be. The trouble is, I can't seem to reach anyone who could do something about it. I'll keep trying, but time matters, Richard!"

My urgency got through, finally.

"Very well." He scraped his hand along his jawline. "I can create a distraction. Sir Mordred hates fire, won't ever let me burn rubbish. If I started a fire of the brush I've been clearing out, it'd smoke pretty badly.

He'd come out of his shop for that, I'll be bound. And I could nip in and make off with a few tools. Not many, mind. He'll come looking for me, to tear me off a strip."

"*Thank* you! I particularly want that vise he was cleaning when he felt ill on Wednesday. You know, the biggest one? It does unclamp from the bench, doesn't it?"

"It's screwed on, I think, but yes, I can remove it. Anything else?"

I thought quickly. "Anything heavy and portable. A monkey wrench, if he has a big one."

Richard looked blank.

"I mean a — a spanner, a — oh, what do you call them? A big heavy wrench — spanner, I mean, that has adjustable jaws — you use them for some kinds of plumbing, I think —"

I waved my hands frantically, trying to communicate in a foreign language. Richard smiled slightly and nodded understanding.

"An adjustable spanner. I doubt he has a heavy one, but I'll have a quick look. I'll be off now to build a bit of a fire." He thrust his shovel into the ground, its handle quivering, and brushed off his hands. "Wait here."

I had no intention of waiting there. I

watched until he was out of sight, blew my nose again, and then, carefully avoiding the workshop, walked through the front door of Brocklesby Hall.

19

"It's all right," I told the girl at the ticket desk. "I'm just going to the library. I've been helping Meg and Susan with their work."

That was almost true, but the important thing was the air of assurance with which I breezed through the entrance hall into the great hall and turned in the right direction for the library. The young woman accepted what I had said and turned back to her book, business being slow today, and I strode past the library to the magnificently ugly main staircase.

I thought what I was looking for might be in the attic. It wasn't in Mrs. Lathrop's rooms; I'd already searched them, and so had the police, much more thoroughly. I didn't think it would have been left in one of the dust-sheeted, disused rooms, because finding it there, by chance, would have given the police much cause for speculation. Too much cause. No, on the whole, the attic was the most reasonable place.

I climbed.

And climbed, and climbed. Brocklesby

Hall ran to high ceilings, and there were three occupied, or once occupied, floors below the attic floor.

On the third floor, what the English would call the second, I got lost. The stairs came to an end, and I had to hunt for attic access. I wandered through the senseless maze of corridors, wishing I'd been smart enough to look at a floor plan of the house before setting out. At this rate I could be here all day, at greater risk of being discovered every extra moment I remained. Once, when I heard footsteps coming up a flight of steps I couldn't even see, I blundered into a closet in sheer panic, but the steps went away after several thousand years, and I persevered.

The attic stairs were behind a closed, but fortunately not locked, door. They were uncarpeted, noisy under my feet even though thickly furred with dust. The dust appeared to be undisturbed, a fact that worried me a little, but not a great deal. Doubtless, in a house this size, there were other attic stairs.

In fact, there were probably many attics, as I realized when I attained the top of the stairs. It might even be that they were not all connected, though I hoped they were. All I could see from my vantage point at the head of the stairs was a vast collection of beams and chimneys, stretching into shadowy corners and even darker distances, and full of dust and stuff.

Lots of *stuff*. Boxes, trunks, old furniture, stacks of magazines and newspapers. The typical attic collection, grown monstrous with time, and with the oddity (and wealth) of the people who had collected it. It was, I thought, exactly the kind of attic where discoveries are made. The forgotten Gainsborough. The lost Jane Austen manuscript. The skeleton.

I sneezed, from the dust or my burgeoning cold, and then shuddered as my eyes met a real skeleton, a pathetic little heap of bones that had once been a bird. I hoped it had died of something peaceful like cold, and not in the jaws of a rat. Thinking about rats was definitely stupid. I attempted to banish them from my mind and looked about in despair. Where even to begin a search?

With the trunks; trunks suggest clothing. I moved to the nearest one, treading carefully lest I go right through the uneven flooring into the room below, blew off the dust, and opened it.

It was three trunks later (curtains, nasty old furs, and a remarkable collection of Victorian-era corsets) that I realized I was approaching my search in a thoroughly dim-witted fashion. Every trunk I had opened had been white with dust. If what I was looking for was up here, it would have been put here quite recently. Hence, the dust would at least be moved around. I needed to look for signs of activity within the last few days.

The light in the attic was none too good; there were plenty of windows, but they hadn't been washed in years, and the day was a dark one. It had been stupid not to bring a flashlight, but it was all of a piece with my other actions. My brain was not at its best; it felt stuffy and distinctly giddy. I was getting a fever.

And my stupidity was prolonging this business far too much. What I needed was to find another stairway, with footprints in the dust leading to and from it, find what I was looking for, and then get myself home, away from any possible hazards.

I looked out a dusty, cobwebbed window and saw, at the edge of one of the gardens, a small curl of smoke rising from a pile of brush and leaves, and then a tongue of flame. Richard was keeping his promise.

After what seemed like hours, but was probably five or ten minutes, I found the other attic stairs, and sure enough, disturbances in the dust. I couldn't exactly call them footprints, I decided, but definitely marks. I stepped to one side of them, teetering on the narrow boards of the subfloor so as not to disturb evidence.

The marks led me to a nest of luggage, generations newer than the trunks I had first explored. There were small canvas carry-on bags, larger suitcases, one very large upright black bag with wheels and an attached handle that I coveted. *How* nice that would be for long vacations! It was quite dusty, however, which made it an unlikely hiding place for what I was seeking. I checked everything else — empty — and then stopped and looked around, deflated. Plainly this was Sir Mordred's own collection of luggage, and the footprints could be explained by his recent trip to London. I hadn't found my cache, after all.

I glanced out the window. The fire was going nicely. Richard was standing nearby, watching from behind a shed, and he was alone. Sir Mordred hadn't yet — ah, yes, here he came, nearly running, looking like a particularly frenzied beetle from my foreshortening point of view, and apparently shouting as he ran. As I watched, Richard melted into the bushes and was gone. Well, looking for him would keep the master of the house occupied for a while, anyway.

I fished for a tissue, blew my nose, and looked around, but there were no other footprints, and I had run out of attic. My hunch had been wrong. I'd have to look elsewhere, or abandon my search. I took one last longing look at the big suitcase, and experimentally tilted it back on its wheels.

Oh, dear, maybe I wouldn't try to find one like this, after all. It was extremely heavy, though well-balanced on its wheels. But if it weighed that much empty —

It wasn't empty. I spied a corner of fabric caught at the end of one of the zippers. Cautiously I laid the case flat on the floor. It wasn't all that dusty on the front, either, only on the top. I unzipped the cover and folded it back.

The clothes were packed in so tightly that they sprang out at me. Suits, dresses, blouses, conservative in cut and fabric, well made. They were of that ageless style that takes forever to go out of fashion because it is never *in* fashion, but they were of recent manufacture. I cautiously turned back corners of the layers. Most of a summer wardrobe was packed away in here, even — I unzipped another compartment — panties, bras, stockings, scarves. They were not in petite sizes, but none of them could have begun to cover Mrs. Lathrop or the cook, Mrs. Hawes.

With difficulty I crammed the clothes back in and managed to close all the zippers, carefully leaving the corner of fabric sticking out as I had found it. Then I stood the suitcase back where it had been and looked at it in utter incomprehension.

I had expected to find one woman's outfit, the disguise worn by the murderer as he had crept into Brocklesby Hall to kill Mrs. Lathrop. I was confronted instead by an embarrassment of riches. Why was there an entire woman's wardrobe in Sir Mordred's attic?

I was very careful as I came down the long flights of stairs. Sir Mordred would be on the rampage, looking for Richard, and might turn up around almost any corner. I had come down the second set of stairs, the nearest ones, and I didn't know where I might find myself when I finally hit bottom, though I suspected I would be somewhere near the kitchen. Backstairs usually lead to the servants' wing. If so, I would need to watch myself; lunchtime was not far off, and Mrs. Hawes would be busy preparing a meal for Sir Mordred and the house staff.

I was right, for once. The backstairs

turned a sharp corner near the bottom and debouched in the hallway next to not only the kitchen stairs, but to a backdoor leading outside. I turned away from the stairs, beyond which I could hear the sounds of meal preparation, and hastened through the backdoor into the kitchen garden.

It was a walled garden, and for a moment I thought I was trapped, but there was a door at the far end, so I trod as quietly as I could past the late cabbages and brussels sprouts, past the parsley and the mint and the great waving heads of dill and let myself out.

I was unfamiliar with this part of the grounds, and could see little, with the garden wall at my back and masses of brush facing me. There was a path going off to the right from the garden door, along the wall. It was rutted with the tracks of a wheelbarrow and was presumably Richard's service path, which meant it would lead to a place where he might be found. That was unfortunate, for Sir Mordred would be looking for Richard, too, and I didn't want to encounter Sir Mordred just now.

However, the path was really the only way I could go, every other direction being barred by high, thick hedges. At least the packed earth was quiet underfoot. I stole along, feeling for all the world like James Bond, alert to any sound, any glimpse of human activity.

The path made a right turn, still following the garden wall. I eased round the corner cautiously and found myself facing a gate, a high, businesslike affair of steel framing and wire mesh. Beyond it both wall and hedges ceased, and I could, for the first time, see where I was. Not far beyond lay the flower gardens, and beyond them the barn and workshop. I could see, to my left, the shed and the dying remains of the brush fire. And up on the hill I could just see Richard's cottage, to which, I hoped, he had safely absconded with Sir Mordred's tools.

I saw all these things, and wished that I could get to them. For the gate was securely locked.

I couldn't climb it. I might have tried, regardless of my unsuitable shoes and my unsuitable figure, but there was a very nasty-looking strand of barbed wire at the top. I did try shaking the gate, to no avail. The padlock was shiny and new and obviously sound. I realized now that part of my mind had questioned why both the backdoor and the garden door were unlocked. Here was the answer. There was no need to lock them, with the outermost defense secured.

I leaned against the wall, blew my nose, and wondered what to do now. If I couldn't go on, I'd have to go back, but —

Someone was coming!

There was no place to hide, but I scrunched down beside the hedge and tried to make myself small. There was no need to try to be quiet; the person, whoever it was, was making a great deal of noise, shouting and singing and —

Singing?

It was unmelodious, but determined, and it was a voice I recognized. I peered cautiously out the gate and there, sure enough, was Bob Finch, stumbling toward me with a bottle in his hand and a patriotic roar on his lips. Somehow he looked more like a gnome than ever. Maybe it was the red face.

" '. . . Britannia, 'tannia rule the waves! For Britons nev'r, 'ev'r, 'ev'r shall be slaves!' " The song ended in a strangled hiccup; he saw me, then. " 'Ow d'ye do?" he said, very carefully. He saluted me with the bottle, spilling quite a lot of its contents on his head, and looked at me owlishly.

"Bob, thank goodness! I need to get out of here. Do you have the key?"

He looked at me blankly, his eyes trying hard to focus. I tried again.

"The gate's locked, Bob. Do you have a

key to the padlock, or can you find one?"

"I found it," he said with immense satisfaction. "Thought they could 'ide the 'All, all those roads, all those corners, but I found it. Can't 'ide from Bob Finch, I said. I told 'em —"

"The *key*, Bob!" I said despairingly. "Can you get the key?"

"Right." He saluted again, and turned on his heel, or tried to, but he kept on spinning and landed on hands and knees in the dirt. He smiled winningly. " 'Ave a li'l lie down first." And he rolled onto his side, his head pillowed on his hands, and began snoring there on the ruts of the path as sweetly and angelically as a child.

I could have cried. Rescue within sight, and as useless as the heap of old clothes he resembled. I shouted and pleaded, but Bob wasn't going to wake up for quite a while.

In the end there was nothing for it but to turn around and go back, with all the skulking to do over again. I had stopped feeling like James Bond. Things like this never happened to him. I just felt frustrated and tired and, I realized as I let myself back into the kitchen garden, definitely unwell. It wasn't going to be long before I reached the why-can't-I-die-in-a-hurry stage of my cold. I hid behind an apple tree, fumbled in my purse, and found a couple of rather elderly antihistamine tablets that I swallowed, with some difficulty. They would make me feel a little better in about fifteen minutes, though they would also make me very sleepy.

I sneaked to the kitchen door, mindful of the windows that overlooked the garden. But it seemed, thank goodness, that no one was interested in my activities as I crept back into the house. I would have hated to try to come up with a convincing explanation for my presence.

I paused for a moment in a shadowy corner, my hat becoming entangled with a coat hook on the wall, and considered my options. The quickest and easiest way out was the most direct: down the hall, a right turn into the main corridor of the north wing, and thence to the great hall and the front door. I would stand the greatest chance of running into people that way, but it wouldn't really matter, not in parts of the house that were more or less public, and where I had been before as an invited guest. What was important was to get away from here, where I had no conceivable excuse to be. I was about to skitter past the stair head to the freedom of the hallway when I heard rapid footsteps climbing the stairs from the kitchen and shrank away, up a step or two of the backstairs, out of sight.

It was Sir Mordred, with an expostulating cook right behind him. Both of them were in a temper. He stood in the vestibule by the backdoor and argued with Mrs. Hawes. "But the wretched man must be somewhere! He's not in any of the gardens, nor in the house. By God, I'll have his skin for this! He knows I don't allow burning of any kind. And unattended, at that. We could all have gone up in smoke, all my work, my house, everything! He deliberately flouted my orders, and I intend to wait, right here, if it takes all day. He's bound to come in for his meal sooner or later, and I mean to . . ."

I didn't hear the rest. Resignedly, and very quietly, I climbed the backstairs.

20

Once I had gained the upper story, I thought I could simply make my way to the grand staircase and down to the great hall. It wasn't as easy as that. The maids were working — or talking and giggling, at least — very near the backstairs. I might have dreamed up a story to tell them if I hadn't felt so tired, or if my head had not begun to ache. I was probably hungry; I couldn't remember if I'd had any breakfast. Food, however, held no appeal, though a bed sounded wonderful. And unattainable. I could sit on a step, though, just rest for a while and wait. They'd leave soon, and —

Ah, yes, they'd leave. Down the backstairs to the kitchen, and their lunch. Wearily, I went up the next flight. I could go on up to the third floor, cross the house, go down, and leave. Not for home, though. Oh, no, first I had to inspect what Richard had procured for me with such trouble. That meant I had to get out of the house unobserved, drive or walk to his cottage . . .

I sank down on a step and blotted my

streaming nose with a tissue. I didn't dare even blow it, with the giggling maids just below. Well, the tablets I'd taken would shut off the spigot soon — I hoped. Meanwhile, I'd rest here where I was for a few minutes until my head stopped pounding, and then go on up . . .

"And may I ask, madam, precisely what you are doing on my backstairs?"

I woke only with difficulty. I wanted very much to stay asleep, and indeed when I came to full consciousness I wished I hadn't. My throat felt as though someone had been rubbing it with sandpaper. My neck, and indeed every part of me, was stiff and sore. My head was as big as a balloon and pounding with fever.

"I don't know," I croaked, and cleared my throat. "I must have fallen asleep. I only meant to rest for a minute, but I felt so awful — and I'd taken those pills —"

"Indeed." Sir Mordred's voice rose on the last syllable, and positively quivered with outrage. "Am I to have an explanation of your presence here at all?"

"Oh." I began, through waves of dizziness that nauseated me, to have some return of memory, and with it dire apprehension. "I'm not sure," I said with a feeble attempt at dissimulation. "I really am not feeling at all well." I peered at my watch. "Heavens, it's after two! I think I must have taken a wrong turn, and —"

"And climbed a great many steps without realizing you were doing so," said Sir Mordred nastily. "Surely you can do better than that, with your talents for prevarication.

"I saw you, you know. I was in the hallway when you came through the garden. You've no idea how ridiculous you looked, peering about you like some sort of spy and never seeing me, behind the curtain at the window."

"I wanted to take a look at your kitchen garden," I said with as much dignity as I could muster. "I'm interested in herbs."

"Perhaps in monkshood, particularly? I've nothing to fear from you, madam. The police already know it grows in my gardens. And why not? It's quite ornamental, you know. And of course it was my gardener who put it there. I had no knowledge of it, myself, until it was pointed out to me."

"I'm sure —" I began.

"No, I have no interest in what you might have found in my garden. What I *should* like to know, as a matter of academic interest, is why you have been trespassing in my attics."

"What a ridiculous —"

"There is nothing ridiculous about it, and I should be grateful if you would not waste my time." He was pouting. "I have already spent considerable time waiting for you to come downstairs, and waiting for that wretched gardener to put in his appearance. Do you not realize that my time is valuable? I have a great deal of work to do, can you not understand that?"

He seemed to expect no answer.

"Really, my dear lady, if you insist on sleuthing, you ought to learn a few rudimentary rules. It is better to do things well, even foolish things. No good detective strews signs of her presence about the scene." He produced from his pocket a folded tissue. "You left this near my luggage, along with the marks of your shoes all over the floor. I found them when I was looking for my gardener, though why I should have expected to find him in the attic, I cannot imagine. I ask again, why were you there?"

My brain was not working. I couldn't think of any reply except the truth. And did it matter, anyway? Maybe if I told him what he wanted to know, he'd let me go somewhere and sleep and sleep and sleep.

"I was looking for the clothes. The woman's clothes you wore the night you came back to doctor Mrs. Lathrop's tea."

"And did you find them?"

"No. I found lots of summer clothes for a woman, and I didn't understand."

"It is a relief to know that there is something you don't understand. How did you work out the rest?"

There was a note in his voice I didn't quite like. When I felt better I'd try to figure out why it bothered me.

"Mrs. Lathrop had too much money. I finally realized she was blackmailing you, though I don't know about what."

He smiled unpleasantly.

"Anyway, I thought you sneaked back from London early Thursday morning, disguised in women's clothes. You'd left a bicycle at the station, and came out to the Hall to put the monkshood in the tea. You left it awfully late; she almost caught you."

"I had read an old railway schedule. There used to be an earlier train. It wasn't my fault."

"And then Claude somehow figured out something. Either that you were a murderer, or else whatever his mother had over you. Anyway, he decided to take up where Mum left off, and you had to kill him, too. Hit him over the head, probably with that little vise of yours. It would make a lovely weapon."

"A perspicacious woman," he commented lightly.

"But I still can't figure out *why* you were being blackmailed."

Sir Mordred laughed with what seemed almost genuine amusement, clapping his pudgy little hands together. "I think, dear lady, that we will allow you to remain ignorant on that subject. Though doubtless you would have reasoned it out, given sufficient time. It is rather a pity that I cannot allow you that time, but you will quite understand that I am not eager for you to convey your ideas to your illustrious husband. They are only ideas, of course. You haven't a shred of proof."

My brain was beginning to work just a little, and I didn't care for the implications of what he was saying. "I've already told my husband everything I know."

"No, you haven't. Your husband is out of town, and if you had managed to reach him, there would even now be hoards of flat-footed bobbies swarming over the place, looking for evidence. They might even find some; who knows? So I think I shall have to work out a way for you to disappear. I should prefer to wait until nightfall, which comes early in November. Meanwhile, this is a large house, and particularly with your indisposition — I do *wish* you would not sniffle, my

330

dear — I shall be able to give you another pill or two and leave you for a lovely little rest until I have decided exactly how to —"

There was a crash somewhere near the bottom of the stairs, and a roar. "Dorothy! Are you there? DOROTHY!"

I stood, swaying a little, and started past Sir Mordred. "I'm afraid you've left it a little late. ALAN! I'm up here! Al—"

Sir Mordred clapped a hand to my mouth and pulled me close to him in a frantic embrace. "Quiet! Up the stairs! Now!" He forced me up a few stairs with a strength amazing in such a soft little man.

I bit him, freeing my mouth. "I won't! Let me go, you idiot! It's no use, they've heard —"

Footsteps began to pound up the stairs two flights below as I struggled to free myself. I got in one blow to Sir Mordred's chest that astounded me; he screamed in pain and I pulled back in horror. "But —" And then we both lost our balance and were falling, falling . . . falling, at last, into the arms of my husband.

There was a terrible pain in my leg, but I had to tell him. "But listen, Alan, he isn't —" And then a garden gnome brushed against my leg and I screamed, then sank thankfully into deep blackness.

21

We were seated around the dining room table almost a week later, with the remains of Thanksgiving dinner, carefully prepared by Jane at my direction, in front of us. The cats, replete with illicit turkey scraps, were sleeping it off somewhere; the rest of us were near that somnolent state. Jane sat back in her chair, her hands folded comfortably over her stomach. My American friends, Tom and Lynn Anderson, chomped absently on some celery. Richard sat with his arm draped casually along the back of Meg's chair, while young Jemima, in the corner of the room, played with my dollhouse, brought downstairs for the occasion. She didn't know it yet, but it was going to be her Christmas present.

Ada and Bob, who had been invited, had declined with thanks, but Ada had sent along a batch of English-style mince pies, the little ones like tarts. "Which," she had commented, "I don't know as 'ow they're the right thing, seein' as it's not Christmas, but I 'ear tell as you 'as 'em for this Thanksgivin' 'oliday, too, and I wouldn't want you to think as I wasn't thankful, though I wouldn't feel right, sittin' down to dinner with you and 'Is Nibs an' all."

I was almost comfortable, my leg stretched out in its cast to one side of the table, my crutches on the floor. I nibbled a mince pie idly and said into the sleepy silence, "And to think that I never realized he wasn't a man, until it was almost too late."

"Almost too late, indeed!" snorted Alan. "If Bob hadn't sobered up enough to remember seeing you, I'd have gone off looking for you somewhere else, and . . ."

"Now, now," I said soothingly, "you know I tried to call you and the chief inspector, and I never intended to confront him — her — I don't know what to call Sir Mordred."

"Might as well call her Morgana," growled Jane. "Her real name."

"Anyway, I was just going to get the proof I knew you'd need before he had a chance to clean all the blood off the vise. It was when I looked at that bloody tissue, you see — sorry, all you English, I'm not swearing, I mean the tissue that had my blood on it from the cat scratch — it was when I looked at it that I realized how much dried blood looks like rust. I knew then that he wasn't cleaning rust off his tools that day. I should have realized, anyway. He was much too good a craftsman to let his tools get rusty. I'm sorry, I keep saying 'he.' "

"I can't get used to it myself," said Meg, shaking her head. "Over a year I worked there, never having the least idea I was working for a woman."

"There were things everyone should have noticed," I reflected, "though I didn't, either. His — her voice got very high and squeaky whenever she was upset, for one thing. And she would never see a doctor. That, of course, would have given the game away."

"Just what *was* the game?" demanded Lynn Anderson. "I've grasped the fact that Morgana Brocklesby was pretending to be her brother Mordred, and had been for years. But why?"

"For the sake of the Hall," said Alan.

"I always said the Hall was at the back of it," muttered Jane.

"I'll explain, Dorothy," Alan went on. "You're still a trifle hoarse from that cold, and there are some details I've not yet had a chance to tell you."

He tented his fingers and went into his lecturing mode. "Mordred and Morgana were in their twenties — there was only a year's difference between them — were in their twenties when their parents died, and they decided to continue living together in Brentford, just outside London. I don't know that they were particularly devoted to one another, but they stayed on in the family home, perhaps out of inertia. Neither was interested in marriage, and they were disinclined to move from a place they were used to. They kept themselves to themselves, their neighbors say, and pursued their own interests.

"The switch happened during a trip abroad together in the fifties. There was a disastrous hotel fire in Venice; many people were killed. Morgana tells us she was out for the evening and returned rather late to find the place engulfed in flames. She realized immediately that her brother was dead, and with him her hopes of living one day in Brocklesby Hall. The inheritance was through the male line only."

"But he — she — hated the Hall!"

"So 'Sir Mordred' would have had us believe. In fact, Morgana's heart, all those years ago, was already given over to the collection of miniatures and to her dream, one day, of establishing the finest museum of dolls' houses in the world. Brocklesby Hall, and the money that would come with it, were essential to her dreams.

"So she decided, on the spot, that she

would become her brother. They were not unlike, physically. He was a soft little man, and she a rather masculine woman. It remained only for her to stay somewhere obscure the night of the fire, buy some men's clothing in the morning, and show up at the morgue to identify her brother's body as hers.

"Italy was rather disorganized for some years after the war, or she probably wouldn't have been able to get away with it. Nowadays fire inspectors do what they can to identify bodies before the families ever see them, with dental records and so on. Even if only bones remain, they can be identified as male or female, at the very least. But at the time, her word was apparently accepted with alacrity, and no difficulties were put in the way of her obtaining emergency identity papers that would allow her a new passport, since she claimed she had left hers — his — at the hotel that night, and it had been burned. (You're right, my dear, the pronouns are confusing.) At any rate, from that day, Morgana Brocklesby vanished, and Mordred moved to another part of London, where no one would be likely to recognize that he was not quite what he seemed, and flourished."

"But Morgana must have resurfaced from

time to time," I put in. "Or else why did she keep women's clothes in the attic?"

"She says she simply grew tired of being a man all the time, and now and then would go as Mordred to her club, which admits both men and women as members, change her clothes, exit as Morgana, and enjoy a day of nice feminine shopping."

"And that's how Mrs. Lathrop found out, I'll bet. She snooped and found the clothes, and then blackmailed her boss, since he — whatever — would do anything to keep from being found out and disinherited."

"Morgana says not. She says Mrs. Lathrop had met her many years ago, at some country-house function when she was a young woman and Mrs. Lathrop a house-maid. There is a small birthmark on Morgana's forehead, mostly hidden by hair, but Mrs. Lathrop had dressed her hair all those years ago and had, unfortunately for Morgana, an excellent memory. Lathrop apparently spotted the mark one warm day when Morgana pushed her hair back. She started blackmailing her a few days later. Morgana has gone on at some length about how monstrous Lathrop's behavior was."

"She seems to be talking an awful lot," commented Tom Anderson with a yawn.

"Oh, yes. She's gone right round the

bend, and is quite proud of her exploits. She's explained any number of times to Derek Morrison that Lathrop was a criminal, robbing the Hall blind. You were right about that at the end, love; Morgana was stealing her own miniatures and selling them to pay off Lathrop's increasing demands. She knew the Hall could be profitable without that drain, so once she had finalized her plans to murder Lathrop she began buying them back, and hiring the staff her beloved museum required. She says she did nothing more than what had to be done to save her precious miniatures, and that she would have got by with it if it had not been for Dorothy. She seems to feel that justifies her being released, with our apologies!"

"Is she right?" growled Jane.

Alan looked amused. "I don't believe Derek has any plans to release her soon." His smile faded. "In any case, her heart is not strong. It's quite possible she may never stand trial."

Jane sighed with heavy patience. "Right about Dorothy."

"Oh. Well, very possibly, as a matter of fact. She had covered her tracks nicely. No one at her London club had any idea 'Sir Mordred' had not spent the whole night there, when she came back to poison Mrs. Lathrop's tea. As for Claude's murder, the staff at a busy pub couldn't say with any certainty whether a particular person had been there on a given night, and any marks there might have been in the grass, from dragging Claude's body to the lake, were nicely erased when you, Richard, mowed the lawn."

"At the order of 'Sir Mordred,'" said Richard.

"Exactly. It's true there were still traces of blood in the jaws of the vise. We'd have spotted that, if we'd had occasion to look. But it seemed that 'Sir Mordred' had no possible motive for either murder, not to mention having been apparently elsewhere at the relevant times. No, without my perceptive wife —"

"'Perspicacious,' Sir Mordred called me."

"Rather high-flown language, don't you think, my dear? At any rate," he cleared his throat, "that is why I have a proposition for you, and I might as well make it quite publicly, lest I ever be tempted to renege."

"Alan, what *are* you talking about?"

"Just this, my dear. We've done some talking, and I for one have done considerable thinking, about your involvement in criminal investigation."

I looked ruefully at my broken leg, which was beginning to ache a good deal. I knew what was coming.

Alan saw my glance and grinned broadly. "No, you will need to be married to me for a good many more years before you can *always* read my mind. I am *not* going to warn you off, despite your tendency to damage yourself. Quite the contrary, in fact.

"You have agreed that the move to Bramshill is a good idea, and that you can accept the temporary oversight of a country manor, though the thought gives you qualms. In appreciation for that generosity of spirit, I wish to state publicly that there is no excuse whatever for my discouraging you from getting mixed up in crime as much as you wish."

I opened my mouth; he held up a hand.

"Let me finish my speech, love, and then you can say all you want. You see, I found myself recalling the reasons I first went into police work, all those years ago."

"I asked you about that once," I said, interrupting in spite of myself. "You said something about not liking crime."

"I understated the case. I detest crime, and what it does to the victims." His eyes moved for a moment to Meg and Richard, and then to Jemima. "They include the whole community, you know. Everyone is hurt by crime, especially violent crime."

"And Bob lost his jobs," I commented. "Even though he hadn't done anything."

"Precisely. And when I was young, and discovered that I had an aptitude for finding out about things, and could be quite good with people, I decided to have a go at police work. I've never regretted it for a moment, not even through budget cuts, and the rise of public indifference — all the frustrations. I've spent forty years doing what I wanted to do, and I've done it well. That's a satisfying sort of life.

"The point is," he went on as I started to speak again, "the point is that you have the same qualifications I had — have. You're good with people; they like to talk to you. You have a positive genius for putting two and two together, and if the answer is sometimes five, it usually turns out that both twos were really two and a half. And you have a strong moral sense that sees evil for what it is, and despises it."

I swallowed. "Oh, come now. I'm no angel, as you should know well enough by now. I have a temper, and I'm too quick to judge people, and I love to feel sorry for myself —"

"You're human, in short. Of course you are. So am I. But if you have the attributes that make a good detective, why on earth shouldn't you be one? You'll never be official, of course. But we don't have enough good men and women in the official police; we never will have. I can see no reason whatever why we shouldn't gratefully accept assistance from a member of the public who happens to be a gifted —"

"Snoop."

"All right, if that's the word you want to use. In any case, I've come to my senses. You go ahead, my girl, and do what you're so good at doing, and if there's any way I can help without running afoul of the regulations, I shall. All I ask is that you look after yourself. I can't afford to lose one of my best detectives."

The little round of applause served to remind us that there were other people in the room. And it was fortunate, because, for once, I couldn't think of a word to say to Alan.

"And here," said Tom Anderson, standing and lifting his champagne glass, "is a double toast. First of all, to a Thanksgiving worth having, with Dorothy safe and another case solved."

"Here, here," said Jane. "Even drink to an

American holiday, when it makes sense."

"And second, to the only amateur sleuth in the world with a professional sidekick. To Dorothy and her new partner, Alan!"

The employees of Thorndike Press hope you have enjoyed this Large Print book. All our Large Print titles are designed for easy reading, and all our books are made to last. Other Thorndike Press Large Print books are available at your library, through selected bookstores, or directly from us.

For information about titles, please call:

(800) 223-1244
(800) 223-6121

To share your comments, please write:

Publisher
Thorndike Press
P.O. Box 159
Thorndike, Maine 04986

DATE DUE

DATE DUE			
JUN - 1 2001			
JUL 0 9 2001			
AUG 2 9 2001			
GAYLORD			PRINTED IN U.S.A.